Praise for *The Sealwoman's Gift*

'A remarkable feat of imagination'   *Guardian*

'An evocative, striking new novel'   *The Times*

'Richly imagined and energetically told, *The Sealwoman's Gift* is a powerful tale of loss and endurance'
                                                      Sunday Times

'An epic journey in every sense: although it's historical, it's incredibly relevant to our world today'
                                                      Zoe Ball Book Club

'A really, really good read'   *BBC Radio 2 Book Club*

'A novel that moves gracefully between what is known and what must be imagined'   *TLS*

'A rich, captivating work'   *Mail on Sunday*

'Engrossing, atmospheric'   *Sunday Express*

'Compelling'   *Good Housekeeping*

'From the first, it leaps from the page . . . I enjoyed and admired it in equal measure'   Sarah Perry

The Ninth Child

The
Ninth Child

Sally Magnusson

First published in Great Britain in 2020 by Two Roads
An imprint of John Murray Press
An Hachette UK company

1

Copyright © Sally Magnusson 2020

A CIP catalogue record for this title is available from the British Library

Hardback ISBN 978 1 473 69660 0
Trade paperback ISBN 978 1 473 69661 7
eBook ISBN 978 1 473 69663 1
Audio digital download ISBN 978 1 473 69665 5

Typeset in Hoefler Text 11/15 pt by
Palimpsest Book Production Limited, Falkirk, Stirlingshire

Printed and bound by Clays Ltd, Elcograf S.p.A.

John Murray policy is to use papers that are natural,
renewable and recyclable products and made from wood grown in sustainable
forests. The logging and manufacturing processes are expected to conform
to the environmental regulations of the country of origin.

John Murray (Publishers)
Carmelite House
50 Victoria Embankment
London EC4Y 0DZ

www.tworoadsbooks.com

To the Reverend Fergus Buchanan

Contents

Part One – 1856
1

Part Two – 1857
85

Part Three – 1858
99

Part Four – 1859
137

Part Five October – 1859
217

Author's Note
317

Acknowledgements
322

About the Author
324

Sir Walter Scott

To proceed to more modern instances of persons supposed to have fallen under the power of the fairy race, we must not forget the Reverend Robert Kirke, minister of the Gospel, the first translator of the Psalms into Gaelic verse. He was, in the end of the seventeenth century, successively minister of the Highland parishes of Balquhidder and Aberfoyle, lying in the most romantic district of Perthshire and within the Highland line. These beautiful and wild regions, comprehending so many lakes, rocks, sequestered valleys and dim copsewoods, are not even yet quite abandoned by the fairies, who have resolutely maintained secure footing in a region so well suited for their residence.

Indeed, so much was this the case formerly that Mr Kirke, while in his latter charge of Aberfoyle, found materials for collecting and compiling his Essay on the 'Subterranean and for the most part Invisible People heretofore going under the name of Elves, Faunes, and Fairies, or the like' . . .

It was by no means to be supposed that the elves, so jealous and irritable a race as to be incensed against those who spoke of them under their proper names, should be less than mortally offended at the temerity of the reverend author, who had pried so deeply into their mysteries for the purpose of giving them to the public. Although, therefore, the learned divine's monument, with his name duly inscribed, is to be seen at the east end of the churchyard at Aberfoyle, yet those acquainted with his real history do not believe that he enjoys the natural repose of the tomb . . .

It is to be feared that Mr Kirke still 'drees his weird in Fairyland'.

Sir Walter Scott,
*Letters on Demonology and Witchcraft,
Addressed to J. G. Lockhart, Esq*, 1830

She is like the Archangel Michael as he stands upon Saint Angelo at Rome. She has an immense provision of wings, which seem as if they would bear her over earth and heaven; but when she tries to use them, she is petrified into stone, her feet are grown in to the earth, chained to the bronze pedestal.

Florence Nightingale, *Cassandra*, 1852

It is with no ordinary feelings of pride and satisfaction that we are enabled this day to state to Your Majesty that we have completed one of the most interesting and difficult works of engineering and, at the same time, the largest and most comprehensive scheme for the supply of water which has yet been accomplished in Your Majesty's dominions.

John Burnet, secretary to
Glasgow Corporation Water Works Commissioners,
14 October 1859

Part One

1856

Nothing ill come near thee
William Shakespeare, *Cymbeline*

I

Alexander should have warned her. Explosions, Issy, he might have said. Puddles, he could have mentioned. Grass of a less manicured variety than the Botanic Gardens, pronounced absence of paths wider than your dress – a hint would have been helpful.

Had he warned her? This morning's compliment on the strawberry bonnet had been, on reflection, a shade less than sincere, but no, nothing had been said. She would have paid attention to that much.

Isabel sank majestically on to a hummock of grass, which is the only way a descent from the upright can be accomplished in a crinoline, and looked around. There were men everywhere: navvies distinguishable by their gay neckerchiefs and hobnail boots sauntering about with armfuls of ironmongery or leading the most enormous horses along the shore; gentlemen guests whooping themselves hoarse around a vast Corporation of Glasgow banner, each boom accompanied by a frenzied waving of hats. By now Alexander would probably be hollering right along with them.

As the only lady for miles and certainly the only woman braving the wilds today in a hooped lilac gown and a bonnet nodding with silken fruit, Isabel had been attracting so much attention that she barely noticed the other figure staring at her from a clump of bright trees. She might not have registered him at all – black coat, something white at the neck, no hat of any kind – if she had not been so struck by the man's eyes, which burned through the faint gunpowder haze with a peculiar energy.

'Hungry' is how she would describe the look afterwards.

'Poor fellow,' her husband would murmur. 'We need to find him work.' Alexander was not easily engaged with a metaphor.

The man was quickly gone, and Isabel, hot and disgruntled in her billow of skirts, had no more inkling of peril than a twinge of anxiety for her strawberries. There was certainly nothing to alert her that here on the banks of hidden Loch Chon was a beginning. Or that this sunny May morning would ever remain for her a kind of ending, too.

2

Out.

Out.

I am out.

The earth erupting in thunder and fire.

Out.

Smoke drifting across the heavens.

Out.

A lady attired in a fine gown and egregiously silly bonnet.

Aye, I hear you. I see her.

Robert Kirke is out o' faery – and one glance is enough.

3

Just start at the beginning, ye say. Tell it your own way, Kirsty McEchern, and forget who's listening. But see, beginnings, endings – it's not always so easy to know which is which. Life's a circular sort of thing most o' the time and so's a story. Those of us at the heart o' this one would likely all tell ye differently where it began, and as for where it ended, well, is it even finished yet? That's what I ask myself sometimes.

It's a long while since I've spoken about Robert Kirke, but maybe it's time. Maybe it's time right enough. I'm the one who knew Isabel Aird best in those years, unless you're counting her husband and there were times I wasna so sure you should. And I'm the one who warned her. 'Mrs Aird,' says I, 'be careful. I've got a feeling about this man.'

I get these feelings. When you grow up in the Highlands and Islands with Gaelic your first tongue, you come away with an instinct for things that are that bit beyond what you might call the natural, though to us it's all one. You see what canna exactly *be* seen in the names our ancestors gave to the hills and the hollows and the brown peat moors and the ancient mounds of the *sìthichean* – that's fairies to you. English never quite catches the idea of any of it. Nor, to be honest with you, did Isabel Aird.

THE NINTH CHILD

You have to remember she was a Lowlander, born and bred in a city. What did she know about matters that Highlanders drink in with their mothers' milk? She thought they were no more than a quaint thing to read about in those fancy books that brought tourists to ooh and aah at the landscape o' the Trossachs. There she came all innocent, with her parasol a-twirl and a background that had bred her useless. Broken inside, though. Awful broken. A woman like that has no defences.

4

Methought I was come into a battlefield. But after the first explosions I paid no heed to the noise. Only lay on my back, hands folded behind my head, glorying in the sight of the water glinting beyond the trees. A great rush o' beauty fell upon my starved senses. I was out, and my spirit exulted.

But there followed thereafter –
quick thereafter,
immediately thereafter
– the knowledge that I am returned a different man. A canker within. A sickness of the soul. Robert Kirke is not who he was.

They spake to me then, filling my head, issuing my commission. A bargain was made. Then I stood up and saw the lady. They told me she was the one.

And I looked upon her with a huntsman's eye.

5

'Engineers,' Isabel had roused herself to protest as the brougham clattered them through the frosty streets of Glasgow that January of 1856. 'Alex, they'll all be engineers.'

She frowned through the front glass at the inoffensive back of the driver hunched over the reins for warmth; his dark coat glistened with spent snow.

At her side Alexander was sitting as stiffly in his black tails as a man will who is more comfortable in a blood-grimed apron with a knife between his teeth; a man, moreover, who is beginning to have doubts about tonight's plan.

In truth Isabel's reluctance to attend Professor Rankine's supper party had little to do with their host being one of the country's leading engineers. Nor was it solely because she had never been a natural in any drawing room, although that was part of it. 'Oh, Isabel, will you not try harder to dazzle?' her mother had used to plead, palpitating with anxiety that her only daughter's too easily furrowed brow and barely disguised preference for her own company were never going to snare a husband. It was a fear that had persisted until the day that Mrs Sarah Gillies, hosting a soirée herself of the tepidly polite kind Isabel most disdained, collared from among the guests a cheerful young medical man with distressingly gingery whiskers but good income prospects. 'Come out from behind the curtain, Isabel, and let me introduce you to the dashing Dr Aird,' she had commanded, stretching the point: never in her life had Mrs Gillies seen so many freckles. Alexander had winkled Isabel from the window seat, made her laugh with a dry commentary on her cousin Josephine's erratic interpretation of the 'Moonlight Sonata' and then engaged her attention for the rest of the evening with the latest trends in surgery. He had understood Isabel's social reserve from the first, appreciating the unfocused intelligence underneath it, sensing both an impatience and an insecurity with the subjects a lady was expected to enjoy discussing. He had envisaged a marriage full of lively conversations about the things that mattered to him and a social life in which they would signal their private reactions across the room and chuckle all the way home.

Alexander cast his wife a sideways glance and blew out his cheeks in a surreptitious sigh. These days Isabel was too listless to want to go anywhere and getting her this far tonight had been a struggle further than he normally ventured. Nor was the subject he intended to air likely to occasion gales of merriment on the journey home.

'You will have no need to talk to any engineers,' he returned with a strained grin. 'You'll be whisked away by some matron in black to discuss preserves, while I offer my thoughts on Rankine's mathematical analysis of the cooling of the earth and take the opportunity of correcting his latest theories on heat and steam.'

Isabel laughed. He could still disarm her. 'Fraud! You no more understand the action of a piston than I care about the boiling point of jam.'

He smiled more easily and slipped an arm around her. 'Our host is an excellent fellow, Issy, although his brilliance might trouble me if I thought about it too long. He's designed harbours, waterworks, railways and heaven knows what else. I'm fairly sure he's even got a Rankine's Method to his name – something to do with railway curves. And he composes songs. And plays the cello.'

'Well, that should enliven the evening at least,' she said, reflecting that her husband had probably been fretting about this man's accomplishments longer than he liked to admit. William Macquorn Rankine was in his thirties too.

Alexander looked vaguely out of the window. 'Anyway, there's something I want to ask him.'

Macquorn Rankine, all amused eyebrows and rioting curls, succeeded in frustrating the worst of Isabel's expectations by proving to be an entertaining host. He regaled the company with his own ridiculous ditties to such repeated acclaim that Alexander had to wait until he rose from the pianoforte and made for his pipe before waylaying him with the subject on his mind. To his wife's chagrin the subject on Alexander's mind proved to be Glasgow's waterworks project.

Water. Alex had inveigled her here to talk about *water*?

The engineer responded with enthusiasm – indeed with such alarming enthusiasm that Isabel feared they were in for a night of it. He expounded at length on why Loch Katrine was a better solution to Glasgow's water problem than any competing source, of which, as everyone knew (an expansive flourish of his pipe was kind enough to include Isabel, who nodded as if she did), there had been many. He had tramped the Trossachs area himself, taking measurements to compare Katrine with arch-rival Loch Lubnaig to the east. Both lakes would require extraordinarily difficult tunnelling – 'Gneiss, Mrs Aird. And mica slate. Both devilish hard' – but Katrine's tunnel through a fairly narrow ridge and around Loch Chon would have the merit of being shorter.

'Loch What?' she murmured. Isabel had heard of Loch Katrine – had not every reader in the land? – but here was a new one.

Rankine obliged with a grandiloquent roll of the throat.

'Chon, my dear lady. Chon. It's a Gaelic word, like so many of the place names out there. You aim for *Hon* with the *ch* of "loch" and out it comes.' He repeated the performance of a man attempting to dislodge a fishbone. 'Dog Loch, in English.'

Isabel smiled her thanks. Why dog? she would have liked to ask. But Rankine was already back on course.

'The purity of the water in those parts is quite unparalleled. It's because the rock is so impenetrable, ye see, and the area so little cultivated. No moss. Traces of potash, soda, some iron. Bit of lead that caused us problems in Parliament right enough, but really you couldn't find a better source of water.'

It was around this point that it occurred to Isabel that a woman may tire of water.

Perhaps sensing it, Rankine remembered his manners and turned to Alexander. 'May I ask why you're interested, Dr Aird?'

Yes, Alex. Pray explain.

Alexander looked quickly at his wife and back again. He should have thought of trying to divert her towards the doughty dowager holding forth on a nearby chaise longue on a subject

that sounded as if it might be gloves. Too late. He hesitated a
moment. Then, flushing red as his hair, he ploughed on.

'Because I feel I'm wasting my skills, sir. I have a house in
Bath Street – the fashionable end, as my mother-in-law would
doubtless have you know – and a decent enough income from
phlegm and constipation.' Isabel registered the querulous note
from a man whose exuberance in medical matters had tended
to the puppyish when they first met. And what possessed him
to bring her mother into this? 'And my training allows for some
dining-table surgery for those who can afford it. But this in a
city that had near four thousand perish from cholera last time,
and as many the time before.'

Isabel stared at her husband with mounting consternation as
he warmed to his theme.

'And you know where they died, sir? Of course you do. Not
all, of course, but most of them were in the stinking wynds that
us in this room do our best to keep away from. Does it not shame
us that in no other civilised country in the world is so large an
amount of filth and misery and disease in one spot as Glasgow?'

Was this what had been preoccupying Alexander behind
his newspaper, then? Was it among these hideous places that
he walked when he was on his own? Isabel was not sure she
had ever been down a wynd, stinking or otherwise, although
the streets in their part of town could certainly be better
swept: sometimes Annie had to scrub her hem for an hour.
She knew about cholera, of course. Panic erupted across the
city every few years and last time, now she thought about it,
Alex had been miserable at his inability to treat it. But the
disease had never arrived at their own front door, and behind
it she had been nursing miseries of her own.

'It's practically certain,' he was saying now, 'that contaminated water plays a part in the progress of cholera.'

Isabel tried to remember if he had mentioned such a thing before. There was a time when she would have been the first to hear it from him. There was a time when she would have paid attention. She watched as he leaned earnestly towards the professor, his eyes alight with the old eagerness.

'You know what it's like, Rankine. The High Street, the Gallowgate, the Saltmarket – all those thousands of folk crammed into filthy tenements – there are such horrors there as the better off among us never see.' He shot another glance at his wife. 'Dunghills that reach as high as some folk's first-floor windows. Pigs wandering the vennels. Wells taking drinking water from the Clyde where it's no better than an open sewer.'

Pigs? There were certainly no pigs in Bath Street.

Macquorn Rankine nodded so vigorously that his dark curls shook. 'Aye, I know, I know. None better. Your husband will have told you that I teach at the university in the High Street, Mrs Aird, amid such sights and smells as would shock you. As soon as another epidemic hoves into view, the newspapers shout blue murder and the orders go out for whitewashing and scrubbing. Down go the dunghills, out with the swine. But once that epidemic is past, what happens? It's the job of all-merciful Providence to spare everyone another visitation – not the ratepayers. That's what those of us who wanted to bring pure water from the Highlands were up against. Quite a battle the Glasgow Corporation had of it in Parliament, not to mention those naysayers back home. But the contracts are out now, thank God.'

He smiled genially at Alexander. 'So that's why you're interested in the water scheme, is it, Aird?'

Alexander looked uncomfortable. He could sense the irritation radiating at his side. 'I heard they would be looking for a doctor up there,' he said.

'Did you?' Isabel did actually gasp.

Alexander avoided her eyes and rubbed his nose, an infallible sign of perplexity and in this case, as she had no doubt, guilt.

Rankine glanced from one to the other, sucked on his pipe and murmured placatingly, 'Well, that's most interesting, Dr Aird. Plenty of work up there for a medical man, I'll wager. And let's see if Loch Katrine water can hinder the next epidemic.'

Alexander blushed again. 'Yes, indeed. Exactly. It's what they're calling public health. The fight against disease and squalor, as you might say.' His ears were now also pink. 'I was thinking I would like to be involved.'

Public health! What about his wife's private health? Alexander knew fine what she would think of this.

The atmosphere on the way home was chilly. Isabel turned pointedly towards the window on her left, obliging Alexander to address his apologies to the back of a fox-fur stole.

'For the tenth time, I never mentioned it because I knew how you would react and I thought we could find out more tonight. I thought . . . hoped . . . you'd be interested to hear from a man like Rankine, who was involved from the start. Intrigued, even, as you used to be by new . . . um . . .'

He trailed off as her shoulders stiffened further.

'But I was mistaken. I'm sorry for springing it on you in public like that. There, I've said it again. I am sorry.'

No movement from the fox-fur.

Alexander tried a different tack. 'But are you not just a little curious, Issy? The Trossachs area is quite the tourist draw these days.'

Isabel continued to gaze steadfastly out of the black window. Every now and then a streetlamp threw out a pool of yellow light.

'How does it go now? *One burnished sheet of living gold, Loch Katrine lay beneath him rolled.* Was *The Lady of the Lake* not on your dressing table for weeks?'

Oh, it was, Alex, it was. Is there anything else to do but read? She had been wallowing in the novels and lengthy narrative poems of the Borders laird Sir Walter Scott for years, while remaining untroubled – as she might have mentioned but could not be bothered – by any inclination to inspect his famous fairy glens personally. She also kept up with the latest blistering caricatures and social satires from the pen of Mr Dickens, although she thought his heroines weak and wished he had a better feel for the inside of a woman's head. Directing a couple of maids and discussing meals with Cook had proved less fulfilling than billed in seven years of marriage.

The horses' hooves skittered on the cobbles.

'Rankine says the works are to be inaugurated in May,' Alexander tried next, reaching, bravely in the circumstances, for her hand. 'There's to be some kind of ceremony, he says. Why don't we go together then and take a look? Just a look, mind.'

Isabel went on inspecting the streaks of Glasgow grime on the carriage window, lethargy settling over her like sleep. What did any of this matter?

'And think, Issy. Moving there for a while would give you

something different to do, to think about. You've said yourself you have too little to occupy you, after . . . Well, anyway. I saw you were interested in what Rankine had to say. Admit it.'

'After what, Alex? After losing every child in the making for six years – was that what you were going to say? And you think a trip to the Trossachs will remedy that?'

He stroked her glove with a tentative finger. 'I only meant it might offer something new for us both. I have wanted to do more with my life.'

'And I have wanted a life.'

'Then what harm can come of taking a look?'

6

Even as late as May the weather on the Isle of Wight could be chancy, but Albert had long ago ceased pointing out that while breakfasting on the terrace could be pleasant on a fine day, it was less so in a south-westerly straight off the Solent. Victoria's own constitution seemed not to register the difference. On mornings like this the Prince Consort wondered about the wisdom of having designed Osborne House's terracing so exactly like a Renaissance palazzo, with every aspect guiding the eye past a fountain or a statue to the sea. If he had foreseen how attached Victoria would become not only to taking breakfast in the open air but to conducting the greater part of their official business out here every morning, he would have built a glass-house.

Seated at the table in as many layers as he thought he could get away with, Albert tried to rub some warmth into his cold hands. Victoria complained that he complained about the cold more than was entirely manly – which was possibly true. His spirits plummeted every time he spied her bustling over to a fireplace in pursuit of an unwarranted spark or narrowing her eyes at the wall thermometer (which, again, he had been the one to introduce, so had no one to blame but himself). At night, windows flung open, he had been driven to retiring to sleep in long white drawers with the feet attached, an ensemble that Victoria said made him look like the Easter Bunny. Sometimes he resorted to a wig. It was a matter of regret to Albert that at thirty-six years old he had not retained more of his own hair, which if nothing else might have helped to keep him warm. *Gott im Himmel*, the balding head and burgeoning paunch in those *Punch* cartoons!

Of course Victoria cared not a jot what anyone thought of her appearance. The gossips might as well be rude about the flanks of the Grampians as carp that the Queen was growing stout in her thirties, or that her lips fell short of a rosebud curve, or that she made such little effort to court admiration with her attire. What they always forgot were those pellucid blue eyes and the nose, that adorably neat nose. But in any case Victoria was never, ever anything but herself. Like her beloved Scottish mountains, she simply *was*. Albert admired her indifference to admiration. He was not particularly vain either – so he assured himself – but he was as punctilious about his appearance as everything else and aware that even the official portraits, in which Victoria assured him he cut an excellent dash, could not conceal the premature toll of overwork, ill health and the strain of keeping his beloved happy.

This morning Victoria presided over the family's open-air breakfast in blessedly good humour. Mealtimes attended by the older children could in Albert's experience be wearing. His wife had a regrettable belief that the role of a loving mother was to be correcting her offspring at all times, ordering them about and generally taking it upon herself to organise the smallest details of their lives. His own view was that it is well-nigh impossible to be on happy terms with people you are always scolding and he was forever sending Victoria earnest notes to this effect, to which she did not, as a rule, respond well.

Nor was she often at her best around the youngest of their brood. The poor *Liebchen* felt wretched when she was expecting and wretched for what seemed an interminable time afterwards, periods which taken together had covered most of their married life and laid upon Albert more and more of the burdens of state she felt unable to face. He was also under pressure to feel guilty – on behalf, it sometimes felt, of the entire male sex – that it was woman alone who bore the consequences of marital passion and had to spend so much of her time feeling like a cow. Albert considered that he had done his honest best over the years to imagine what a cow went through, and to sympathise, but he did draw the line at conceding that any of this was exclusively his fault. Victoria was as much a force of nature within the bedroom as out of it.

But Albert did feel that their married life had been sailing in less turbulent waters of late. And the reason, it seemed to him, was perfectly obvious: it had been a whole three years and one month since Victoria was last delivered of a child.

After the breakfast and the children had been cleared away, Victoria summoned the leather despatch box newly arrived from London, and side by side they set to work. Beyond the parkland the sea shifted and a whiff of salt reached them on the strengthening breeze. Albert had an anxious moment envisaging his finely honed epistle to the King of Prussia being whisked towards Calais, but his long experience of judging paperweight deployment in relation to wind velocity stood him in good stead.

'Here is the correspondence I drafted for you last night, my dear,' he said, passing along a sheaf of documents and adjusting the glass weights to secure it. Each bore a royal profile that neither had glimpsed in the mirror for some years. '*Lese aufmerksam*, if you would.'

'Of course I will read carefully.' Victoria glanced at the papers. 'But I do hope, Albert, that these letters are resounding enough. You can be rather stilted with the grander emotions.'

'You need have no fear about the tone. It's important to be lucid and, as I always like to remind you, diplomatic, but I should hope I know your style by this time. You might run your eyes over the English, though.'

Victoria looked at him with one of the sudden rushes of undisguised affection that never failed to beguile him. When she smiled, her face shed the dourness that people so often criticised and those eyes that looked so well in the island light danced.

She laid her pen down and breathed deep of the sea air. 'Oh, Albert, I cannot bear to think of returning to London.'

'*Liebchen*, you always say that. And then you spoil the remaining days of the holiday for everyone else by reminding us how few of them are left. We'll take the horses out for a canter soon and you will feel better. And before you know it, off we shall go to Scotland. Really, Victoria, we do quite well for holidays compared with—'

Her attention snapped back. 'There is no possible life to whom ours can or ought to be compared, Albert.' He sighed. Must Victoria always sound so peremptory? 'But my spirit shrinks to think of Buckingham Palace in the summer heat, with the Thames so frightfully unpleasant. It's like living on the edge of a cesspool.'

Albert replaced his own pen in a straight line beside the Cabinet minutes and gave himself wholly to the pouring of balm. 'Well, we shall be at Windsor too. You know how pretty you find the walks there, and the flowers will be in bloom.'

'Gloomy Windsor. Why can't you design us something nice inside, like some decent plumbing?'

'Oh, Victoria, I am quite busy enough with Osborne and Balmoral and writing your speeches and responding to your ministers and performing opening ceremonies when you're indisposed. I must be the possessor of more silver trowels than any man in the world. And you should know that I blame this' – he patted the straining waistcoat – 'on all those dinners you refuse to—'

'You look very fine, Albert,' she said, regarding him with a hint of the appraising look he remembered from early in their marriage. In those days merely watching him scrape a foamy razor down his cheek had excited her in a frank way immensely flattering to his self-esteem. While shaving did not produce precisely the same effect today, Victoria could still be flirtatious and touchingly loyal when he least expected it.

He laughed. 'Now sign this letter to the Prime Minister, while I see what our noble press are complaining about today. And then we shall have that ride.'

They read in silence for half an hour. From the shore came the shriek of an oystercatcher. A chaffinch alighted on the patio and was waved off by the nearest footman. The breeze had lessened, although it still brought stray petals of may blossom fluttering past and made careful handling of the newspaper necessary. Reading *The Times* outdoors in every mood of the British weather was another skill Albert had perfected in sixteen years of marriage.

Without looking up Victoria murmured, 'Is there anything one ought to know about in there?'

'Nothing you won't already have in your box. One thing only, perhaps. I see the works are to begin on a public water supply for Glasgow. The bill took an age to proceed through Parliament, but it seems the construction will start at last.'

'Waterworks, you say? Is this a briefing, Albert, or merely part of your obsession with drains?'

'It has nothing to do with drains. Except in the sense that the water will run into pipes and ultimately, one hopes, into decent water closets for people – which you are just as much in favour of as I, so don't pretend otherwise. Especially at Windsor.'

She gave no reply, and his mouth twitched. 'You may also recall, my dear, that you approved the legislation.'

Victoria barely paused in the penning of a V. 'One approves so very many laws.'

He smiled at her bent head. 'The water is to come from Loch Katrine in the Scottish Highlands. It will go through tunnels and aqueducts for – let me see, *wo hab' ich das gelesen?* – twenty-six miles, to a reservoir to be built on the edge of Glasgow. And from there another eight miles into the city. Descending by gravity alone all the way. The engineering challenges quite take one's breath away.'

'Ah, Loch Katrine.' Victoria looked up at last and put down her pen. 'Such a romantic place. Sir Walter Scott wrote most affectingly about the scenery there. It lies somewhere about Loch Lomond, does it not? Will we pass anywhere near on our way to Balmoral?'

'I think not, my dear. I cannot imagine it is possible to pass the site of these works on the way to anywhere at all.'

7

The Airds set out from Glasgow early in the morning. In the months since Professor Rankine's supper party Alexander had put some effort into assuring his wife that the spangle of lochs around Loch Katrine popularly known as the Trossachs was not really the Highlands; or at least not much the Highlands; or at the very worst not far into the Highlands. Admittedly it was something of a journey to get there and by all accounts the area was not what you might call civilised· barely populated at all, he did acknowledge. But really when you thought about it, the site of the waterworks was not much more than thirty miles from Glasgow. 'Nearer than Edinburgh as the crow flies,' he proclaimed, as if that would settle the matter. Only after she got there would Isabel be in a position to point out that crows were not required to spend hours trailing from carriage to Clyde steamer to train to Loch Lomond steamer, nor to rattle over country tracks that had no business being described as roads while feeling prodigiously sick, nor skirt puddles in enormous petticoats.

They were travelling as guests of the Corporation of Glasgow, genially led by the city's former Lord Provost, Robert Stewart. The Airds peered curiously at the portly figure who had led the waterworks campaign and been so monstrously demonised over the last few years that Isabel half expected a pair of cloven feet. Among their group were engineers and local landowners, a few pressmen, an aged kirk minister thin as paper and an extravagantly costumed piper.

Sailing up Loch Lomond, Isabel experienced a moment of anxiety when the smell of bacon assailed her over breakfast, but the waters were calm and the famous banks and braes as bonnie in the sunshine as ever poet claimed. The road between Loch Lomond and Loch Katrine tested everyone's breakfast, however. The coach had no sooner hauled them uphill from the Inversnaid pier than the horses were on a wild descent, surely out of control and – 'Isabel, will you stop that squealing!' – about to topple them into a peat bog. Even Alexander, whose complexion was bleached at the best of times, went pale. When the road straightened out a little, he began exclaiming at how empty and solemn the scenery was, and, look, could she see the peak of Ben Lomond behind them, clear against the sky? All Isabel could think of was making it to their journey's end with her buttered roll still roughly where it should be.

A glimmer of water appeared ahead. 'There you are,' Alexander shouted. 'Loch Katrine!'

It was all they saw of the burnished sheet of living gold. Although the water gleamed tantalisingly close for a while, they lurched to the right before reaching it and set off up (and down and up) a new-made works road. From the direction of the invisible Katrine a cheerful line of flags and banners could be seen descending towards the road through a knotted jumble of summer trees. There was more greenery on this one hill alone than Isabel had seen in her life, or had ever much wished to: Glasgow's Botanic Gardens had quite enough of it.

'A lot of grass, would you not say, Issy?' Alexander teased.

He was nervous, though. She noticed how he fingered his cravat and kept adjusting the brim of his hat. It reminded her that her husband had no idea what to expect today either.

The carriage swung to the right, bounced a little further and finally halted some way above what appeared to be a different loch, although little could be seen of it from here through the many trees. Alexander leaped out to assist her and Isabel glided down the step in full rigging. On reaching the ground she felt it yield damply beneath her feet. The tip of her parasol disappeared entirely and emerged stained with mud, its tiny bow arrangement flattened.

It was quickly apparent that the path they were invited to follow had been cut to accommodate the girths of stout men, possibly horses, maybe a wheelbarrow or two, but emphatically not a woman in an inflated lilac dress. Isabel swished through banks of weeds, briars snatching at her gown's expensively tailored panels. Alexander plunged into the undergrowth to lend an arm, but her ivory kid bootees slipped and scurried on stones shiny with last night's rain. The ponderously fruited bonnet was making her hot and its ribbon kept chafing the underside of her chin. With reckless disregard for the security of the silken strawberries Isabel untied the bow. Her cheeks flared with effort and rising irritation.

She was feeling unexpectedly exposed here. An eye-catching hat and dress were supposed to bolster her spirits, and in a Glasgow park with nice wide avenues and any growing things safely contained inside a glasshouse, they usually could. Isabel wondered sometimes if clothes were all that kept her afloat these days: a drowning woman clinging to fashion like a spar in a swirling flood. The choosing, the touching, the delicious changing of mind could absorb her for hours. She could while away a whole morning at the Arthur and Fraser's fabric counter, poring over folds and crinkles, animated by the feel of crisp linen or the floaty airiness of muslin. And after all there was not a handier subject for ladies' conversation, when required, than the aesthetic merits of a Bertha collar or a Mancheron sleeve – just as long as nobody expected Isabel Aird to sew one. There was even an ambivalent satisfaction, sweet and hollow as a cream puff, in showing off a waist that never took long to return to tight-corseted slenderness and looked so well in a crinoline.

But that was the city. Here the spar felt more precarious. Isabel clutched Alexander's arm and smouldered silently at him for having badgered her to accompany him where she did not belong.

The path curved around the hillside and deposited the stream of guests in front of a wide trench of exposed rock, above which the bunting straggled to a halt. Behind the trench an enormous cloth banner bearing the arms of Glasgow was being held steady by four leathery navvies, two to a pole, who beamed affably at the arriving gentry. Then began a modest ceremony to mark the start of what would one day be hailed, not so modestly, as the greatest engineering marvel since the construction of the aqueducts of Rome.

The flags, it was explained, marked the line on which the first shafts would be sunk to make a tunnel carrying water from Loch Katrine on the other side of the hill, around Loch Chon here and on to Glasgow. All by the force of gravity, declared the chief engineer, a Yorkshireman with exuberant facial hair by the name of Bateman. The water would descend at the rate of ten inches in every mile and the engineering challenges, which involved boring through nearly thirteen miles of hill and some of the hardest rock on earth, would be very *toof*. The antique minister then invoked divine blessing upon a great number of people involved in the scheme, including the citizens of Glasgow who were to benefit from it, and prayed that the workers might be protected from sickness, fatal injury or serious accident, which, quite unexpectedly, made Alexander's heart swell.

The former Lord Provost was fervently introduced as the saviour of Glasgow. Robert Stewart's dome of a forehead glistened as he described the works that would begin today as one of the greatest undertakings Great Britain had ever witnessed, and required further mopping when he touched on the insults and obloquy he had suffered for years from the many vested interests who had tried to stop it. Then he stepped forward with a cere- monial hammer and drill to strike the inaugural blow of the Glasgow waterworks, after which a pair of navvies set about pouring gunpowder into a line of holes already drilled in the rock.

'There's to be a salute to Her Majesty,' Alexander whispered, laying a hand on Isabel's arm. 'Stand back.'

The hillside exploded and they both missed a heartbeat. Shortly afterwards it exploded again. And again. The sky began to dim.

'You mean there are to be twenty-one of these?' Isabel yelled.

After the fifth explosion she had had enough. Skirts seized in one hand, muddy parasol in the other, she gestured to Alexander that she was leaving and stamped off down the hill. Public health? She could no more live here than eat the grass.

At the moment when Isabel noticed the bare-headed man among the trees, she was sitting on a tussock of grass judged free of insects and had just completed an inspection of the damage to her shoes. He fixed her with his fierce, hungry stare and was quickly gone. Then she saw something else. It was as if, she thought later, the man had whisked aside a curtain, or stepped away from a window, to reveal what she was actually meant to see. Framed by the copse where he had stood lay water: shining water glimpsed through trees.

Isabel's breath snagged again. When they arrived she had been facing the other way, up the hill towards the banner and the trench, towards the dignitaries in rhetorical flood. This was her first proper look at Loch Chon. The shore, she saw now, was lightly fringed by more trees, their spindly limbs silvery in the sun. Birches, she supposed. It was all she could have told you then about any kind of tree, that birches were silver. The smoke had not drifted as far as the loch, and the vaulting sky above it remained a peerless blue. On the surface of the water the trees on the far bank met their double. The lake was not still at all, she realised, but shimmered here and there, teasing the reflections. It felt quiet – *quiet!* she thought, as the gunpowder bellowed – and perhaps even a word like modest. She wrestled to pin the impression. Beside such unshowy beauty the earlier charms of Loch Lomond seemed almost gaudy, a touch too much ankle on display. There was a mind here, a soul, a heart, a spirit – what was it? – communing with hers in the oddest way. It's only sun on water, she told herself. A few gangly shrubs. There will be smoke along any minute. But still her chest ached with the loveliness of it, the intimacy, the wonder, the solace. It was a joyful, muscular ache, and she had no idea what to do with it. The Botanic Gardens had not had this effect at all.

In a cool corner of her mind Isabel did understand that this idyll was set to become an industrial wasteland. The signs were there already: bald, brown patches sprouting iron on the far hill, timber construction nearer the shore, and these explosions of course, ripping through your head so shockingly that all any sensible person could think of was escape. Isabel recognised all this well enough, yet still the water drew her. Hauling swathes of dress and petticoat into a standing position again, she abandoned the parasol and teetered further down the slope. The fragrance of bluebells reached her next. The tang of pine hung in the air. She filled her senses with comfort.

Comfort. Could it be that she had lived so long with her body in turmoil, preparing itself over and over for new life and then expelling it before the child ever had time to be ready, that she had forgotten what comfort felt like? Certainly nothing else in the routines of her life supplied it. Not reading, which she liked; nor paying morning calls to admire the charms of other ladies' infants, which she certainly did not. Not practising on the pianoforte, for which she had as little flair as cousin Josephine; nor embroidery, which bored her even more than having to calculate the butter order and discuss with Cook how much flour would be required this week. Fashion pleased and clothes fortified, but they could not comfort. Not even the wordless refuge of Alexander's arms provided consolation, and nowadays she seldom sought it there. Last time she had barely even wept, merely turning away as Annie cleared up the mess.

Turn away. Avert your eyes. Close your mind. Linen or lace. There is no other way.

Now there was life growing again. It was only weeks started, and there was no telling how long it would last. Isabel had trained herself not to hope and steeled herself not to care, which is to say she was no longer in the habit of feeling very much about anything. Yet here she was, stunned by a glimpse of water.

As the piper on the hill behind launched into a catchy reel to mark the end of the ceremony, Isabel's spirits soared as they had not for years. What in the world was happening to her? Was it too ridiculous to believe that this place was at some inscrutable level beyond thought itself actually calling her?

Yes, it was ridiculous.

Most definitely.

And yet.

She eyed the pulled threads on her dress. Might the solace of still water, this overpowering offer of comfort, count for more than ruined clothes? Might it be possible to get used to mud and knee-high grass? She had become used to worse in life and Annie was good with a brush. Social opportunities in these parts would be limited, yes, but – be honest, Isabel – would that not come as a relief? And after all were some kinds of loneliness, her kind of loneliness, not the same anywhere?

Afterwards Isabel could not put her finger on a moment of decision, recalling only the rush of questions and the sensation of hopefulness that followed, new and astounding and intoxicating as the scent of the bluebells. She carried it with her as she turned from the water and began ploughing inelegantly back up the slope.

8

'Tis thin, this place of water and stone and tree.

Here meet north and south, Highland and Lowland, Gael and Scot. Here are mountains made too trim for awe; burns that idle over-prettily, the maist o' them, for the making of grand waterfalls; lochs rendered so gay by silver-green woodland that a man could forget – aye, and a woman too, my lady of the billowing dress – the depth of their blackness.

The most profound separation in all existence is at its most thin here as well. Perilously thin. This have I also discovered.

And so will she.

9

Having armed himself for debate, persuasion, inducement and *in extremis* an improbable plan to cajole his mother-in-law to join them, Alexander was relieved to be informed that Isabel had decided in the space of about five seconds that she liked the place.

Well, obviously he was relieved. He was also sceptical. The slightly giddy mood in which his wife rejoined the group at the end of the ceremony was so unlike her that he spent the journey home sneaking worried glances in her direction. There was a glitter in her eye that he found vaguely alarming. Alexander wondered if being instantaneously charmed by a place might be a symptom of pregnancy the medical books had missed, or whether it was merely the latest of the bewildering moods he blamed for grinding down their marriage.

In the steamer he resorted to biting his nails to check if it would still annoy her. Which – not that he could work out whether this should be celebrated or not – it did. He kept asking if she was sure.

'I thought you wanted me to come, Alex.'

'I did. Do. I'm only worried that you agreed so quickly, on the strength, as far as I can gather, of a few ripples on a loch on a sunny day.'

Since this was exactly what had happened, Isabel was hard put to answer. How do you explain to someone else what you cannot explain to yourself?

Her mother was no help.

'Mark my words, Isabel, you will last a week. What will you *do* with yourself on a building site, surrounded by uncouth men and mud and . . . and' – Mrs Gillies cast about for a suitably rural horror – 'nettles. And I imagine you know there will be no *facilities*?'

Which had not occurred to Isabel: surely they had water closets in the Highlands?

'And you are so often indisposed. What will you do miles from civilisation if anything should go wrong again?'

'Mother,' Isabel said wearily, 'I'm married to a doctor.'

Over the next few weeks she supervised the packing of her more serviceable gowns and went to some trouble to assure a reluctant Annie of courtship possibilities among what was sure to be a host of brawny navvies. She read *The Lady of the Lake* again from cover to cover, twice, until she could almost smell the eglantine embalming the air and see the warrior oaks anchored in the rifted rock of the Trossachs.

It was pleasant to have something to look forward to. Alex had been right, she told herself: it would be an adventure. When had she last had the taste for one of those? When had she ever, come to that, had the opportunity?

10

In London once I ate a pudding made of bread soaked in finest Canary sack. It had cream in it, and eggs and nutmeg and sugar. I ate and ate till I vomited it up. Then I wanted more.

What are ye trying to say, Robert Kirke?

That faery sickened me.

You are thinking more than that, Robert Kirke.

II

The pair o' them moved into a very nice stone house not far from the loch. I was about to get all too familiar with that house myself, though I didna know it the day I saw a horse and carriage come clip-clopping along the works road and this pale-looking lady float out, the way they do, and stare around as if she maybe had to remind herself what she was doing here. We were well into the summer of '56 by then, but the wind was having a right good wintry moan to itself and it was spitting rain in that half-hearted way that makes you wish it would just get on and soak you and have done with it, and the funny-looking hill behind was looming over the house in what to my way o' thinking was an awful eerie way. Well, you can smile all you like. I don't like to see a hill that's round as a ball and too perfect by half. We all know what it means, which is likely why the folk in these parts called it Fairy Knoll.

To my mind, you'd need to be away wi' the fairies yourself to build a house so close to a mound like that. I mean you could practically bid good-evening to the *sìthichean* trooping past your back windows. But there you are: I don't suppose the incomers that built it knew any better. The rest of us were living further along the road in a camp that sort o' straggled along the shore

36

and up the slopes behind. Some wag that was not long back from blowing up Russians in the Crimea called it Sebastopol. I suppose the explosions put him in mind of it. Anyway the name stuck.

If you want to see what that place was like in your mind's eye, you've got to imagine Loch Chon in the middle of everything. Pretty in places yet, where there were still trees bending over it, and further away you had the bog cotton rippling on the moor and the broom still flowering where it could. There were burns all over the place, and the way they would come haring down the sides o' these hills around the loch, and the bubble and gush o' them, fair put me in mind of home sometimes, though James said they were going to be nothing but trouble to bridge when the time came. Loch Katrine, where the water was to come from, was over the other side o' the ridge that went up behind the house where the Airds were staying, and there were, oh, five or six hundred men it must have been by the time it got going properly, out there day and night to make a tunnel from the one loch through the ridge and right the way round the other. There were likely thousands more folk working beyond that on the sections further south, but I never saw any o' that. Thinking back it was a bonnier place than many I've stayed in, but it was fast becoming as big a mess o' mud and iron as any building site the country over, and I've been in a few of those in my time, I can tell you.

You'll likely want to know how those of us were living that didna have big stone houses to bide in. A navvy that had left wrote to the newspapers to tell how the workers lived. Said we stayed in caves, so I heard, and how disgraceful it was. Well, he maybe had a point: nobody's saying it was Buckingham Palace (which James saw once, by the way – he said the streets around stank to high heaven). But what yon navvy maybe wouldna ha' known – I never heard where he came from himself – is how our people lived before. The wee bit o' stone and turf James and I had on the isle of Mull was a hovel itself, if you're minded to use the kind o' language this fellow did, though it was a home for all that, and it was the piece of earth that tied our hearts to each other and to all the generations that went before.

When we got to Loch Chon we found the navvies up from Yorkshire had bagged the wooden huts lower down the hill. I wouldna ha' wanted one o' them anyway, to be truthful with you. Bunk beds three or more high all round the walls and up to the rafters, two men to a bed, or a man and his wife and bairns if he'd a family, all wheeched in together with a place for a fire in the middle and frying pans in a circle around it. Yon navvy wrote that folk were packed in worse than an emigrant ship. Anyway, navvies are clannish and we're better keeping ourselves to ourselves – Highlanders, Lowlanders, Irish, English folk – since there's aye fighting when the men are in their cups. Rough lot, most o' them. The Irish are the worst, I can tell you. The stramash on pay night! So I preferred to be that bit apart wi' my own kind further up the hill.

I'm not saying it was exactly perfect, especially before we got a window in, but we had a roof over our heads and it kept the worst o' the rain out, so that was fine. James dug it from the hill so that the back and side walls were ready made, if you can imagine it, just needing some heather for lining, and he made a front wall in no time from the turf that was dug out. Then all he had to do was buy a few planks and spars from the contractor for a door and some rafters to keep the whole thing from falling on top of us. Which it nearly did a few times. We got a brick or two for a chimney and an old powder firkin for the can on top, and it was cosy enough with some wood on the fire. No shortage of wood in those parts, I'll say that, though I had a hankering now and then for the smell o' peat. But when winter came round not even a smoored fire in the night would stop the cold eating into your bones till you thought you would die, and your heart was pounding in your chest if there was a bairn hard to waken in the morn. Och, but there were times on Mull when you woke wi' your eyelids frozen too, and at least the navvying gave us a payslip and there was food to be bought with it from those crooks at the site store that charged too much because we had nowhere else to go, but still . . . we ate, and eating was something you didna always get to do at home. I still remind myself of that when I think o' the blackbird singing its heart out in the morn or the lapwing tumbling about our island sky like a mad thing. Funny how it's always summer when you think back, and your stomach's aye full.

Anyway, James would ha' told you navvying is not the life for a family man. You never met James, did ye? Not properly anyway. But when the landowner decides he can earn more from breeding wool for the cities than collecting rent from island crofters that can't pay it most o' the time anyway, where's your choice? If you don't leave, they'll take away your cow and starve you out. James reckoned it was either the Tobermory workhouse for us, a ship to the other side o' the world, or trailing to Glasgow and beyond to seek navvying work. He was strong and could put his hand to anything, so that's what he did.

He went for the railways first – no shortage o' work building those in the fifties. That's where he learned earthwork, embanking, boring and the like. I always say you won't find an engineer or contractor who knows more about soils and rocks than my James did, and the number of blasts it'll take to split the rock and how much water this bit of earth or that will hold. Nor one who'll work sixteen hours wi' less complaint, day or night.

Then James heard they were paying for navvies to go and build roads in the Crimea, so off he went to London to sign up. Came back a hero, everyone saying the navvies had won the war for them. Forty miles o' railway track they built from the port at Balaclava to the camp at Sebastopol in six months. James said those navvies did more work in a day than yon British regiments managed in a week. The bairns and I near enough starved when he was away, mind. Stayed wi' my sister's lot and another family in a room in Glasgow that was more like a dungeon. I was never so glad to see the sky again when he came home wi' money and we got back on the road.

When he heard there was tunnelling work starting in the Trossachs we got ourselves there in the boat, walked over from Inversnaid and James signed on right away. They were needing boys to run messages as well, taking sharpened drills and the like from the smithy to the shaft heads, so that was half the family in work.

And there you go, I've worked my way round to the day Isabel Aird turned up outside my house, which is what you'll really be wanting to know about if I'm right. Ach, I'm an awful blether. Why don't you give the fire a wee poke for me and I'll tell you how we met.

12

The lady is come back.
They told me she would.

13

Fresh from her dousing in *The Lady of the Lake*, Isabel was delighted to discover that the giant mound next to the house Alexander had rented went by a local name that could itself have been plucked from Scott's pages. She declared it a perfect name for the house too, and Fairy Knoll the dwelling instantly became, although there was nothing remotely enchanting about living in it. The gabled stone cottage was cold. Velvet curtains – ordered and sent on by her mother in response to an urgent letter – took weeks to arrive from Glasgow. Fires in the main rooms banished neither damp nor creeping draughts, and the winds banging rain against the windows at night made it necessary to huddle closer to Alexander than had been her habit of late.

As the works grew around them, he threw himself into setting broken limbs and binding mangled flesh, returning home weary but exhilarated by the medical challenges of a construction site with enough risks to last any doctor a lifetime. There was disease to treat as well. Typhus, flourishing in the shared beds and unwashed clothes of the navvies in their overcrowded, noisome huts, was a greater challenge than any broken arm.

Isabel envied him his exhilaration. With nothing to do, she

spent the summer missing the daily routines of excruciating dullness that had at least given her life in Glasgow a focus. She indulged fond thoughts of elegant ceilings, raucous streets, cobbles underfoot, the rustle of taffeta, fresh provisions and largely interesting meals. She even missed her mother, who would have been appalled to learn that nettles were the least of the sensory hazards facing a daughter brought up at a civilised distance from the living quarters of the lower classes. The untidy cluster of whitewashed, turf-roofed wooden dormitories was only a few minutes' walk along the rough works track that led past the loch from Fairy Knoll. The smell of frying meat and outdoor toileting was a shock for which Sir Walter Scott had not been in a position to prepare his readers.

Above the shore were the burrows that the Highlanders and the Irish called home. As Isabel was aghast to discover on the day she set out to explore the slopes and happened upon a ruddy-faced navvy's wife sunning herself outside one of them, these dwellings were dug into the very hillside itself. The most presentable home in the camp belonged to the young minister, whose wooden house expanded by dint of judicious partitioning into a schoolroom and reading room and on Sundays transformed, like water into wine, into a church. Every time she passed the place she learned to call Sebastopol, Isabel felt like sinking to her knees with gratitude that the doctor was not required to live there too.

But the Fairy Knoll house itself was too close to the tunnelling works to escape either the sights or the noise. The hills rang all day with gunpowder blasts and the screech of machines. Along the projected line of the tunnel an alpine range of excavated rock began to rise in a muddle of hills and indentations, as the land itself was formed anew before her eyes. Men and horses crawled over the scabrous slopes like flies. In the waters of the loch horse gins and great turning wheels shimmered where there had once been only trees. And sometimes there was carried from the lochside camp the howls of the mastiffs chained inside the huts of the English navvies in readiness for the next prize-fight, the distant echoes of their keening carried far and wide on a darkling wind.

Now and then a terrible cry would reach as far as Fairy Knoll. Isabel wondered then if Alexander would come home that day morose with failure or, since it could go either way, talking too fast, eyes flashing, elated that he had got there in time, had stopped the bleeding, cauterised the wound; or it might be that he had sawed a couple of fingers off, this being the only way to save the poor fellow's hand, Issy, but it worked, it worked, and if only there was no infection he might recover yet. And Isabel would try to be glad for him or sad for him as the occasion demanded. But mostly she was sad for herself because she could think of nothing to say in return, had nothing to offer before the parlour fire except to mention that she had found an intact clump of meadowsweet – 'You know, Alex, those frothy white blossoms like wool caught on a spike' – and had realised at last what the fragrance reminded her of. She had been puzzling it over, wondered about honey, but, no, it was marzipan. And he would try to look interested, though he was not really and she knew he was not, and he would have teased her for even knowing the name of a wild flower if she had not been looking daggers at him, daring him to mock.

The truth was that she was waiting for another child to leave her, and trying not to think about it, and finding it harder in this place to stop herself feeling it, because although her life in Glasgow had been so very unsatisfying, there were social rituals there to keep feelings at bay and clothes to play with. She might have told him that. Whereas here she was feeling all the time – couldn't help it: curiosity and disgust and wonder and loneliness and comfort – oh, all sorts of things, Alex; and through it all dread, a growing knot of it in her stomach that she thought had been left behind two pregnancies ago. Another day passed, Alex, she might have said. And if she had, she might have learned that he was counting the days himself.

As the works took shape, it was not only the acute medical challenges awaiting his attention that drove Alexander to the saddle every morning, but a powerful sense of why he was here. Guiding his pony through the foul clutter of Sebastopol or along the stony lochside paths to the latest accident, he liked to picture this industrial stage to himself as the setting for a great drama in which the villain cholera would receive its comeuppance in the last scene. Alexander had no heroic illusions about his own role. He was a spear-carrier, no more, or at most the decent physician in Shakespeare's *Cymbeline* who advances the plot by preparing a sleeping potion instead of poison. At any rate he was someone with a modest part to play in an enterprise far greater than himself.

Cholera had entered the country for the first time as an epidemic in 1832, wreaking panic and death the length and breadth of Britain. In 1848 Alexander had seen another one at close hand himself as a student doctor: nigh on four thousand deaths in Glasgow that time, mainly in the poorer areas honeycombed with subdivided tenement houses which relied on polluted water from public wells. Five years later the city succumbed again. He had watched patients dehydrate with terrifying rapidity, seen floors and beds soaked with diarrhoea as clear and thin as rice-water, listened to screams of agony as the abdomen cramped. On those who received any medical attention at all he had tried the usual hopeless treatments – bleeding, burning – resorting in the end to merciful opiates. When water began to be implicated and a fresh public supply from the Highlands was eventually mooted, Alexander became gripped by the hopes and the arguments filling the tight-printed columns of the *Glasgow Herald* day after day.

His wife was at the time gripped by the loss of their first baby. Fully formed at six months gestation, gone from her in three hours. Medical treatment had been useless there too.

Neither one of them was aware – and indeed only in hindsight could it be seen – that Alexander's rising interest in the waterworks project coincided with the withdrawal of Isabel's interest in almost anything at all. By the time William Macquorn Rankine had submitted a detailed proposal to the council for a public water scheme controversially funded by ratepayers, Isabel had already miscarried a second time, at a late stage again, and the news passed her by. She was grieving. She wanted Alexander to grieve with her.

There was a third child stillborn not long after the Corporation of Glasgow appointed Halifax-born John Frederic Bateman, fresh from designing a water scheme for Manchester, to survey different lochs and possible routes for a tunnel. A fourth pregnancy ended in the August of 1853, just three days before Bateman presented his conclusion that Loch Katrine was the best long-term solution for Glasgow. Alexander thought it wiser not to mention at home how excited, how hopeful, how seized of new possibilities this made him feel.

Sometimes he found it hard to recall that theirs had been a marriage founded on easy conversation and a teasing respect for one another. They fitted, Isabel had said to him early on as they slipped towards sleep with his lips in her hair and his long legs wrapped around hers. She had even confessed to being pleasantly surprised that the business of making children should be so much less trying than her mother had led her to believe. Within the bedroom or without, he knew how to make her laugh. He had been sure-footed in bantering away the irritations and dissatisfactions of a constrained life without making too light of the intelligence that lay fallow between them. He had always loved the hint of gravitas in that hazel eye, and the frown where her eyebrows met, which could give her face a resting air of sulkiness but usually meant – used to mean – that she was thinking. These days the sulk was sometimes all he registered.

A fifth pregnancy was gamely flickering into life in December 1853, when the council, undaunted by vigorous opposition from testy ratepayers and private water companies, endorsed the wording of a proposed bill to Parliament. As a Westminster committee convened the following March, Isabel was still pregnant. There were arguments (inconclusive) about the effects of lead. There were objections from the Admiralty that the scheme would silt up naval anchorages on the River Forth. Alexander pored over the newspapers and Isabel stared out of the window. Lord Provost Stewart rallied opposing opinion, but the bill ran out of time. So, not long afterwards, did the pregnancy.

Next year Mr Stewart tried again. On 16 November 1854, the

Faculty of Physicians and Surgeons in Glasgow declared itself ready to endorse publicly the link between foul water and cholera, and offered to mount its own supportive petition to Parliament. On hearing the news Alexander could not restrain himself from tossing his hat in the air on his way along Bath Street. Isabel would remember it as the day she found blood in her underwear again.

On 2 July 1855 the Glasgow Corporation Water Works Act received the royal assent from the Queen. Isabel was pregnant for a seventh time that July, although not for many weeks longer.

Now, a year later, there was construction under way and another life in the making. Alexander bandaged and treated, rode and walked, worried about infection and collapsed exhausted into his bed at night. Isabel waited.

The works never rested. When darkness swallowed the loch, everywhere else woke up and the sky blazed orange with watch-fires. Paraffin lamps capered over the pitted surface of the earth like fairy revels. Smoke swirled across the face of the moon, under which the silhouettes of man and beast toiled on. Isabel could watch the drama from her bedroom window. Sometimes the night-workers' songs drifted into her sleep and joined the unceasing thuds in some fitful dream. Waking, she would ask herself what had possessed her to follow Alexander Aird into hell.

Only, she knew. Just as he did, Isabel always knew why she was here and why she stayed. Along the shore beyond Sebastopol there were still trees. While summer lasted, the foliage made a kind of curtain to frame the loch as she had first glimpsed it that May morning. Here she found herself able to lay her small ghosts to rest and claim the promised comfort. Sometimes she saw them in the haze on the water, and would count them, one to seven. There's Johnnie, she would think, and here comes Sarah, named for her mother though she never told her. After those two there had been no more names. Sometimes the children could be found budding from a young tree or blethering to one another in the burn's rush. They were not phantoms, these lost children. They had no shape but the thing itself: the heat shimmer of a July afternoon, the blossom on the hawthorn bough. Later on she would find them in the snow's dimple and those sticky springtime leaves she would never have guessed could bring such delight.

It gave Isabel a peaceful feeling to see her children, even as she agonised over whether they were alive or dead and waited for another to join them. Could you be dead if you had never been alive? Might you still be alive if you had never been dead? Sebastopol's Reverend Clark, while eloquent on the subject of heaven's many mansions, had never mentioned the dead being all about us, nor suggested even the vaguest possibility that babies who had never taken breath and could not be christened might even now be chasing each other in the lush grass.

Only after she met Kirsty McEchern, the big-boned navvy's wife with a raw, red face and more children than she could lay hands on at once, would Isabel learn of another way of experiencing that chimed with her own.

'Ach, mistress,' Kirsty said comfortably when Isabel had nerved herself to explain, 'I'll tell ye what any Highlander would. It's no' always so obvious who's the more alive – those of us who're living (or what passes for it in some places), or those who've been this way once and are about us still. If you ask me there's never as much difference as folk think.'

Listening to the navvy's wife, Isabel could almost persuade herself that enjoying the company of your children in a downy leaf was the most natural thing in the world. She was not quite six months gone with the next one.

14

So here's how we met. I'd put some clean rushes on the floor and was thinking I would cook up a bit o' meat for the dinner. James used to come home awful hungry. Oatmeal fills your stomach nicely and you could get a turnip easy enough, but sometimes we were able to afford some mutton or beef from the store to boil up over the fire and those were fine days, I can tell you. But when I was out dumping the old grass I thought I might just sit in the warm for a while. It was one o' these summer days when there's not a cloud in the sky – just a bit wispy wi' the gunpowder maybe – and the sun on your face puts you in mind of a wee nap. The boys were at work and I had a girl at the school the minister chappie had started. The rest were running around somewhere.

I sat down on a scrap o' grass outside. There was hardly a thing to be seen o' the green slope it was before – not with all those shelters cut higgledy-piggledy into the hillside and everything trampled. I suppose there will have been some blasting going on, but it's funny how you stopped noticing that.

I must ha' nodded off right enough, because I opened my eyes to find this lady looking at me. She was the one I'd seen getting down at the fancy house not so long back, but you always know a lady anyway, even when she's got mud on her dress and her hair half out her cap. Something about the way they look at you as if you're an insect, or an interesting variety of potato. Don't you be laughing – it's true. This one did seem pleased enough with her inspection, though.

'I had no idea there were women living up here,' says she, peching from the climb. She put a hand to her hair as if to tidy it, and gave her dress a wee pat, then shrugged as if it wasn't worth the bother or I wasn't, one or the other.

When I said nothing, being just as surprised to see her and if you can imagine it a wee thing tongue-tied, she said, 'You'll have to excuse the mess of me. I don't bother much, living out here.'

Which I dare say I could have taken amiss, her being in a nice lacy cap and the prettiest dress I'd seen up close in all my days and me . . . well, ye can imagine what I looked like. But och, I could see she didna mean any harm by it.

She had the kind of accent you'll hear in the posher parts of Glasgow, meaning no discourtesy, of course, since you've got one yourself and I've no doubt it's easier on the ear than my own mongrel speak. Her hair – nice rusty-brown colour it was in those days – had escaped its coils at one ear, which gave her a bedraggled look right enough, though who was I to think it that last took a comb to my hair the day I was wed. Her cheeks were sore flushed from the climb. I remember thinking that wi' her costly blue dress and that rosy face on her she looked like a lost butterfly that had landed in the wrong bush. She had a bairn on the way, too, if I was any judge. Which it turned out I was.

I could tell she was taking it all in – the smoke dribbling from the chimney can, the dark inside, the door nailed together all rough, with a nice, fresh branch o' rowan fastened above to keep the *sìthichean* from bothering us. She put a little white hand to her mouth, and I couldn't say if it was disgust she felt exactly, or if she was just taken aback. The smell might not have been all that pleasant either, come to think of it, wi' the midden so close. I suppose she would be thinking that if her own house was not up to Glasgow standards, it was at least nothing to this. Hers was better than even the minister cobbled together in Sebastopol by a long way.

'Are you . . . comfortable here?' she asked then, a bit hesitant, as if she was choosing her words.

'Och,' says I, 'it's fine,' says I. 'We'll see what like the winter is, but I've known worse. And you'll no' be finding a house up here that's cleaner.' I always did like to keep a place swept, though it was a struggle, and there were many that gave up. 'What brings a gentlewoman like yourself to a place like this?'

'I'm the doctor's wife.' She said it in an offhand way, with a shrug.

'I'll warrant he keeps busy here?' I said, to be polite.

'He does indeed. We were hardly here a week when he had his first leg to set and a man's hand blown clean off. And there's disease in the camp already.'

'It's aye the same. So many living close together, bringing their ills from all over. Will you take a cup o' tea?'

She shook her head faster than was maybe altogether mannerly. 'I must get back,' she says. 'I've wandered far enough already today and Alex will scold me. He thinks I should be resting all the time.'

'I'll say *chì mi a-rithist thu* then,' says I, and was about to shut my eyes again when I saw that instead of leaving she had stooped nearer.

'You speak Gaelic?'

'Aye, mistress, I've been on the road so long I'm handy wi' Scots, English, a bit of everything, but Gaelic's where I started. I was only bidding you farewell.'

'I was just wondering,' says she. 'Someone told me this water is the Dog Loch.'

'Aye, that's so. *Loch a'Chon*, we call it in the Gaelic. Loch o' the Dogs, the Dog Loch – whatever takes your fancy.'

'Do you know why it's called that?'

She turned to look back down the slope as she spoke. I mind the water that day was looking quite cheery.

'I know a lot o' stories,' says I. 'You come back some day and I'll tell you. That one's no' so pleasant, though – it's about a dead bairn.'

At that she whipped back to face me where I was sitting looking up at her from my wee bit grass. She had a fiery light in her eyes for a moment. Then it just faded away and, 'You're right,' she says. 'Another time.'

Many's the time Isabel Aird dropped by after that. It was clear to me she didna have a thing else to do. She never had a lot to say for herself, but by and by she did tell me about losing a wheen o' babes in the years before she came to Loch Chon. Well, it's a trial for a woman to have children, and I'd ha' been glad of a bit more say in the matter myself, but I dare say it's as sore a trial not to if your heart is set on it. Maybe it's what made her more open to those other things I was mentioning, the *sìthichean* and suchlike – I'm never happy calling them fairies, which has an awful tame ring to it in English – albeit she had no idea how to handle any o' that.

She had a sad, distant air about her most times, but something about the place seemed to make her more peaceful. She said to me that she kept seeing her lost babes as she walked around, so maybe that was it. Said she would talk to them and maybe scold them for this or that or sing them a wee song as the light went down and the birds stilled their blether. I mind how she had to work herself up to tell me about that, as if there was a shame in her seeing what's there for the looking. I wouldna be surprised if she never let another soul know about it – and maybe it's not right I should be telling ye now, not even after all this time. But there, I've said it. It made sense to me, as I told her straight off. The water and the trees comforted her – that was the main thing. And, poor woman, she was aye looking for comfort.

15

Only a couple of miles in length and not so much as five hundred yards across, the Dog Loch lay within a bowl of wooded hills. Shafts were already being sunk along the slopes on the southern bank, marked by thunderous explosions that sent up plumes of smoke to be carried wherever the wind chose. But on this side there remained slender stony beaches, tree-girt oases where the loch could still enfold Isabel in its charms.

It was on one of these beaches that Isabel was idling, counting explosions to divert herself from the insistently cheerful flutterings beneath her dress, when there came from behind the sound of feet on shingle. She swung around to see a man approaching, arm stretched towards her, palm outwards, as if in entreaty or perhaps to forestall retreat. Isabel recognised him as the figure who had made a fleeting appearance on the day of the ceremony, who had seemed to draw open the curtain on her first view of Loch Chon.

Plainly encouraged that she did not shrink away, he came to a halt before her. With no cap to remove nor a gentleman's hat to doff, he hovered there, twisting his hands.

'Good afternoon,' she said pleasantly.

He was tall, this man, and so tremendously thin that he made her think of a heron, hovering like that, not exactly on one leg but poised all the same and absolutely alert, gazing without a blink. Weeks earlier she would have struggled to name a starling, so Isabel was glad to know about herons and thought she might ask Kirsty if you could get black ones.

'Good afternoon. I hope I have not startled ye.'

If anything did startle her, it was his voice, too rich and deep for the weedy frame, too assured for those nervous hands, which continued to twist and rub. He spoke in a plain Scots brogue, beautifully modulated and mellifluous.

'You have not,' Isabel said, relaxing. She was becoming used to being addressed by workmen of every demeanour and degree of civility, and managed most encounters with more aplomb than the stiff social gatherings she was in the habit of avoiding in town. Yet this man did not carry himself like a social inferior, despite the disreputable coat and knee-breeches, which were shiny with wear and very much soiled. About his neck he wore a grimy cravat of sorts, which might once have been white.

'I believe,' she added for politeness, 'that I saw you not far from here once before?'

'Aye, that would be richt,' he said in that slow, rolling voice. 'I am glad to find ye so well and blooming.'

Even for Sebastopol manners this was excessively forward. She drew back frostily. 'I don't believe we've been introduced, Mr . . .'

'Kirke. Robert Kirke. Forgive me, madam. I forget my manners.'

She did not offer her hand. 'I am Mrs Aird. Isabel Aird.'

At that the man's jaw tightened. He swept over her a gaze so fierce and yet so oddly tender – this she registered with surprise and a frisson of alarm – that she took another step backwards and began after all to consider a means of retreat.

'Isabel,' he said softly.

There was no one else at hand. She was so far along the shore that no cry for help would ever be heard in the camp.

The man seemed to remember himself and offered a faint smile. 'Pardon, madam. 'Tis a bonnie name. I meant nothing more.'

Isabel melted a fraction. Compliments were thin on the ground in these parts.

'It comes from the Hebrew. Perhaps you knew this? It means pledged to God.'

'Does it?' She glowed. Pledged to God.

'Do you live nearby?' she asked, mesmerised by the strangeness of this man who spoke with such directness and said he liked her name, whose long fingers fidgeted restlessly but whose eyes did not once move from hers, who looked like a tramp but had the self-assurance of an educated man: at any rate he seemed to know his Hebrew. She wondered how old he was. For all his antique air and clothing, his hair and beard were only lightly touched with grey and he neither spoke nor moved like an aged man.

'I stay hereabouts,' he said. 'I grew up in the parish of Kirkton by Aberfoyle – not lang from here if you know the paths.'

'I can't say I've ventured that far. Well, it's been a pleasure to meet you, Mr Kirke, but I fear if I delay longer I shall be missed at home.'

'Perhaps ye would let me gang with you?' He offered her a grubby arm. 'There are many iron impediments about and I have stumbled myself. I would have ye safe, madam.'

The faint tingling of alarm returned. Isabel felt pressing on her some need of his, some assumed connection that made her wish of a sudden to be gone. 'Thank you, but I know my way home.'

'Of course,' he said, and stood aside.

As she moved past him, Isabel caught the faint whiff of an odour about the man's person that, while not wholly unpleasant, struck her as obscurely strange. It was only as she was hurrying home that she realised it was the smell of autumn, which in early August had not yet arrived.

16

Isabel.

Her name, o heart, is Isabel.

17

When she told me she had met this Robert Kirke character, an awful funny feeling came over me. Honest to God. I'm not saying I recognised the name or knew one single thing about him, because I didna. If I'd really known I'd maybe ha' said something and who can tell what heartache might ha' been turned from our path. So I'm not talking about the clever thinking you're so good at. But there are other kinds o' knowing come to those that are open to it, and that's more the thing I'm meaning.

We were in her kitchen at the time, I mind. I was on my knees with a scrubbing brush, which is where I spent half my time at Fairy Knoll. She'd got me helping out at the house by then. Told me she couldna get the staff out there and her serving-girl was aye complaining about how much work she had to do. Mind you, I had the idea that Mrs Aird was as pleased to hear me talk as clean her floors. She always said it made a nice change from gloves. She liked to hear about the jobs James had been on before and where we'd come from first, though it was news to her that folk had been starved out their homes by blight and famine or served notice by the factor to make room for sheep. 'Have ye never wondered why Glasgow is so full o' Highlanders?' says I. Turns out she hadna noticed.

Anyway, this time she pipes up suddenly, 'There's a man walks about here. Very well spoken. Dresses in black. He doesn't look like a navvy. Have you ever noticed such a one?'

'Would it be Mr Bateman, the engineer? He's round here a fair bit. Enough whiskers on his cheek to stuff a pillow. Speaks funny?'

She shook her head. 'No, this man looks more like a tatty minister.'

'Och, that will be the Reverend Clark.'

She smiled then, and suited it. That smile o' hers was slow in arriving, but when it came it cleared her brow and freed up her whole face. She was pleasant to look at, Mrs Aird, I'll say that – and kind enough, too, when you got talking to her – but she was inclined to come over a bit tight.

'Mr Clark is most certainly not tatty,' she says. 'He would die to think it. No, the man I have in mind is a Mr Robert Kirke.'

And that's when I got this feeling.

'No,' says I out loud, 'I can't say I've heard that name before.'

So why, I'm saying to myself, have I got this wee quick shivery thing running up and down my bare arms to hear that Robert Kirke is walking? If I'd grown up thereabouts I'd likely ha' known right away what it meant, but I was as much an incomer as she was.

'I hope, mistress,' says I then, taking a bit of a risk because no matter how well she seemed to like my company she could get uppity if I forgot my place, 'I hope,' says I, 'that you keep yourself safe when you're out and about.'

She was halfway out the door by then, but she took a step back into the kitchen and stared at me. 'Safe? What do you mean by that, Kirsty?'

'Och,' says I, light as feather, 'I just mean you can never be too careful wi' these characters ye meet around the place. Ye never know what they might be after.'

She bristled a bit at that. 'Thank you, Kirsty. If I happen on Mr Kirke again I'll be sure to request his credentials for you.'

And with that she swung on her heel and was off.

Well, that was me told. I got to my feet, picked up the pail and went to throw the dregs out the back door. And I'll tell you this for nothing, I was glad to see the sun.

What happened next put Robert Kirke right out my head. And hers too, I'm sure I'd be right in saying. Before August was out Dr Aird came rushing through the camp looking for me. His face was so pale the freckles jumped right out at you and his voice was all tense.

'My wife asks that you come to her, Kirsty,' he says. 'She's in labour.'

I was glad she'd asked for me. Nothing wrong wi' having your very own medical man to hand, I dare say, but a woman likes to have a woman around at these times and it warmed my heart that Mrs Aird trusted me to know what I was about when it came to delivering bairns. Not that there was much delivering to be done by either him or me, as it turned out.

Though I'd never liked to ask just how far gone she was wi' this bairn, I knew as soon as I saw the doctor's face that it was too early. I followed him back to the master bedroom at Fairy Knoll, my heart thumping away inside me, and there she was on the bed looking awful peely-wally and the only way I can describe it is out of herself. That's what I remember the most

– this sense coming from her that it was all happening to some-body else.

When I went over and asked leave to touch her belly I could feel ripples under the skin. And that was the sadness of it: the mite was still doing fine in there. Trouble is, her body couldna hold on to it, which was aye her problem. Here she was again, having to push this bairn out that she wanted sae badly to hold safe inside.

Soon her waters started to seep away and after that the move-ments just died. As I say, it's a sad thing to watch, even when you've seen a few births go wrong in your time.

When the bairn came, Mrs Aird turned her face to the wall and refused to look at it. Neither then nor after did I see her weep a single tear.

But I mind to this day how her husband stood still as a post looking down at the wee lifeless thing. It fitted right inside his palm, the head not much bigger than a fair-sized conker. Everything formed just right, though. Just perfect. A wee lassie it was. The doctor's face was that grim when he looked at it, stern and closed but sort of anguished at the same time. I didna know where to put myself, if I'm honest wi' you. So I just got started on the cleaning up and nobody said a thing.

By and by the doctor asked if I could find something to cover the child in. I took it from him and wrapped it in a napkin. He leaned over the bed and made to stroke his wife's head, but she kept it turned from him. His hand hovered there a while, and then he took it away.

Just before sunrise next day I buried the wee thing under a rowan tree near the house. Mrs Aird had no idea how a stillborn's soul could be rescued for heaven, but I thought it would be nice to tell her that I'd kept her bairn safe from wandering homeless among the stars. She thanked me for that. Said it was the first grave any bairn o' hers had ever had.

A few days later she got herself up and went back to walking about the place the way she'd done before, with not another word said.

18

There she stands on the same scrap of shore as before.

She looks different this time. Sae different I would scarce recognise her if I did not know fine she is the only lady between here and Aberfoyle. Pale as the moon she is today, and thin. Her eyes have lost their life.

I see what ails her. Can tell it at a glance. And now is my mind in a whirl o' doubt and despair. Is she not the one after all?

Be not so impatient, Robert Kirke. 'Twas aye your weakness. One of your weaknesses.

But I thought—

Bide your time, Robert Kirke. Bide your time. She is young enough yet.

19

All Mrs Aird did the rest o' that summer was wander hither and yon. I'd see her sometimes loitering along the shore and my heart fair bled for her, though to my way o' thinking if she'd had a flagstone floor to scrub and her own meals to cook it might ha' helped. It's a daft thing about the gentry, begging your pardon, that the very things that keep a body going when you canna bear to think and would forget to breathe if you only could are so far beneath their dignity that all they can do is sit and wait for someone else do it. In those days, mind, ladies were hard put to sit down at all in those puffed-out dresses that were the style. Och, they could hardly walk past a candle without going up in flames. Mind, Mrs Aird had stopped wearing the silliest ones by then and she could walk about and sit down and stand up nearly as easy as I could. But I did used to think she should try setting her own fires sometimes, or running a bodice through in the burn. A life o' leisure's all very well, and I'd have liked to try it myself now and then, but when there's a grief on your heart you need something to do and folk depending on you, and Mrs Aird had none o' that.

Of course she claimed she had nothing to be grieving about. She said once – the only time I mind her mentioning it at all

– that the thing had happened to her too often to care. She said it in a throwaway voice as if she had mislaid another of those fancy combs she was aye dropping about the place. But not for a minute did she fool me. I saw the spots o' colour high in her cheeks and the way her nose went all pinched and the grazed look in her eye. She cared all right.

And so did he. I couldna get out my mind the look on his face when his wee lassie was born, though I'm not sure she noticed.

20

Bide your time, they say, smooth as you please. But time is an agony. Time is a trick.

I was ta'en into faery in the year of our Lord 1692 and have come out in 1856 to find my beloved's grave pocked with lichen. One hundred and sixty-four years I was away, yet it passed below as days or weeks. Weeks of abiding horror, but weeks none the less. Not a year older am I now than the forty-seven I had on me when I was removed.

Perhaps 'tis nature's way for time to pass at different speeds above and below. I have thought much on this. Mayhap it goes faster for the stars than the sea, the eagle than the mole, or by infinitesimal amounts for the tall man than the short. I have even wondered if every man's head lives longer than his feet. 'Tis a notion to contort the mind, like so much else since my return.

But what does a man do with time to bide?

He walks, Robert Kirke. He walks.

And whither should I walk?

Far and wide, if it please you. Were you not used to be a curious man?

Must you ever mock?

Walk where you will, Robert Kirke. As long as ye return. Be not so foolish as to forget our bargain.

21

Balmoral Castle, on a quiet bank of the River Dee, was where Albert and Victoria were at their happiest. Rebuilt and expanded to Albert's design and decorated in tartan (for her) and deceased stags (for him), it had become as cosy and intimate a home as a household teeming with every rank of servant and a constant stream of guests is likely to be.

Jibe though she might at her husband's obsession with plumbing, Victoria was the first to appreciate fourteen water closets and four baths. The sole disappointment was that so few of the local Highlanders wore tartan, a dereliction that offended her sense of the picturesque. Her own enthusiasm for plaid had been expressed across such an extensive expanse of wallpaper, carpet, tablecloth and upholstery that at least one ungrateful guest complained of the effect on the retina. As for wearing it, what the locals failed to don by choice her family and staff were required to do by edict. Albert acceded with good grace to the exposure of his knees north of Carlisle. Although breezy at times, the kilt was a small price to pay for contentment.

Out on the hill Albert could put aside the strains of trying to defuse international discord, defuse ministers, defuse Victoria. No need to steel himself here for the next would-be assassin's shot at their carriage or wonder if some demented English mob was going to attempt to carry him off to the Tower of London as a foreign spy. To stalk a stag across the moor was to feel himself no longer the royal consort, husband, protector, private secretary or diplomat, the interloper always minding his English and guarding his ideas, always wary, always polite, always punctiliously busy with this task or that – but only a man with a gun in a landscape too big for him, breathing deep of the clean Highland air with every sense alert in a different way. And he needed the release that followed, the explosion of tension when the trigger was drawn back. Walking back down the hill with the carcass strapped to the pony and the rifle limp at his side, admiring the bounding grace of a mountain hare or the breath-catching glide of an eagle, Albert of Saxe-Coburg and Gotha could truly say he was a man at peace.

Victoria too was unfailingly restored by the moors and mountains around Balmoral, for which her husband had particular reason to be grateful that autumn of 1856. With life's unerring ability to deliver just what you are congratulating yourself on having avoided – or in Albert's case, just as you have allowed yourself to believe that eight children will prove the totality of your bountiful blessings – Victoria was with child again. She would be confined in April. More misery for her, more work for him: he was quailing already.

In the early weeks of pregnancy her emotions were particularly prone to turn on a sixpence. Even the presence of Miss Florence Nightingale, who stayed on the estate for some days and supplied a stream of hair-raising stories about her nursing experiences in the Crimea, left Victoria feeling low. Greatly taken with the nurse, she asked some keen questions over tea and gave every appearance of enjoying herself, but then she grew wistful and fell into what Albert, an experienced judge of atmosphere, categorised to himself as an ominous silence. As they were preparing to retire that evening he asked what had been amiss.

'Dear Miss Nightingale,' his wife returned bleakly. 'She has no children.'

'Indeed not. It must be a great loss never to have married.'

'That is not what I meant,' Victoria snapped, tossing her head so sharply that the lady-in-waiting almost dropped the hairbrush. 'Have you never thought what I too might have achieved without children?'

'My dear, you are the Queen,' Albert ventured, with the damp feeling of a man sinking into sand. 'It is hard to think of a—'

He caught her expression in the dressing table mirror and hazarded no further. How preposterous for his *Liebchen* to feel her achievements confined, when she enjoyed the highest station in the land and influence to which even the indefatigable Miss Nightingale could never aspire. This was just the sort of irrational outburst he dreaded from Victoria.

Preparing to wrap up for bed, Albert drooped at the thought of the months of tiptoeing among maternity eggshells that lay ahead. *Gott sei Dank* for the distractions of Balmoral. Tomorrow the landscape would surely work its magic on Victoria's spirits again, as it always did. As, gloriously, it always did.

Autumn fair in the sunshine, the day was the kind that showed Balmoral to best advantage. The trees on the hill opposite their bedroom were all fired up and the River Dee positively glittered its way past the house. It took only one beatific glance through the window for Victoria to announce that this was the perfect morning for a ride to the Glas Allt stream. A party was assembled – servants, ghillies, children, ladies-in-waiting, a couple of lords – and off they trekked. When they reached secluded Loch Muick, they dismounted from the ponies and began climbing the path to the waterfalls. It was rough from recent rain and very steep, but the pregnant Victoria was neither abashed nor wearied. In fact she tackled the ascent with considerably more energy than Albert. Her physical resilience never ceased to astound him, not least at a time when she was so easily wearied by everything else.

They took luncheon a little way below the summit and opposite the Glas Allt Falls, in a spot Victoria pronounced romantic. Before them the valley was laid out in purples and browns around a silken loch. A lone walker, no more than a dark smudge on the lower slope, was the only human but themselves for miles.

Settling herself on a tartan rug, Victoria took out her sketchbook. Albert smiled fondly to see her sitting so contentedly, gazing down at the water and then back to her page with a look of such ardent concentration that he was contemplating dropping a kiss on her head when, like a clap of thunder from nowhere, she banged down the book, declared that the frolicking children were making it impossible to draw and issued so terrifying a scolding that little Helena burst into tears.

'My dear, must you speak so sharply?' Albert muttered. The children had needs be well behaved and orderly, of course, but he hated to see Lenchen cry.

Victoria arose and let fly. Could Albert not see that he was the one who did not discipline the children as a father should? It was unfair that he always left everything to her. It was wholly insensitive of him to upbraid her in this way and ignore the tender condition that put her nerves on edge.

'And do not write me a note later, detailing all my faults. I have quite enough to read from the Prime Minister.'

Albert was stung into what he would normally have been the first to judge an incautious reply. 'Why must you always be like this when you are with child?'

'And whose fault is that, pray?' Victoria had now raised her voice.

Albert noticed a couple of servants staying the hands that were packing the luncheon utensils into the baskets. Beady Lady Toplady, who had already made it clear where she personally placed the blame for Victoria's condition, gave him one of her deathless stares from a neighbouring rug. He swallowed carefully and held out his arms.

'*Komm zu mir*, my dear,' he said gently. Poor love, she was very het up. 'You are quite right, quite right. Forgive me, and let us sit down over here and enjoy this beautiful view again. See, the children are quiet now.'

Huffing a little, Victoria allowed him to help her sink on to a grassy outcrop of rock. The loch shimmered below.

'And see here,' he said, pulling an empty seltzer bottle from his pocket in the hope of consolidating his gains. 'Why do not I leave something for posterity?'

Albert had never outgrown his boyish delight in hiding an object to be discovered later. It tickled his fancy to leave a message in a bottle and wonder who might discover it by chance some day, perhaps far in the future, and what this person would think, and what mysterious connection might spring between strangers across the ages.

'Come, *Liebchen*. What shall I write?'

'Whatever you care to,' Victoria returned icily.

But she did turn to see which bottle he meant – and her wrath vanished.

'Albert, are you quite well?' Victoria was now in a panic of solicitude. 'Your stomach does not pain you again?'

'Hardly at all.' All that Albert felt at this moment was pleasantly giddy at the sudden recovery of his fortunes.

He summoned paper and pen, and his wife leaned in to watch him write. Balancing the leaf awkwardly on one knee, he wrote: *Here we sit in the sunshine, surrounded by our dear children and another to come. Albert and Victoria, September 1856.*

'Or would you prefer "Victoria and Albert"?'

She shook her head. He folded the paper, squeezed it through the narrow neck and buried the bottle deep among the thick roots of a heather plant. Victoria watched him lovingly, all remonstrance forgotten.

'My dear, dear Albert,' she murmured, and took his hand.

'Come, *Fräuchen*,' he said, expanding with relief. 'Let us enjoy the rest of the afternoon.'

22

The castle has turrets and its own clock. The home, as I learn, of the sovereign herself when pleased to visit her northern kingdom.

'Tis but the latest surprise of my journeying. Every day has brought the wonder and shock of this new world I am fallen into. Methought only lochs harboured monsters, but nay, they have come shrieking across fields and over rivers, breathing smoke, red-eyed in the night. When first I felt the earth shudder, I thought faery was come for me again and almost fell in a faint. But it was only a machine, a wondrous coal-eater which carries goods and people o'er the land faster than any horse.

In the towns are now too many people, ill-looking and ragged the maist o' them, and so few folk left in the country places as can scarce be credited. Small farms are joined into one, the families gone to cotton mill and coal mine. Sheep piddle around in places where I thought to see cattle, or people. The number of turnips grown is very remarkable.

I have been drawn north and eastwards by a longing to see taller peaks than those I grew up among – Doon Hill the least majestic of them all, rearing up betwixt the Aberfoyle manse and the flatter lands beyond the Forth like some overweening pimple. I walked the drove roads through lang, shadowed valleys, passing cattle on their way to the markets in the south and sleeping alongside the drovers on the grass beside their beasts. Ofttimes I shivered the night long, for I have no covering but the coat in which I walked up Doon Hill on the night of my life's great calamity.

O'ertaken by autumn I followed one rubbled river after another among layers of balding hills, until the winding Dee brought me to this most excellent castle. There are trees of every species on the slopes above and along the river behind, some already so prodigal with their leaves that they give them away at the first hint of a breeze.

There was a woman on the throne when I was taken also: Queen Mary, reigning o'er our troubled isles with her husband, the Dutch King William. The servants here, not slow to answer the questions of a harmless wanderer with a pulpit voice, tell me this Queen's husband is no king but a consort merely. That a man should be ruled by his wife is another peculiarity of these new times. But they interest me, this Victoria and Albert. I have been observing them closely.

The great house serene behind me. The late afternoon sun breaking the river into shards and flinging great shadows across the folded hills. Its beam strikes so low that I must squint to read again the words in the strange-shaped bottle that I picked up on the hill beside the falling water.

Be not diverted, Robert Kirke. You have a commission.

'Tis no diversion. I was but thinking the commission might be fulfilled in a different wise.

23

Albert, Prince Consort, to Christian Friedrich, Baron Stockmar

Balmoral Castle,
September 1856

Mein lieber Freund,

I must seize a few minutes to describe a most odd occurrence. Yesterday evening Toplady, whom you will recall as quite the most irritating of Victoria's ladies, regaled the dinner table with reports of an uncouth man loitering in the grounds. As usual I was paying her as little attention as possible, devoting myself largely to the conversation of our delightful guest, Miss Nightingale, who is staying on the estate with her father and has impressed everyone with her modesty and straightforwardness, especially in the manner with which she describes her nursing role in Scutari. As you would expect, Miss Nightingale and I were in complete agreement about the want of system and organisation that so blighted our Crimean war effort and scandalously ill served our troops, and it was sobering to be reminded that ten times more of them than succumbed to any bullet, shell or

The Ninth Child

sabre thrust perished from disease. She spoke of witnessing a most distressing amount of cholera, which she maintained was carried in a miasma of foul air. Here I believe the lady to be mistaken, although one supposes that her view, in which she is by no means alone, derives from her experience of the general benefits of cleanliness in treating the sick and wounded. I was in the midst of drawing her attention to the recently begun water scheme for Glasgow, which has been undertaken on firm expert opinion in Scotland that contaminated water and not air is the culprit, when the rising shrillness of Lady Toplady's narrative forced me at last to attend.

In answer to some question from the other side of the table she was shouting that the loiterer in question had been wearing black from top to toe excepting a pale cravat at the neck, and had waved at her in what she described, that sharp beak of hers a-quiver, as an 'unpleasant' manner which had given her 'a dreadful turn'. Victoria interjected briskly that it had probably been a shepherd down from the hill, but that Brown, one of the most robust of our Highland ghillies, should be ordered to search out any intruder. Toplady begged Her Majesty in tones verging on hysteria to brook no delay from Scotch attendants renowned for putting off whatever must be done at once until next week at the earliest.

This afternoon I proposed to Brown that he and I walk about the grounds in case such an intruder as Toplady had described could be espied. You may remember John Brown. He is a strapping Highlander with a forthright tongue, which Victoria tolerates with as much equanimity as his excessive fondness for whisky. Brown advised that I should not, as he put it, 'fash' myself with matters that could with confidence be left in his own hands. But it was the hour when afternoon yields to evening at this time of year and the sun bathes everything in a most pleasing light of the kind that always draws me outdoors. Brown and I climbed Craig Gowan, the hill opposite the house from which one may with ease survey the scene around. We walked about a while, scanning the countryside. The outdoor servants had ceased their labour for the day and the air was filled with such tranquil drowsiness that all anxieties drained from me and I was feeling perfectly relaxed, when Brown suddenly beckoned.

'Look yonder, Your Royal Highness. Down by the river. Do ye see that?'

I saw nothing for a moment, and then caught it: a flash of light, followed soon after by another.

I should tell you that in light-hearted spirit I planted a bottle yesterday at the Glas Allt Falls. As a physician you will like to know it had contained seltzer! When we descended the hill after luncheon I left it hidden in the heather and thought no more about it. I cannot tell you how I knew it was the same bottle today, refracting the sunlight from a spot by our home, many miles from the Glas Allt. I say only this, Stockmar: I knew it, and it produced in me the strangest feeling. As a man devoted to scientific progress and rational thought I am not prone in the slightest to uncanny imaginings, as you will be the first to attest. But the thought of my bottle being turned this way and that by a pair of hands far below gave me an unexpected turn.

Brown and I descended the hill, and I cannot disguise the fact that I proceeded with reluctance. As we made our way past the house and turned along the river, my steps became ever more heavy.

'Will ye no' go inside and leave this to me, sir,' said Brown, eyebrow arched. I dare say he thought me afraid.

'Certainly not,' I returned.

We moved closer to the glinting light. The hill was in shadow now and the air, as it seemed to me, heavy with threat. I recall once watching the hair rise on the arched back of an affrighted cat, and marvelling at how nature responds to a threat. I felt like that cat. I grasped tight to my staff to still a sudden tremor; my skin prickled; sweat gathered on my brow; my heart beat too fast.

We came at last upon the intruder sitting on a verdant spot by the Dee, which curves at that point close to the house. On seeing us he rose at once, and I saw that in his hands he did indeed hold the glass bottle that had given away his presence. The shadows had reached him before we did and the bottle now lay dull in his grasp. He was a ragged man with unkempt hair, dressed in dirty, old-fashioned attire, although a more educated bearing revealed itself when he opened his mouth. In pleasing Scotch tones that were almost soothing to the ear, startlingly so in view of the aura of subdued menace he exuded at the same time, he volunteered at once that he had read my playful note. He proceeded to question me with breathtaking directness upon the date when Victoria was to be delivered.

Had I made a sign, Brown would have struck him at once, as he was clearly itching to do. But the man's demeanour was so mild, his speech courteous with yet something behind it that I may describe as restrained urgency, that I stood rooted, my thoughts in confusion. I remained in the grip of those sensations I have just described to you. I shivered. I could believe the very hairs on my back to be standing upright if such a thing is physiologically possible, which you will doubtless tell me it is not. What I am trying to convey is that I was at one and the same time both powerfully attracted and most horribly repelled. I make no sense, Stockmar. I write only as the scene unfolded and remains with me as I write.

The man professed himself a church minister, which seemed likely enough from his antique clothing and educated demeanour, *although it was obvious he had come upon hard times. Then he desired to know where our child would be baptised. At that my whole body was suffused with what I must describe as horror. I know not why, since the question, while scarcely appropriate (as could be judged by Brown's intake of breath at my side), was delivered without insolence or overt threat. Yet threat there was.*

'The baptismal arrangements of the monarch's family are no concern of yours,' I said tightly, hardly able to bring the words to my tongue.

'But that fine kirk across the bridge will be the place, will it not?' he persisted. 'I have observed you and your Queen worshipping there.'

The feeling of menace was growing upon me by the minute. I wanted to flee – flee, Stockmar; to whom but you might I confess it? – yet I felt compelled also to protect my family. From what I knew not, and know not now, but I was seized by such an apprehension of peril as I have never known in my life before.

'It will not take place in Crathie Kirk,' I said, quietly and I hope with some remnant of dignity. 'Her Majesty is head of the Church of England. No child of ours will ever be baptised in Scotland.'

At that I observed a ghastly paleness overcome the man's cheeks, and knew my words had struck a blow more injurious than any Brown could have delivered.

The man fell silent. Then, very slowly and without another word, he turned away. I signalled to Brown to suffer him to proceed, for the relief of his departure was immense. He walked with head bowed, staggering a little as he made his way along the rough path by the Dee and away from the house. Watching him, I was overcome by the sense of having escaped something unutterably malevolent yet also, in the strangest way, sad. Left behind in his wake was a faint smell of decay. I hope I never encounter the fellow again in my life.

The Ninth Child

My dear friend, I have prevailed too long upon your patience. Let me assure you that my next letter will confine itself to forestry plans.
I remain your faithful friend,
Albert

24

What meant you by that piece of folly, Robert Kirke?

An end to the waiting. I wanted an end to the waiting. I canna abide the waiting. I thought—

You were ever too prone to thinking. And to hopefulness.

May you rejoice then, fiends, for each is broken now.

From Balmoral am I come among the Cairngorms, sae different from the mountains of home that I stand before them in awe. They reach to infinity, these crystal peaks, jagged with precipices and buffeted by winds that can knock a man to his knees in an instant.

And of a sudden I ache, ache with the devout longing of the auld Robert Kirke, for heaven. And I wonder what might have become of me if I had lived my life among mountains such as these, and kept my eyes on the heights, and never thought to look below where human happiness is nowhere to be found, nor ever can be.

No room for pity either, Robert Kirke. Least of all for thyself.

Snarl not in my head again. Not in this holy moment.

Then would ye pipe down about crystal peaks, man, and have patience until the lady is ready.

Part Two

1857

Fear no more the heat o' the sun

Cymbeline

25

Mrs Aird was that floored by losing her bairn that for long enough she hardly said a word to me. Months went by without much more than a 'Do this for me, Kirsty. Fetch that, would you.' Said nicely enough – I'm no' suggesting otherwise – but she drew right back into herself and went a long time without asking me about things the way she'd started to do. Trees, birds, stories, nothing. And before you ask, no mention was made o' Robert Kirke either. Neither hide nor hair o' him did she report after that first summer. Then one day she comes on me washing through some bits and pieces in the loch, and all of a sudden she's wanting me to talk.

'Tell me about the Dog Loch,' says she straight out.

It was a good drying day, as I recall it, with a decent wind making little waves in the water. Not that anything ever got what you'd describe as properly dry. They say the Highlanders are dirty, but you might ask yourself how easy it is to make a floor that's no more than the earth itself shine like marble and how little you'd be caring about honeysuckle round the lintel if you barely had a door. Anyway, I washed where I could all the same – I have my pride – and I'll tell you it was pure joy to have a stone floor to scrub in the Airds' kitchen and scullery. Many's the time I was glad to see the doctor come in from the site wi' his boots covered in muck so I could start over. You can smile all ye like, but that was the way of it.

I was in no hurry to tell her about Loch a'Chon. There's hardly a loch in Scotland hasna got its monster and I wouldna be so sure about the half o' them. But when the night is that dark that all you can see is black outlines o' nothing, and the wind is up and the clouds are fleeing across the sky as if they're running from the devil himself, and yonder are the waves, I can see them now, thrashing about the loch like some great body is stirring them, well, you can't help being put in mind o' the time a tinker threw a bairnie in. A young boy it was. The Dog raised itself out the water and swallowed him whole, poor mite, and folk say he ended up in faery. They'll tell ye the Dog is always there, lying in wait beneath the waves to do the bidding o' the *sìthichean*. It makes your bones go tight in your chest to think about it on a night when the moon's in tatters. And when all's said ye never do know what's down in the deeps waiting to come for you.

So I told this to Isabel Aird. Silly girl, what was she expecting? Some fluffy pup that would tumble in the shallows with her lost bairns?

'Oh Kirsty,' says she, all bleak, 'you've ruined the loch for me. Where am I to turn now?'

See, that's what happens when you get sentimental about a place, the way I get with the isle o' Mull if I'm not thinking straight. The bad's as much a part of everything as the good, and every bit is written in the land and sung through it. Those that know how to look and listen will hear a warning in the corbie's croak. They'll see the last breaths of a body that's coming to death in the shapes the air makes around them, birled about like wildfire.

'You turn to your husband,' says I. Which was forward of me, as she made plain, and came out without thinking. Right enough, if it was comfort I was needing myself I'd have preferred a cup o' tea than to go looking for my James. Steady as you'll find in the navvy world, but not what you'd call tender. Still, out it came: 'Will ye no' turn to your husband?'

Well, Mrs Aird was black affronted. I can't mind if she said anything, but she stalked off soon enough. None of my business what went on between her and her man, ye might say, and you'd be right. But I had a soft spot for Dr Aird. He had all that flame-red hair without the temper. Mild and quiet he was as a rule – milder than she was anyway when her dander was up. I always say you can't have two tempers in a marriage or there's trouble, though that pair had trouble anyway so I don't know what I'm havering about. He had big hands that made you feel safe somehow. I mind noticing when he got their bairn delivered that time how the wee dead lassie fitted right inside them.

It was obvious to anyone they were strained with one another. It was as if that last stillbirth had closed the door between them good and proper and neither one could get through it to the other, or maybe cared to any longer. Who am I to know? As the weeks and months went on the doctor was out in all weathers, and at times it would be after dark when I saw his lamp quavering through the camp and up to Fairy Knoll, since you have to understand these works went on as much by night as day, and the accidents too.

Oh, these accidents. You wouldna believe the different ways a man can hurt himself in a place like that. James saw a navvy walking head down on a day when not a thing could you hear for the wind, and this man was hit right slam in the chest by the arm of a gin. The gin was where they had horses walk in circles turning the windlass so the men could go down the shaft in a bucket. Broke his back. James said he gave one awful squeal and fell down and the next horse around went right on and trampled him. I never heard if there was anything the doctor could do there, but James was gey shaken. I havena thought o' all this for a long, long time.

I recall there were limbs mashed under the hammer too. They had to drill into that rock by hand to make a hole big enough to set the gunpowder and it took a fair nerve to hold steady the jumper, which is what they called the drill. The jumper was a sharp pole nearly as tall as me, and one or two would hold on to it and the rest of the gang take turns to strike it wi' the hammer. That rock was hard as hard. Down came the hammer with a great swing behind it and you'll know as well as anyone what was like to happen if they misjudged it. The surprise is you didna have more injuries that way. These men were skilled workers and could strike true time and again. Sometimes they had to work wi' the jumper for hours, boring away till the hole was ready to be primed with the powder. What happened then, James used to say, was that many a time the shot passed straight out, clean as a cannon, and you just had to hope you weren't in the way. I mind one boy had an eye blown out that way.

Aye, I could go on. James used to have me all shook up wi' his tales. He did all right himself, though my heart was in my mouth when he was down that tunnel. Once he had a hot rivet fall all the way down the shaft on his head, and Dr Aird said it was only his cap that saved him. Big Kilmarnock bonnet it was that I'd knitted myself. Had his tobacco and a nice piece for his dinner inside. I canna bring to mind what was in his piece that day but it must ha' done the trick, though the doctor said James was lucky to remember my name after that. Mind, he took his breakfast next day quite the thing.

Couldn't ha' been easy for the doctor, I used to think, though I suppose medical men are used to the sight o' blood and that. He told me once, when he was sort o' loitering in their kitchen and Mrs Aird as usual nowhere to be seen, that he'd found his training on the grisly side. Ran once from the dissection room to be sick, he says wi' that big grin of his. I always thought he had the nicest smile I've seen on a man, Dr Aird. Took up half his face. But he had broad shoulders that could wield a saw quickly, he said, if it came to it.

'Quickly is the thing, Kirsty,' he says. 'If we can't get a man to Glasgow in time' – and that was a palaver, let me tell you – 'then it's me,' he says, 'that's got to amputate and the patient won't thank me for hanging around.'

It used to bother him how many died afterwards, even when he thought he had cut well. He was a sensitive soul in some ways, Alexander Aird, though maybe not in the way his wife wanted him to be. He was aye fretting about how he could make an operation safer or sort a gangrene or stop the cholera, whiles I'd be thinking, man, have you asked your wife how it feels to have your breasts fill wi' milk – if you'll pardon an old woman's bluntness – and no babe to relieve them? Have you asked yourself how you get over a grief when you have no work to be lost in, not even your ain fires to set?

She might ha' done better to tell him anyway, but, no, she just drifted around, more and more distant. I overheard Mr

Clark saying to the man collecting up the Bible one Sunday that Mrs Aird reminded him of Ophelia, whoever she might be. Och, away you go, says I to myself. Isabel Aird needs no fancy name. She's a woman wi' hurts that nobody gives the time o' day for and not enough to do.

It's what made her such easy prey when Robert Kirke came back, which I'll get on to by and by if you'll give me a minute. We could do with another pot o' tea here, don't ye think, unless it's maybe time to get that flask out your pocket? Think I didna have my eye on it, did you?

26

St Andrews by the sea. I know not why my steps have turned hither. Ach, but I do. When the voice stays silent I hear the echoes of a different self.

I was a student at the university here after a divinity degree in Edinburgh – which city I have no wish to see again, since I cannot think it will be one whit less dirty and uncouth than it was then. One boon of Edinburgh, though, I should not decry: I made a good friend of the university principal, who helped mak Robert Kirke what he was.

Robert Leighton reminded me in some wise o' my mother, for all that she was barely educated and he a fine and subtle thinker. My mother had a talent, light as a butterfly and without one sign of intending it, for drawing attention to the absurdities that involve men in near ceaseless argumentation over very little. It aye made me laugh. And Robert Leighton, an ordained Presbyterian minister o' the Scottish Kirk who yet allowed himself to be appointed an Episcopalian bishop by King Charles II – making him no better than a papist in the eyes o' many – had the same bent as a theologian. He had me weigh every allegiance judiciously and dispassionately, as he did himself. As our auld country tore itself apart in bloody struggles for religious dominance, he sought to reconcile Presbyterians and Episcopalians in a united Church o' Scotland. He taught tolerance, and with full heart I followed.

St Andrews cam next on my path to Christian ministry, and glad am I to discover the place sae little changed today. Here stands the college of St Mary's, calm and graceful yet. Here flap the same scholarly gowns in the same east wind. It pleases me to sit beneath a flaming sunset, waiting for the waves to trickle up the sands and between these same toes, my back to the warm wall, the salt sea breeze on my face and the gulls crying overhead. I mind how often I used to come here to think on the lectures, seized by the ideas that aye made sich lively music in my head: Descartes' notion of an immortal, spiritual soul separate from the body; the metaphysical insights of the Greek master Aristotle, laid out side by side in my notebook with the arguments o' the moderns who disagreed with him.

'Twas another time then and a different Robert Kirke: one who believed every form of enquiry a good in itself, as if all things in life could be reconciled. Thus was I set for my soaring flight to the sun. This mind o' mine, opened to different ways of understanding God and tolerant approaches to the beliefs of men, would prove fertile ground for the idea – sich a tantalising idea when first it cam to me – of a faery commonwealth.

Not all things in life can be reconciled, nor should be. I found it out too late. Icarus fell to the sea and died beneath the waters, tangled in his sizzling wings. The fate of Robert Kirke was worse.

27

Albert, Prince Consort, to Christian Friedrich, Baron Stockmar

Buckingham Palace,
June 1857

My dear Stockmar,

I write to tell you that the christening passed today without incident. Why I should have feared incident is a matter on which neither of us would wish to dwell. I will merely confide that I did spend some foolish moments glancing anxiously towards the door of the chapel, until Victoria caught my eye and I heaved my attention back to the ceremony, which was as correct and orderly as one could wish until Victoria's dear mama, the Duchess of Kent, who had the honour of publicly naming the child, made an error that threatened catastrophe.

'Beatrice Maria Victoria Feodore,' she declared in ringing tones. Dear God, Maria! The child might have been some Spanish infanta.

Whereupon to our horror the archbishop, despite having the correct names written boldly on a paper in front of his nose, proceeded to christen her so. Victoria, who I may say was looking

most fetching in her wedding lace, cast thunderous looks at both duchess and cleric. The child was intended to be Mary, of course, a name we had earlier most assiduously impressed upon my mother-in-law.

I fell to mulling over what would be required to correct the record afterwards (a task which, Gott sei Dank, I am now able to report has been successfully accomplished). As I did so, the anxiety receded that I was at any moment about to glimpse a stooped figure in black stealing in at the back, like Rumpelstiltskin returned to claim his wicked payment from the Queen. Or at least I no longer had the leisure to indulge the feeling, which may amount to the same thing. By this you will understand what imaginings have perturbed me since my encounter with that chilling figure at Balmoral last autumn.

Our youngest daughter behaved impeccably throughout, sounding only the smallest note of complaint at the moment of christening, and in this she continues the most complaisant of infants. Since her birth in April she has proved nothing but a delight. Unusually, indeed I am tempted to say uniquely, Victoria is entranced with the child. You may imagine my relief! I suspect it may be to do with her being so very pretty. Although one's offspring do rather blend in the memory, I believe Victoria is right to suggest that Beatrice asserted more or less instantly her claim to be the most appealing of our children. At eight weeks she has large blue eyes and every sign of a winning temperament. Victoria has even taken to supervising her bath. I cannot tell you how exceptional this is.

I have sometimes wondered if the administration of chloroform for a second time also predisposed Victoria to take more quickly to this child. She declares that it makes the experience of delivery very much less painful and distressing. Many physicians remain to be convinced, as you will certainly know, and the public are as suspicious as they always are of anything new. The Church of England is decidedly not in favour, and you may be assured that the mode of Beatrice's entry into the world did not form part of my conversation today with the Archbishop of Canterbury. But after her first experience of the drug while giving birth to young Leopold, Victoria was most insistent on receiving it again. It was administered by Dr John Snow, a medical man with admirably wide interests. You must have heard of him, Stockmar. He has been conducting research into cholera epidemics in England for a number of years, taking on the authorities in robust fashion over the need for clean water, although I fear he has as far to go to convince his medical colleagues of the source of cholera as the efficacy of chloroform.

As far as the latter is concerned I can only attest, two months after the birth of our princess, to a relatively relaxed and preternaturally motherly wife. Now that Vicky is to leave us this winter for married life in Prussia – how I will miss my beloved firstborn! – there has come upon me a tremulous premonition of happiness surrounding this our ninth and, may it please the heavens, final child. My foolish fears and fancies now proved baseless, I look forward to enjoying little Beatrice as she grows and flourishes.

Ever your constant friend,
Albert

Part Three

1858

Nor the furious winter's rages

Cymbeline

28

Before flitting to the Trossachs Isabel Aird had indulged what she now, these two years and more later, regarded as a gentle-woman's spoiled fancy for snow. Certainly Glasgow snow could be an inconvenience when it delayed the coal delivery or had Cook attempting something adventurous with last night's left-overs; and naturally, if you really had to venture out, there was no pleasure in wading through horse ordure disguised as slush. But by and large snow was a pretty thing to watch lacing the lamp posts and swirling around the Bath Street chimneys for as many hours as Annie kept the fire stoked. When it descended with more serious intent, so heavy and fast from an oyster sky that it smothered the clatter of stagecoach and tradesman's cart, hansom cab and omnibus, it had only served to muffle her own thoughts too, stilling the dismal clang of them and suspending her in as airy a state as the poetical romances she had so liked to read.

At Fairy Knoll there were no such cosy interludes. The house was nearly as cold inside as out, and she was more likely to while away the hours by the kitchen hearth than loiter before a window whining with draughts. But mostly she would go out, and will-ingly at that. The same Isabel Aird who used to weigh up the risk to her footwear of navigating seven steps between front doorstep and waiting brougham thought nothing of swaddling herself in shawls like a navvy's wife and billowing out into whatever the elements flung her way.

By now she knew what to expect from winter. When November knifed the chest you would find frost covering the grass like a caul. By December the trees would be stripped so bare you could see their bones, stained white on the wind side when the snows arrived, gathered about the loch like a host of skeletons. Then the navvies, who this winter were building small but intricately engineered aqueducts on the far slopes of Loch Chon, would appear black as demons on the bleached hillside. Alexander was kept busy with falls from icy gangplanks or accidents caused by frozen hands that refused to clasp the hammer tight enough and sent the jumper awry. Isabel would wait until he had left to attend a call and then sally forth herself.

Her habit was to skirt the Sebastopol camp and make for the quieter end of Loch Chon, sometimes walking as far as tiny Loch Dhu or further along the chain of waters to Loch Ard. After the ending of her last pregnancy the emptiness of these places attracted her, even in the harsher seasons that followed. How little formed for human pleasure were the untamed wind and rain when they swept down the hill and whisked the water into a frenzy; how careless of her feelings were the flaying cold, the insupportable dark. Isabel strode into the winds and screamed her loneliness. She walked her pain to exhaustion, licking rain from her lips, picking hailstones from sagging stockings. She wiped her streaming nose with the back of her glove, let sweat freeze on her eyelashes. The breath steamed from her like some stamping horse. For the first time in her life Isabel

Aird relied on her own mettle to steer a course and return safely, and knew what it was for the blood in her veins to surge with energy and her limbs to stretch. The novelty of being able to do this, the damp, messy muscularity of battling forward with head bowed and cheekbones aching, were exhilarating for a woman so long constrained by crinoline, hobbled by failure.

Accompanying her to the wild places were the lost children. For all its fetish for mourning, society offered no rituals to dignify her sorrows: no funerals, no graves, not even a black dress to alert the world and remind Alexander that there had ever been eight lives made and eight lives unmade. But in the raindrop trembling on a blood-red hawthornberry Isabel cherished the sight of her last child, whole and smiling. Facing down the rain itself, soaked to the skin, she cried and she laughed for the freedom of being nothing, and everything, and only herself.

On Loch Chon's stony beach she drew consolation from ruffled water and austere winter trees. Sometimes, watching at the lochside for her children, she was reminded of the strange figure she had met here before, and the conflicting impressions he had left behind. At these times the memory of Robert Kirke – she had not forgotten the name – returned to her like a small itch, or a story lost before the end. When she thought of him at this distance it was as an indistinct creature of the landscape itself, ambiguous as her beloved loch was ambiguous in its ability to dispense both comfort and (thank you, Kirsty) the image of a slavering dog with mouth agape.

All was as it had to be, Isabel understood now. For with the passing seasons and her own stripped-down sense of self had come a bleaker but perhaps truer feel for her surroundings. She drew into herself not just springtime balm but a wintry strength, and a resilience she took to wearing like armour. When Alexander drew her to him in the night, she told him plainly no.

She had also discovered the Sebastopol reading room. It took nerve to negotiate dog mess, horse dung and beery vomit in ankle boots you hoped to wear again. But Isabel learned where to divert and what to skirt, holding as close as possible to the lapping waterline until she had passed the navvy dormitories and could make a beeline for Mr Clark's stock of improving volumes, miscellaneous journals and out-of-date newspapers. These had been sent up by charitable organisations in Glasgow in the hope that an exhausted labourer might prefer intellectual and moral enlightenment to a few hours' sleep or a dogfight – a hope that could not have been entirely forlorn, because she came upon books thick with grease and smeared red with iron rust. Wrapped to the ears, Mr Clark too busy on the other side of the partition to attend to a fire, she settled down at the table in a hard chair with a new kind of reading material spread before her. Amid ragged chants from the schoolroom and the exasperated thwack of leather, Isabel immersed herself in social argument and old news.

For a time she became engrossed in the progress of a parliamentary bill to create new London sewers that would mitigate the piles of excrement heaped along the banks of the Thames and the effluent that was poisoning the river. During the oppressively hot summer London had suffered such a Great Stink, as the press dubbed it, that no citizen could breathe properly. Her Majesty and Prince Albert had themselves been so overcome by the noxious smell that they were obliged to abandon a pleasure cruise on the Thames.

Isabel also read of a London physician by the name of John Snow, who had died in June at the age of forty-five. This Dr Snow was reported to have tried to demonstrate that most of the people in the Soho district who fell ill in the cholera epidemic of 1854 had been taking their water from one single pump in Broad Street, which in turn was drawing it from a well next to the cesspools of nearby slums and drains. Plainly the doctor had not proved his case conclusively enough, because his conviction that cholera was carried in polluted water was still being heartily ridiculed.

Isabel raised her head and attended for a moment to the clank of machinery beyond the thin walls of the reading room and to the gunpowder thuds she barely noticed these days unless paying deliberate attention. What did they think of this enterprise, then, these snide critics? Did this bold and costly championing of clean water as a city's best hope for the health of its people not give pause for thought in London? Isabel was soon steaming with indignation at the obituaries of John Snow, so grudging in tone, so dismissive of his attempt to track down the source of cholera that some, confining themselves to his similarly dubious interest in chloroform, managed not to mention it at all.

Among Scottish commentators she observed no such rush to denigrate John Snow or perpetuate the notion that you could catch the disease by breathing noxious air. It was on noticing this that another desiccated emotion began to kindle. Pride: that's what the feeling was. Pride in the waterworks. Pride that it was being constructed by the citizens of Glasgow. Pride that she was one of them and her husband a ratepayer.

These forays to the reading room were exhilarating in ways not unlike the physical effect of the outdoors. The experience

of engaging her mind with a complex subject was difficult, frustrating, demanding, satisfying. She wanted more; looked forward
to what she would find out next; fretted about what she was
going to do when she had read everything (while deciding she
might even then draw the line at the entire complement of *The
Railway Magazine* since 1835). And when the process brought
her face to face with a few of her own prejudices, as it began
to, she did not look away.

One view in particular now struck her as embarrassingly
shallow. To the extent that she had thought about it before at
all, she had assumed that the diseases breeding in Glasgow's
reputed tenement filth must be the fault of improvidence among
people who had not the wit to better themselves and mind their
own garbage. How very much more complicated it was. She was
beginning to see why Alexander had been so keen to associate
himself with the waterworks and what he had meant all along
by public health. Isabel wondered why she had not asked him
more about it at the time. And then she remembered that the
knack of talking and the habit of asking had eluded them for a
long time now.

Yet she used to ask him questions all the time. How was it
to learn medicine, Alex? Did you dream of it as a boy? What is
university like? How does it feel to open a live body? Are the
patients afraid? Such pain, Alex – how do they bear it? What is
blood for? Why are veins blue? Thinking about it, the eager
questions had all been hers, the eager answers his, but she could
not recall resenting it, since the gruelling tedium of her own life
had held such little interest for either of them. The plain fact
is that she had liked to learn from him, had relished the glint
of admiration in his eye when she caught an idea quickly. But

then the pregnancies began to be lost, and the only questions that mattered then, the ones that nibbled at her self-worth and came to obsess her, were different ones entirely. What am I doing wrong? Why can I not make whole children? What should I do if I cannot do this? Alexander could not answer them. He shied behind his breakfast newspaper and hurried through supper. He asked nothing about the grief that came washing over her afresh year after year and, like the tide, sucked away with it every interest she had ever sustained. Perhaps, she reflected – thinking of Mr Dickens, too, who drew attention to complexity everywhere except in his meek maidens and grotesque matrons – men were simply not equipped to penetrate the interior life of a damaged woman. But of course neither was her mother, who recommended sea-bathing. Wherever the fault lay, the questions Isabel might once have asked – about the spread of disease, about the point of the waterworks, about why Alexander's well-to-do medical practice no longer satisfied him – had bobbed away on the tide like everything else.

Kirsty McEchern had her own notions of comfort.

'Will ye not try a sip of this, Mrs Aird,' she would say of an evening, brandishing some foul-tasting herbal concoction.

During the summer Kirsty was in the habit of wandering the heath herself with the youngest of her brood whooping about her skirts. She had great faith in the plants that still flourished near the site: this one for bruises and that for coughs, a stalk here or berry there for itches, sore feet or eye pus. She insisted her children were the more spritely for them and James had seen his indigestion right off with a couple of holly berries –

upon hearing which, Alexander declared that she would kill them all. Before long she was drying her herbs from a pulley in the Fairy Knoll scullery, explaining she was 'a wee thing short of space at home, Mistress Aird'. Annie grumbled in vain.

'Drink this and you'll sleep like a bairn,' Kirsty would say, advancing with an infusion of valerian root.

And whether it was the herb or the reading or the fresh air, there would sometimes be conjured enough evening warmth for Isabel to welcome Alexander home and ask him how his day had gone, and he would stretch his legs on the footstool before the fire, banked so high they had no need of gloves, and tell her his news. On one such evening he said Mr Bateman had been up inspecting the works with some Glasgow councillors and they had walked right down the tunnel from the Katrine end where the water was to run in.

'He seemed pleased, Issy. Says it's going well, although progress through the rock has been slow. Sixty drills at each face, day and night, can you imagine it? And they've been getting through no more than three yards of rock a month, he says, it's that hard.'

At these times Isabel found she was glad to hear him talk again, glad to see him tilt his head into the wing of the armchair and look over with the old grin, enthusing about a world of which she could not be part, though it trundled and exploded around her all day, too. An idea had been growing in her mind, encouraged by the interest that the reading room had ignited, emboldened too, perhaps, by the awareness of new strengths.

'Could we not go about together sometimes, Alex?' she said, seizing on the improved mood. 'I'm interested to see the works at closer quarters. And – oh, Alex, I would like this – I could watch you at work. Even' – this came out in a rush because it had just this minute occurred to her – 'even help you.'

Alexander rubbed his nose for a full ten seconds and frowned into the coals.

'That's impossible, Issy,' he said at last, not looking at her, although he felt the intensity of her own gaze. 'You surely know the work I do is not for a woman to observe. These are men I'm attending, for a start. It would be quite improper. And some of the sights are . . . well, I'm trained to it and I find them hard to stomach myself at times.'

'What about Florence Nightingale?' she flung back. 'How can she have saved all those lives in the Crimea – to great acclaim, as you know fine – without encountering blood and observing a man's body? Or Mrs Lister. Did you not tell me yourself that she helps her husband?'

Alexander's cheeks, already hot from the flames, fired up further. 'Nursing is not for ladies, Isabel, however much this Miss Nightingale is declared a favourite of the Queen. If you could see the slatterns on the wards of the Royal Infirmary, you would not propose it. They're drunk, the lot of them. I couldn't bear to think of you among them.'

'I'm not proposing a ward round at the Royal, Alex. I was just thinking I could assist in your work here.'

'And I'm telling you it is not right for a lady. From what I hear, Dr Lister's wife merely writes up his experiments and takes care of the frogs. It's not the same thing at all.'

Another strenuous nose-rub. Isabel closed her eyes and the flurry of enthusiasm ebbed as quickly as it had arrived, swept away in the returning tide of apathy. He reached for her hand and patted it.

'If I ever take it upon myself to dissect some amphibians in our own kitchen, you may knock them out with one of Kirsty's tinctures and help me all you like.'

Alexander was not by nature pompous, but when pomposity called he could rally with the best of them. Isabel did not ask again.

29

On the day that Robert Kirke reappeared, Alexander had been called to an accident close to home: a navvy injured at the point where the tunnel from Loch Katrine was almost ready to break through to join the first of the Loch Chon sections. He seized his bag and rushed out, barely pausing to button his coat against the ferociously chilly air.

Isabel watched him prompt his pony in the direction of the nearest shaft and then slipped out herself. It was too captivating a day to stay inside. Snow had fallen in the night, and the sun was picking out diamonds of ice in the hummocks beyond the garden. She was soon striding from one patch of shingle beach to the next, the bottom of her dress sopping already, her cape wet from the shrubs she brushed past on the way. Out of breath and dishevelled, she was filled with the elation of physical exertion under a hyacinth winter sky.

The tall figure was standing very still in almost exactly the same place as they had parted before, only closer to the water's edge. He was gazing so intently into the shallows that he barely acknowledged her arrival. A glance up, a brisk nod. And in truth Isabel felt little surprise to see him either: it was as if

– was this true? – she had always known he would return, always half expected to find him here.

His eyes were fixed on a clump of slender grasses growing up through the water nearest the shore. Further into the loch little gusts of wind were troubling the surface, but here the water lay unnaturally still, as if imprisoned under a skin of ice. Movement had been suspended – so it seemed to Isabel, following his gaze – in the moment of change from flowing liquid to something other. And there was music. Ting. Ting. The pure, high sound of bells.

'Look, madam,' he said softly. Anyone would think they were resuming a conversation from the day before.

She moved closer, noticing as she did that each of the feathered grasses had a tiny collar of ice around it where it met the unmoving waters of the loch. And as the wind brushed over them, the necklaces were touching each other, ringing out like tiny bells.

'Oh,' she said. 'Oh, it makes me want to dance.'

And so it did. Unexpectedly, improbably, so it did. Isabel was seized with such a longing to twirl and spin to this unearthly ice melody that she might have thrown all propriety to the easterly wind and seized the hands of this odd stranger with whom she had not so much as exchanged a polite morning greeting, and invited him to join her in a reel – such was the intoxication of air and sky and chiming ice. It made her think of life. It reminded her she was young yet.

Kirke wheeled around. 'You will do nothing of the kind! There will be no dancing, do ye hear?'

The moment was fractured, the mood altered in an instant. What was wrong with this man?

'Do ye hear me, madam?' He was angry. That was clear

enough. But there was something else too. 'Do ye hear what I say?' he growled again. 'No dancing.'

Panic. Was that it?

'It was only a figure of speech,' she returned stiffly and not entirely truthfully, feeling deflated. But she had no intention of wilting under this unprovoked glower. She would turn and march away, with her head (even if currently encased in an unprepossessing shawl of Annie's) held high.

She did not move. 'The ice bells made me happy,' she heard herself murmur instead.

The eyes that held her own softened. 'And you are not often happy, would ye say?'

With baffling swiftness the tempo had changed again. His voice had regained its measured roll. The note it sounded was sympathetic. Isabel was suddenly as near to tears as she had been a moment ago to dancing. When had anyone last asked her about being happy?

'Really, Mr . . . Kirke, was it?' she said, catching herself in time. 'That is a very impudent question upon such a short acquaintance. Might I ask who you are to ask it and what you are doing here again after all this time?'

'Aye, madam, it's a while syne I was last here. I won't be inconveniencing ye for lang. I merely had a mind to ask if ye were keeping well. I saw before I left that you had been indisposed.'

His mode of address was as direct as last time, and as disarming.

'I am never ill these days, thank you,' Isabel blurted, returning his gaze and wishing she had not given up on her winter bonnet. It was always easier to command the conversational high ground in a bonnet. 'As it happens I am in excellent health and have put a stop to the indispositions that plagued me. Indeed I intend never to be indisposed in that way again.'

Goodness, what was she telling him? The man's bluntness was having the most incontinent effect. An image of her mother swooning in a flounce of petticoats rose before her, and she might have smiled if there had not entered Robert Kirke's eyes a look of alarm, passing strange, which she could tell he was struggling to control.

'I am obliged to you for your concern,' she added hastily as he composed himself. He must consider her very forward. 'Perhaps you would tell me why you have once again sought me out – I a stranger and a lady alone?'

'I believe, madam, that it was you who sought me out this fine day, did ye not?' he said, and smiled.

And what a curious thing his smile was. Uncertainty or discomfiture of some kind remained about the corners of his mouth, but his face also conveyed a vulpine eagerness, some hint of the predatory look that had marked him out before and vaguely unsettled her. Yet the creases around his eyes had deepened at the same time with something else – sympathy again, amusement even – which seemed to speak of older, kinder smiles.

She tried once more. 'I deduce from your attire that you are a minister?'

He fingered the frayed cravat arrangement around his neck. A spectacularly grubby shade of white, it was housing today a couple of crumbling twigs and a small grey feather. The folds of cloth were roughly stuffed between the high lapels of his soiled black coat.

'Indeed. I served in the same kirk where my father was

minister before me, near the clachan of Aberfoyle. And before that I was twenty years in Balquhidder when I finished with the university. Ye will maybe know where Balquhidder is – yonder to the north of Katrine?'

Isabel shook her head.

'Bonnie place, you'd think if ye saw it. From the kirk ye could hear the rushing o' the falls day and night. Every silence had the surge and the tumble of them underneath – like the music o' these reeds here, just tinkling away to themselves.'

His voice had a music of its own and rumbled on pleasantly. Now and then Isabel caught the autumny smell again, carried between them in the lightly buffeting air. She waited for the latest boom from across the loch to finish its reverberations, and listened again for the bells.

'Well, they're not ringing now,' she said, glad to get the better of him.

'Aye, you're richt enough. The wind is dropping. And do ye see how the sun has begun to melt the ice?'

The tiny collars had indeed shrunk. The grasses at their feet were also beginning to shake themselves free with small slushing sounds. As she watched, a few lone umbrellas of dry cow parsley surrendered the ice from their spokes in a stately procession of drips.

Kirke observed her a while. 'You must be ganging home, my lady,' he said at last, 'or ye'll be catching a chill from these wet vestments. Your husband would be vexed to find you so. He is in good fettle, I trust?'

Isabel inclined her head curtly, discomfited again by the assumption that they were on terms that could permit discussion of Alexander's constitution.

'Well, I will not be delaying you then. Ye must be there to welcome him hame as a good wife should.'

'I *beg* your pardon, sir—'

But Kirke was holding up a long-fingered hand for silence.

This made her bridle even more. 'How dare you presume to—'

'Wheesht, woman, will ye!'

Then she heard it too. A raucous voice calling her name. 'Mistress Aird. Mistress Aird, are ye there?'

And there was Kirsty McEchern ploughing towards them through the tussocky snow, skirts hoist in one hand, the other clutching her side, face ablaze.

As she reached them in a cloud of breath, Kirsty flung Kirke a swift, appraising look. But it was to Isabel alone that she spoke.

'Would ye come at once, Mistress Aird,' she panted, bent double, breast heaving. 'Your husband is hurt.'

30

And what were ye about there, man, grinning like a gomeril?

Winning her trust. As my commission demands.

You acted the part too easily, then. Ice bells! That part of you must die, Robert Kirke.

Oh, 'tis dying all right. You have taken care of that.

Ye will end up liking her and what will happen then?

I have no thoughts o' liking her.

Aye, ye do, Robert Kirke. You like the life-wish that bursts forth when she forgets herself – even though she spake of dancing.

Do not mention dancing! I warn ye. Do not speak of it.

Warn us, would you? La di da.

Her spirit puts me in mind o' my own Isabel. 'Twas all I was thinking. 'Love and Life' I sculpted on the gravestone at Balquhidder. 'Love and Life' I had the blacksmith forge on the kirk bell. Expunge them from my soul and ye will mak me forget why I do this. And I say back to you, what will happen then?

Do not equivocate with us, Robert Kirke.

What hope now of success in any case? Two years have I walked and waited, only to hear from the lady that she means to keep herself chaste. She is indifferent to her husband.

Robert Kirke, Robert Kirke, ye never did see clearly. Her face when there cam ill tidings of her man – did it not tell us a very different tale?

31

He stood barely a step behind her, close as a moth to the light. And I knew. I knew the minute I saw him. The very minute. The funny feelings I'd had when she mentioned his name before came rearing back and I knew right away he was a bad one. The pair o' them turned towards me as I came through the snow shouting her name. Mrs Aird was looking anxious: she could tell something was amiss before I reached her. But he just stood there, very tall and alert and bending forward with his neck like a long, curious bird, eating me up wi' his eyes. He had this thing about him. Folk have asked me since, was it an aura? Well, I've never been sure just what an aura is. Something to do with the colour of the soul around a person, they say. But I'd have to confess I was in too much of a sprachle to notice whether he had muddy airs about him or not. All I'm saying is that I saw Robert Kirke that first time down by the loch, and as sure is sure I felt him. But I had other things to be bothering about in that minute, so you'll understand it was only later that I thought all this through.

Oh, what a fright I'd got when our Lachlan came running to find me. 'You'd better warn Mistress Aird,' says he. 'They're bringing him to the house.'

When I get to the house, she's not there of course, never is, but I tell yon minx Annie to get a fire on in the bedroom and some water boiling, and off I go looking for her, slithering about in the snow that was just beginning to thaw after a cold spell, and fine I remember it because the burn was so quick to get brown and swollen that it nearly cawed the feet from under me.

I told Mrs Aird what had happened and she went lolloping on ahead o' me, stumbling as she went because the snow made the ground look flat where it was full o' holes underneath, but fast on her pins for all that. She was used to walking for miles in any weather by then.

I got back to the house a bit after her, and found her upstairs already with the doctor. What a mess that man was in. Gave me quite a turn to see him lying there on the bed, his clothes soaked wi' blood and his face without a speck o' colour. Well, not a speck o' skin colour any road – it was smeared over wi' dust and smoke and goodness knows what else. Muck in his hair too, which was standing up like he'd seen a ghost. Eyes shut – I'm seeing it now. Lips inked purple and his eyelids so white and delicate-looking in all that dirt. There was a curl o' vapour about his lower legs too, a whitish wispy movement of the air from his feet to his knees that gave me a turn because I know what it means to see the shroud. He looked like a corpse already, if I'm honest.

And she – well, here was the surprise. She'd thrown off her outdoor cape and the old shawl she'd taken to covering her head with – 'There's nobody here to see or care, Kirsty,' she used to say, 'and I'd rather stay warm' – and she was issuing orders calm as calm.

'You there' – to one of the men that brought him – 'would you go and see if my husband's medical bag is found. And you, Annie, fetch me the spare bandages – you know the cabinet where he keeps them – and some scissors. Ah, Kirsty, there you are, would you help me get these clothes off him.'

Just rat-a-tat like some army major. I'd been thinking I'd have to take charge myself and I'd been going over any bit herbs I had and if there might be anything useful. All the way from the loch my heart was hammering in my chest, me thinking, right, she'll either go to pieces like any lady would and howl and cry and I'll have to get rid of her somehow, or she'll go that cold, distant way she does when she's feeling things but wants to keep them at arm's length, which is going to be all the harder because she'll be in my way and I'll feel like slapping her for not showing that man more fondness. Which I often did feel.

So you can imagine my surprise when I see her take charge like that, her face a bit harrowed-looking – the shock o' seeing him, I suppose – but her eyes the very opposite o' that dead way they could be sometimes. They had a quickness in them I'd not seen before.

She and I started to ease away his coat and Annie came with the scissors so we could get his shirt open. Dear God, it was sodden.

'First we need to stop the bleeding,' she says, cool as if she was the doctor herself.

I suppose she must have picked up a few things, being married to him and hearing his tales. I used to hear him say this happened today or that, and he'd had to turn this man on his side or pump this other one's heart to get him back breathing or whatever it might be. He told me himself once to be sure and wash my hands before I delivered any more babies. Bit of a cheek, I thought, me that's helped dozens into the world, but he said to try it anyway before I went poking around the cord o' the next newborn bairnie. Anyway, she grabbed a bandage from Annie and pulled it tight across where the skin was gaping.

'More, Kirsty, we need more,' she says, for each bandage was fair blooming with blood. No wonder his face was paler than an egg – there can't have been a spare drop left in him.

Mrs Aird pushes her two hands down hard on this pile o' dressings and holds fast, and while she's doing it she's calling out to the other navvy who helped carry him in, 'What happened, man? What's caused it? Is he hurt anywhere else?'

He's standing by the door, this fellow, twisting his cap in his hands as if he doesn't know where to put himself, his eyes shining out a queer bright blue from his grimy face, young Irishman as I recall with a funny thick accent, and he says the doctor had gone down the shaft in one of these bucket things at the end of a rope. That's how the men always went down to the tunnel, one leg out and the other in, kicking out at the side o' the shaft to keep themselves from being dashed against it while the thing swung its way down and down to the darkness and a horse went round and round the top to work the rope. It's not a mode o' transport I'd have fancied myself. Anyway, the doctor went there to tend a man that had got himself injured in a rockfall, leg pinned or something, I don't recall exactly, and one of the workers had met him down there to light him along to the injured mannie. But seems this fellow didn't tell somebody he would have to halt the detonating further along, or whether Dr Aird went slower or faster than the other team had thought, always possible, I couldna tell you. It was a fair while ago when all's said, and James was on a different shaft or I'd ha' heard the whole story from him.

All I know is, they were under an awful lot o' pressure from the contractors to get that rock blown up and every firing had to be done time and again to get anything moved, so they were maybe not always so careful. That was James's view of it anyway. But the upshot was, the next blast went off and Dr Aird was where he wasn't expected and he got blown clean off his feet. Goodness knows what happened to the injured man stuck there. Terrible to-do. They had to wheech the doctor up in that scrap of iron again and get him loaded into a cart. And here he was. Just about alive and no more.

Well, Mrs Aird got the bleeding stopped and we cleaned him up nice and gentle and covered him with blankets. But there was a grey sheen to his face after the grime came off and he was breathing awful quick and shallow, like a body does when there's no air to spare. 'I'll sit by him,' says Mrs Aird.

Annie was for getting her to change out those wet clothes. She was shivering the way you do when you've had a shock and only now the chance to think about it. But no, she would stay there. He'd lost a lot o' blood, she said, which was a bad thing if a heart was to keep beating. I offered to go and see if I had a bit hawthorn left over, but she said he was too far gone for herbs. She was in more of a state now than before, Mrs Aird. No hysterics, though, nothing like that, but she was weeping in a quiet, gathered way. Not once did she put a hand to the tears, and her face was soon glossy with them. Made me wonder when she'd last had a good cry and if she knew any longer what to do wi' tears, though that sounds silly now I say it. I blinked myself a few times, if I'm honest, and it was as much for her as for him I was so fond of.

By then the sun was shining wild and hopeful through the window, and I remember noticing how dollops o' melting snow had begun to slide away from the glass on the outside. Sloosh, is how the sound of it comes back to me. Sloosh, another slab away. I got to thinking how lives can go like that. They're loosened and they're slipping and sometimes there's nothing can stop it. In my mind's eye I kept seeing that shroud o' vapour curling about his feet. And on and on went Mrs Aird wi' the silent weeping.

32

It was already dark outside, the window flaring fitfully with distant lamplight, when Alexander Aird came briefly to himself on the evening of his accident. By the glow of the bedside candle his eyes in their pale sea of freckles found Isabel's. He watched them brim with relief. He felt his fingers raised to her lips. Smiled at her. Passed out again.

When next he flickered into consciousness, he took in not just his wife in a chair but the shadowy outline of his own bed, the hiss of a damp fire, the faintly acidic whiff of carbolic soap. He raised a hand to his chest and felt the bandages. He looked a question.

'The bleeding's stopped,' she said, adding as an afterthought: 'And I washed my hands.'

He squeezed the one clasping his and closed his eyes. An hour later he was awake again, able to speak a little. He begged her to lift the dressings and prod about in his torn flesh for any foreign matter.

Foreign matter? Her stomach lurched.

'Bring the candle nearer, Issy. Look for anything that shouldn't be there.'

Even while panicking that she had no idea in the world what

should or should not be lodging inside her husband's chest, Isabel felt a swoop of pride that he trusted her to look. At her touch he so nearly fainted again that she thought she could not do it. And then, concentrating on the wound, shutting out the thought of his pain, ignoring every wince and stifled cry, swift and careful, she found she could do it after all.

'The wound looks clean,' she reported, affecting a confidence that would at least put his mind at ease. 'Now, my love, you can sleep.'

Next day, changing the dressing in the same deliberate fashion, she told him, 'As soon as you can bear the journey to Glasgow we will have you removed to hospital.'

Alexander grasped her wrist as if she had signalled an intention of carting him there personally. How little Issy knew of hospitals: the choking stench of the wards; the drunken nurses who had to be hefted in on stretchers to start their night duty; the wounds foul with suppurations that no doctor knew how to prevent. And Glasgow's Royal Infirmary on the High Street, right next to a graveyard overflowing with corpses from the last cholera epidemic, reeked not just of bodily fluids but of putrid death itself.

'For God's sake, Issy, keep me here if you'd have me live.'

Alexander knew that infections killed most patients with open wounds. Again and again he had watched the deterioration that followed injury or surgery, and it had long distressed him that he could neither stop people dying nor tell why this patient did and the other did not. This he explained to Isabel as she sat at his bedside in Fairy Knoll, the bony winter light upon them and the fire sighing in the grate. He urged her only to keep his own wound clean with good local water, in which he had developed a touching faith. She was to wash the bandages frequently and pray for what sounded just a little bit like luck.

And he did begin to recover. Colour crept back to Alexander's cheeks. The gash in his chest showed signs of healing cleanly. Within days he was managing a few shaky steps across the room and back to bed. Isabel had no means of telling whether this was down to the mysterious protections of Providence or had anything to do with her sickroom care, but she basked in the novel glow of accomplishment.

She sent Kirsty scurrying off for a lavender tincture to help him sleep and instructed Annie, who was not slow in deciding that she preferred a listless mistress, to polish floor, hearth and windows twice a day and see what the Sebastopol shop might yield for broth.

'You're good at this, Issy,' Alexander said.

Before the year's end he was feeling well enough to moot a return to Glasgow to convalesce. They could see out the rest of the winter there, and Isabel might like, he intimated vaguely, to go and buy a dress.

'I can return when I'm better able to tend my patients,' he said. 'And you too, of course. But, Issy, I won't ask it of you. You may prefer to stay in Bath Street.'

They were downstairs before the fire in the parlour, both swathed in blankets against a screaming draught, more at ease in each other's company than for a long time. It seemed to Alexander that the muffled air between them had been cleared and freshened by his wife's surprisingly energetic and (surely) loving devotion. 'You can sleep now, my love,' he kept hearing her say, as if from far away. 'You're good at this, Issy,' she hugged to herself. The one felt loved, the other validated. Both allowed themselves to be hopeful.

Alexander took a breath before going on. He wanted to say something, but was out of practice and fearful of either inflaming Isabel or depressing her spirits. Speaking of their losses generally resulted in one or the other.

'You've already gone to more lengths by coming here,' he began carefully, 'and by staying here, than I had the right to ask of you.'

He rubbed his nose and ran his fingers through his hair, which sprang to wiry attention. As did Isabel, knowing the signs. She listened warily as he took her hand and murmured, 'Nor have I always known how to talk to you of our sorrows.'

Isabel's head shot up.

'*Our* sorrows, Alex?' Bitterness flooded back. The old resentments surged the stronger for having been diverted by trauma and held at bay by companionship, and in an instant she was engulfed. 'What sorrows are these, pray?'

The suddenness and force of her fury shocked them both, although Isabel offered no resistance. Have my pain, she thought. Try it for size. She was glad to see him flinch.

The blow of her words so winded Alexander that when he tried to speak, he found he could not. Isabel continued to find that she could.

'You take your pleasure and see the fruits of it spat out a few months later and what do you do, Alex? You get on with your work. Off you go with your stethoscope and your knife to mend the world. Oops, was that another baby of ours gone on your way out? Never mind, here's an arm to set or a leg to chop.'

Her voice rose. 'There really is so much else to think about, isn't there? Water. Cholera. Public health. Oh dear, was that another baby? There, there, Issy, don't cry. Let's just make another, shall we?'

Alexander's hand dropped hers, leaving her arm to dangle between the two chairs. She snatched it back.

'You don't ache for a way to grieve for them, do you? You don't see them playing in the grass. You don't wonder who you are and what in God's name you're supposed to be in this world without them. Do you, Alex? Do you?'

She paused to see if he would answer, though she knew he would not and suspected he could not. Which is what made her reach, coldly now, for her worst accusation, her saddest suspicion, the one she had always balked at placing before him in case she was right. 'Do you even remember how many there were?'

A high flush rushed across Alexander's cheeks, which had been very pale. His eyes in the firelight were hollow.

'No, Issy,' he managed at last, in a voice as flat and dull as hers had become shrill. 'I have not kept a tally. A doctor who can't save his own bairns, nor discover why they never live – you think it helps to count my failures?'

'Oh, it's about your pride as a doctor, is it? I see. Eight, Alex. There were eight. Do you remember Johnnie, the first kicks of him? A bonnie fechter, this one, you said. No, I don't suppose you remember that either.'

'Aye, I remember.'

Alexander stared into the fire with his empty, dark-rimmed

eyes. Isabel waited. The clock on the mantelpiece ticked into the silence.

'And the next birth I attended – Lady Montgomery, it was, who had every sort of complication and was like to die herself, and the babe the least of it. By God, I fought to deliver that bairn whole. I fought like a lion. I was not going to grab its head with the forceps and crush it like a hazelnut. It was what the rules would have me do – get it out fast, save the mother. But I wouldn't do it. I would not do it, I tell you. And I won that bairnie in the end, and the mother too. It was a tiny thing with a squeak like a sparrow chick, but she had a beating heart and blood pumping and lungs taking in the air like the most perfect human being in all the world. I won that babe to life and I did it for our lad's sake. I can't experience all a mother does, Isabel, but never tell me I have not felt.'

Isabel frowned into the fire.

She had thought that nobody could feel like her.

33

I had a wee hope that Mrs Aird would maybe visit Nancy while they were away in Glasgow. That was my sister I'd not seen in long enough. Annie nearly split her corset laughing when I told her. Who did I think I was? As if a lady was going to call on the relatives of a navvy's wife to say how do ye do. But as I said to myself, Mrs Aird is that flighty and restless you never know what she'll do next. Granted that a stroll down the Saltmarket was on the optimistic side.

Such a yearning I had for tidings o' Nancy. She was younger than me and blithe as a blackbird when we were growing up on the island. But her man lost his croft and that was them on the boat to Glasgow, same as us. She sank an awful lot after that, stuck in a tenement wi' all those bairns to mind and a husband that sickened from just about the day they arrived. Our youngest sister Mary landed on her feet. She got a job in a shipbuilder's scullery in the west end and a bed in the attic, but our Nancy never had a chance to better herself or make it out that tenement. I used to wake at night worrying about her. After I stayed wi' her when James was away in the Crimea, I used to send her a wee something from his pay packet when I could get hold of it, but I couldna tell ye to this day if it ever got to her. I'm not even sure Her Majesty's postal service made it as far down the High Street as the Saltmarket.

I suppose there was mischief as well in me suggesting that Mrs Aird should seek Nancy out. I thought it would be good for her to see what like it was for others in that braw city o' hers she had such fond thoughts of as soon as she was gone from it. Oh, Kirsty, she'd be saying, how good it will be to have tradesmen delivering decent provisions again, how nice to dress properly for a change. Well, I thought to myself, you're welcome to yon petticoats that make your backside look like the rump o' Tam o' Shanter's mare and we'll see what you think of our Nancy's fashion sense.

When I bided wi' Nancy that time I couldn't get away fast enough. Those tenements were grim all right. Crammed wi' Highlanders and Irish, migrants the lot o' them, fleeing black-faced sheep, bad harvests, rotten potatoes, the starving cold, you name it – all wi' their bellies fired by that wee flame you've a feeling might be the same thing as hope. There's work in the city, you think, bound to be. But nobody mentions there's going to be hundreds of you living in the one tenement, fighting over the same pump for water the colour o' port wine and the one privy in the back court. And maybe it's as well they don't tell you, because where else are ye to go? The landlords had left those places to rot and folk just kept pouring in.

Aye, I can see what you're thinking. What have you got to be smug about, Kirsty McEchern, who never had a house o' your own much better? Well, you're right there. The navvying life was no picnic, and our bairns had never seen a pair o' shoes either and had rags on their backs and often as not the floor for a bed, but at least we had a place to ourselves and we saw a bit o' sky now and then, and a tree or two, and the hawthorn blossom thick as cream in the spring. Which mends your spirits somehow, as Isabel Aird found herself.

I was thrifty wi' the details when I spoke to her about Nancy, seeing as folk in the posher parts would never imagine in a month o' Sundays what goes on in their own city. I just had this feeling that as long as she didna know the worst of it, Mrs Aird might take it into her head to go. She'd started asking questions about how folks like me lived if work was hard to come by or your man got ill. That was a new thing with her, and it didna take very long to tell her: your bairns die, you get sick yourself, you live for a slug o' gin, you end up in the worst room in the tenement, you trail off to the poorhouse, you die – it's one o' these things or all o' them. And oh, I was suddenly heart-sore to think about Nancy and that's when I blurted out could she maybe go and see her for me when she went back to the city. And Mrs Aird said, 'Well, tell me where your sister lives and we'll see.' I don't suppose I really thought she'd do it, and Annie made me think I was being daft anyway, but still, I hoped, ye know.

So anyway, at the turn o' the year I waved them off in the carriage that was to take them to Inversnaid for the steamer, and I did wonder, seeing her clad in her city finery again and looking fair excited for once, if Mrs Aird would come back at all. And I wasna just exactly sure what I felt about that. The doctor, sweet man, would miss her, and so would I in a way, but at least, I caught myself thinking, she'd be safe there.

Safe, you're saying to yourself. Safe from what, Kirsty? (See, I always know what you're thinking when ye wrinkle your brow like that. There you go again. And now you're smiling.) But the truth is, I can't rightly say. It was no more than a flash of a thought, and it took me by surprise myself, seeing as I'd only ever laid eyes on Robert Kirke the once.

34

The stone kirk at Balquhidder, up the steep pass of Strathyre, has windows shaped like praying hands. Full twenty years of my auld life it held me fast. 'Tis sad to see the roof wearing through and wandering weeds where once I spoke out God's word to the sounds of the burn outside chasing itself from the hills to the Balvaig river.

Today there stands a new church hard by. But my bell hangs yet in the auld tower, the bell I presented to those good folk when I left for my new parish. Upon it John Meikle, bell founder, had forged at my bidding the words: 'For Balquhidder Church – M Robert Kirke Minister – Love and Life – Anno 1684'.

The bare rowans by the grave are shining with moisture and the river rushes past white and wild, just as it did on the December day I buried my Isabel and called, in an agony of aloneness, on all living things to mourn her loss.

Mayhap the waiting will go quicker here, as time ever does higher up.

Part Four

1859

Nor no witchcraft charm thee

Cymbeline

35

Isabel returned to Glasgow's west end with a benign perspective on doughy tea shops, broughams for easy summoning and rooms capable of heating up. She was less enthusiastic about parks so well groomed you had to hunt high and low for a crocus. She had also forgotten that ladies did not walk, God forbid, but strolled. On her first ramble in the Botanic Gardens her legs practically quivered with frustration, and relearning how to manoeuvre a cage of crinoline around a room without knocking over a lamp was immeasurably tedious. But she was also aware of the energy that her life in the wilds had given her: more aware of it here than in the place itself, where she had begun to take it for granted. Among her pallid peers she savoured the sensation of physical well-being and spent so much time outdoors that her mother feared for her complexion, which was already a regrettable shade rosier than appropriate in a lady.

On the other hand, Mrs Sarah Gillies was thrilled to discover that her daughter was sometimes in the mood to accept with moderately good grace the kind of invitation ('Fanny Montrose is most insistent, my dear, that we call next Tuesday') that she used to avoid at all costs. Isabel even offered to preside over a

supper party herself at Bath Street. Tipping an imaginary hat
to Alexander, she made a point of inviting at least one engineer.

As Alexander regained his own strength, a tentative spark of
camaraderie sprang between them again: a tease attempted, a
chuckling reminiscence about Kirsty's herb pulley shared. While
nervous of the misjudged step or intemperate word that might
chase the other back to their fortress, each tried to understand
better. Sometimes, under the stuccoed ceiling of their Bath
Street bedroom, they found a route back to tenderness.
Afterwards Isabel stroked her husband's back and tried not to
worry.

Sometimes Alexander pushed his luck. Proposing that she
accompany him to Edinburgh to take tea with Dr Joseph Lister
and his wife – the men knew each other already and had found
much in common – he could not resist adding cheerily, 'I seem
to recall you had an interest in their frogs.'

Isabel was too enamoured of the idea to notice.

Joseph Lister had a splendid house in Edinburgh, a city that was
enjoying a trailblazing surgical reputation under the formidable
Professor James Syme. Since arriving in 1854 the young
Englishman had established himself as a popular university
lecturer, a talented assistant surgeon to Syme and, in short order,
his son-in-law. The graciously proportioned Rutland Street was
situated well away from the black tenements of Edinburgh's Old
Town, which teetered into the sky behind the Airds as they
bowled along Princes Street from the station, the stench ripe
on the east wind.

'Where did I go wrong?' Alexander muttered as they were

ushered into an infinitely grander drawing room than their own. 'Remind me not to mention Fairy Knoll.'

Agnes Lister, Syme's eldest daughter, welcomed them with unaffected manners. She was dark and delicate of feature with an infectious vivacity that put Isabel at her ease. Her tall husband – distinctly dashing, Isabel thought, with his wavy hair and classically straight nose – seemed to be in a constant motion of nervous energy. He would leap to his feet as a fresh thought struck, sit down and rise again two minutes later. Laughing, his wife said he had never finished a cup of tea yet, but his demeanour was unassuming and he seemed as eager to hear Alexander's thoughts on why some inflamed wounds became septic and others did not as to hold forth himself.

At times Isabel felt Mrs Lister's lively eyes upon her. When the men retired to inspect Lister's current batch of dissections, she poured again from the teapot and confided merrily, 'These doctors! I never thought I could become so interested in a blood vessel. You know he brought his microscope on our honeymoon and simply could not restrain himself from collecting up some frogs.' Agnes giggled. 'They escaped. You can imagine the mayhem in the house. The servants were at it for hours trying to catch them.'

It occurred to Isabel that she would have embraced an entire house of rampaging amphibians for the excitement of a mission.

'I hear you work with your husband in the laboratory here yourself?'

'Yes, he dictates notes as he's cutting and you'll find me still writing them up by night while he's out at Duddingston Loch catching the next consignment.' Another tinkle of mirth. 'I may tell you that even during meals we discuss little else. I can now discourse upon the workings of the central nervous system with the greatest authority, I assure you.'

A memory, startling in its clarity, returned to Isabel of a time when she and Alexander had spent meals like that. 'Chloroform, Alex? What is it? What can it do?' She remembered him laughing across the table and saying she should slow down, slow down, he didn't know much himself yet. 'You'll be the first to know, Issy, when I find out.'

Isabel had loved these conversations, looked forward to them, initiated many herself. Was it she who had sunk them in lethargy?

Collecting herself, she found Mrs Lister watching her again. 'But are you not too busy directing the house?' Isabel asked, a little flustered. 'Too busy with the children?'

Perhaps Agnes Lister detected the hesitation; perhaps she merely sensed the other questions hovering beneath that one. In any case she spoke frankly: 'I have longed for children, Mrs Aird, but they have not come. We have not been married many years so that may change, but I am readying myself.'

Isabel felt the prickle of tears and could not speak. Agnes glanced at her with those friendly brown eyes.

'I tell myself there is more to womanhood than being a mother or planning meals and directing servants. Or even drinking tea, which I must say Joseph is also very good at when he remembers.' She raised her china cup towards Isabel in a mock toast: 'And in sharing this work of his I have found the thing I can do.'

Isabel gazed at her, still without a word to say in return. Her heart was very full.

'Find the thing you can do, Mrs Aird,' Agnes Lister said, rising from her chair. 'That is what I would urge you.'

She was younger than Isabel, the curve of chin and cheek still rounded with youth. Yet she carried herself with the easy grace of a woman who knows herself. She led her guest towards the door through which the men had earlier sauntered. 'Why don't we join the others and you can have a look at our microscope.'

Before opening the door she placed a hand on Isabel's arm. 'Are you all right with brains, by the way? Not everyone is, I've discovered.'

Isabel said gaily that she was sure she would be quite all right with brains.

On the train back to Glasgow she asked Alexander what he thought about the role of the central nervous system in inflammation. He raised an eyebrow and folded his arms. Now that she knew more about it than most people, might he suggest that Isabel offer him the benefit of her own opinion? After all, she had just received a personal tutorial from Joseph Lister, and nobody in the land understood as much about the subject as he.

'Except Agnes Lister,' Isabel murmured, raising him an eyebrow in return.

Alexander laughed and said he was exceedingly glad she had come along.

Her nights were often restless. Nothing stopped Alexander – it never had – from tipping into sleep with indecent haste, which annoyed her. And it annoyed her for annoying her because there was no conceivable reason for objecting to your husband sleeping just because you could not. She often lay half the night listening to the clop of hooves on cobbles, the lone rattle of the late coach, a door banging shut down the street, a slurred altercation beneath the window. After Sebastopol all these sounds seemed amazingly subdued. How strange to come from country to city for peace in your bed.

But her thoughts were less subdued, and they it was that night after night colonised the cloudy spaces between wakefulness and oblivion.

Sometimes it was Robert Kirke who appeared, inviting her to listen to the tinkling winter bells and asking her to dance, no, not dance, he hadn't wanted her to dance, why had he not wanted her to dance, but she would dance anyway because she felt like it and she hadn't felt like dancing for such a long time. Look, my dear Mr Kirke, how I can dance for you.

A plague of frogs visited too, capering up an imposing staircase with a great hullaballoo behind. And there at the top of the banister stood a dark-haired young woman, laughing good-naturedly and shouting down to Isabel, yes, it must have been to her, 'Find what you can do. We must all find what we can do.'

Nothing so substantial as a plan, or even an idea, arrived in those half-conscious reaches of the night. What did come was more like a phantom parade of possibilities, gone before she could grasp them but vaguely recalled on waking with a heart-skip of optimism.

And then there was Nancy.

She had contrived the visit without telling her mother why she needed the family carriage, which would have entailed an explanation unlikely to receive a sympathetic hearing. Social calls in Glasgow normally stopped well short of the Saltmarket.

But Isabel had a better idea of what to expect than she would once have done. These days she knew what a wynd was, in theory at least, and a vennel. She knew they were overcrowded. She knew they were full of disease. She had dared herself to imagine a dungheap two storeys high. She knew the landlords had abandoned the tenements in the oldest part of the city to build new houses in her own part of town and the suburbs. She knew that Nancy had been displaced to Glasgow with children and a sick husband and nowhere else to go.

'Don't drink the water, mind,' Kirsty had made sure to advise when she was urging the visit with a hint of pleading that was surprisingly touching. Kirsty could be insouciant to the point of overstepping her place, but this time her eyes had watched carefully for the reply.

The stone tenements were so high and so close that they almost kissed each other above the wynd. It was a miracle the sky squeezed between them at all, Isabel thought, stepping down from her grotesquely out-of-place carriage before an audience of filthy children. But it did. A lone shaft of sunlight had penetrated the street and splashed itself across a patch of black wall. Hatched from the closes with sleeves rolled to the elbow, a dozen or more women were leaning where the sun had pooled. They watched her sailing towards them.

'Mrs Nancy Donald?'

One of the women nodded to the nearest entrance. 'Along there. Down the stair.'

For many nights after that Isabel would see again, keep seeing, the dark close and the winding stairs she fumbled her way down to reach the cellar. She would remember the damp cold that went straight through her clothes, the suffocating stink of urine. She would press herself into the dank wall again as a man with beer on his breath lurched past and made a lunge for the purse she had made sure to leave in the carriage. She would hear the wailing of some child on the stair above and the coughing from behind nameless doors. She would find herself once more on the threshold of Nancy's room, registering that there were shadowy people on the floor, and not a stick of furniture in sight, and no window, and no light (not really, though there must have been a candle somewhere for her to see at all), and a sour smell of mould and sweat and illness, and more coughing, and a dog, dear God, a dog as thin and mangy as everyone else, which growled as she put her head round the open door and, swallowing the sensation of rising bile, asked for Nancy.

There was a look of Kirsty about the woman pointed out to her in the corner. The wide mouth in the big-boned face was instantly familiar and for a moment almost comforting, until Nancy looked up at her visitor from the floor and smiled. Oh, that smile. All lip and bone. As terrifying, in a face so white and ravaged, as a clown's rictus.

Isabel shrank back, breathing fast. Then she forced herself forward again and crouched down until her face was on a level with Nancy's. Her dress swept a man's feet and she drew it in with a flustered apology.

'I've brought greetings from Kirsty,' she said.

When Nancy heard her sister's name, her eyes lit up, as luminous in the shadows as the twin orbs of an owl. And at that the toothless grimace became a human smile, as it had been all along, eager and a little shy.

This was the other image that would return to Isabel in her long stretches of sleeplessness in the Bath Street bedroom. It was not just the reliving of a nightmare that kept her awake, not just the squalor beyond imagining of an alien land in her own city. What she saw, and what she would encourage herself to remember for the rest of her life, was the incandescent humanity that had somehow survived.

There was no sensation of optimism when she woke in the morning after a restless night with Nancy. She experienced something else, though. It floated just beyond conscious thought, evaporating as soon as she reached for it. The merest puff of possibility is all it was. But it was there.

36

Professor William Macquorn Rankine to Dr Alexander Aird

Glasgow,
April 1859

My dear Dr Aird,

It was a pleasure to attend you yesterday e'en and I bid you thank
your good wife most kindly for her hospitality. I thought Mrs Aird
looked exceedingly well. She spoke very enthusiastically of Dr Lister's
work in Edinburgh, and I was struck by how affected she was by
her recent visit to the Saltmarket. She seemed, moreover, a good deal
more interested in the waterworks than I recall from our first
meeting. Or perhaps she merely feigned more artfully an enthusiasm
for my engineering monologues – such enthusiasm as I am regretfully
the first to find encouraging!

It has indeed been warming to see the works progress so well
when all the problems are considered, not least the number of
contractors who have pulled out at one stage or another and the
variegated nature of the rock itself, which is obdurate enough to

make an engineer's eyes water at the northern end but full of whin-stone further south. Your wife listened more patiently than I deserved to my description of the substantial water ingress before the tunnel enters the reservoir at Milngavie, which occasioned the departure of Adamson the contractor in financial disarray. Ah well, at least Bateman remains optimistic that all will be finished in good time later this year, even the aqueducts, which have proved almost as challenging as the tunnels. The five between Loch Chon and the Endrick Water look set to be magnificent beasts and, if I am any judge, even the three minor cast-iron troughs across the Chonside burns are like to prove much admired. In the north of the city the laying of pipes is also proceeding apace. As you will have observed yourself, it is nowadays hardly possible to traverse a street that is not being dug up!

By the by, you can expect to see me in military guise 'ere long. You must have heard of the Volunteer Corps, which are bruited about the land in response to the perceived ambitions of France. These suspicions of our ally do seem distinctly over-egged, but I confess to being rather taken with the idea of a citizens' defence corps, which must at the very least make men of a few students I might mention.

Mrs Aird asked me if I had composed any more ditties of late, and I promised I would look one out to make her smile. Since she was also kind enough to enquire if there were not a Mrs Rankine in the offing I thought I would take the liberty of appending 'The Mathematician in Love', hoping she will agree that this foolish rhyme explains everything.

May I add, in more sober vein, that you are fortunate indeed to have found a life's partner of such spirit and sympathy and indeed, if I have judged aright from your wife's most engaged conversation yesterday, such keen understanding of the public health endeavour

*you have set as your professional goal when you return to Glasgow
at the conclusion of the works.*

*I send my heartiest wishes to Mrs Aird and wish you a quieter,
not to say safer, professional time of it as you return to Loch Chon.*

I remain your friend,

William Macquorn Rankine

*PS: You will discover herein, Aird, to what lengths a man may be
driven by the tides of academic solemnity lapping ever upon the
shores of his emotions – although I do try to convince myself that it
addresses not merely the age-old failure of man and woman to
understand one another but the modern tendency to imagine that all
things of value may be reduced to the rational. Pray be a merciful
judge of the literary quality, which cannot be said to exist.*

THE MATHEMATICIAN IN LOVE

*A mathematician fell madly in love
With a lady, young, handsome, and charming:
By angles and ratios harmonic he strove
Her curves and proportions all faultless to prove.
As he scrawled hieroglyphics alarming.*

*He measured with care, from the ends of a base,
The arcs which her features subtended:
Then he framed transcendental equations, to trace
The flowing outlines of her figure and face,
And thought the result very splendid.*

THE NINTH CHILD

'Let x denote beauty, y, manners well-bred,
z, Fortune (this last is essential),
Let L stand for love,' our philosopher said,
'Then L is a function of x, y, and z,
Of the kind which is known as potential.

'Now integrate L with respect to d t,
(t standing for time and persuasion);
Then, between proper limits, 'tis easy to see,
The definite integral Marriage must be:
(A very concise demonstration).'

Said he, 'If the wandering course of the moon
By Algebra can be predicted,
The female affections must yield to it soon.'
But the lady ran off with a dashing dragoon,
And left him amazed and afflicted.

37

It must have been the April of '59 when I heard they were coming back. I mind the worst o' the frosts were past and the days were getting longer. Annie got sent ahead to air the rooms and stock up on coal, and it was no time before she had me hauled in to clean out the range, which I'm sure she was supposed to do herself but no matter.

When they got back I rushed straight over to see if there was news of Nancy. I was that touched when Mrs Aird told me she'd been to see her right enough and brought me her loving wishes. That was all, mind you. She just said Nancy was pleased to hear from me, was happy to know James had work and sent her sincere regards back. To be truthful with you, she looked a bit lost for words when it came to Nancy, which was not like Mrs Aird at all. Most o' the times she had nothing to say it was because she couldna be bothered saying it. But I was right thankful to know Nancy had heard my name and knew I was thinking of her and was well myself, which would make her just happy as a lark.

Mrs Aird was looking well herself when she came back, I will say. Said being in Glasgow had been a learning time in a lot o' ways, but she could hardly wait to be striding out in the wind again and watching the sun on the water. Which I wish I'd had the time for, by the by. Thinking about her being out and about again got me worrying, though.

I'd not seen hide nor hair o' Robert Kirke in the months she was gone, nor felt my skin prickle at some wickedness stealing forth in the night from the mound behind Fairy Knoll – which I was always half expecting, to be honest with you. The second sight is a special gift that I wouldn't claim for myself *as such*, but I do get my feelings and they're nearly always right is all I'll say. Anyway, she was back, Mrs Aird, and from that day on the wee twinge o' worry wouldna go away.

38

She is returned.

And I am ready.

'Tis to be hoped ye are ready, Robert Kirke. Ye spend a sight too much time drooling o'er the past.

I was only thinking I had the gift o' happiness once . . .

Fie, man! Have ye nothing better to think?

Happiness. I remember chasing my brothers up Doon Hill when we were lads, running through oak groves glossy with rain. I always had to stop and look at the polish on the leaves, and then I ran on with a song in my throat. 'Twas the way I was made. Others get a sackload o' glooms that is never emptied however hard they try, others the taste for contention or dissatisfaction which canna let them be at peace with anyone. But I had my mother's easy temperament. Love and life cam naturally to Robert Kirke, mild-hearted Episcopalian in the glowering Scotland o' the seventeenth century.

In those times we had papists on one side and on the other the hunted hillside Covenanters, worshipping their Presbyterian way under the open sky. Looking on from my quiet kirk in Balquhidder, I saw two opposites tied together at the tail by suspicion of error and denial of liberty to everyone else. For my ain part I could never bring myself to ill-like another man for his doctrine alone. From a simple reading o' Scripture it seemed plain that this world was given us to prepare for a better one, and zeal for pursuing your ain interests without a care for how it affected another was the wrong way to go about it.

Tak care where ye go wi' this, Robert Kirke.

The irony screams loud enough in my soul, thank you, but 'tis what I thought.

My ministry at Balquhidder was so far from disputatious that I spent a deal of it translating the metrical Psalms into Gaelic for the ease of my congregation. That was a contentful time, too. For all the worldliness o' my university education I felt at home among simple folk. Their ancient traditions, though not always lying too snug wi' Kirk teaching, awoke in me as sympathetic a curiosity as the ancient lore of the Greeks or the Hebrews. Nay, more. For the supernatural beliefs of my parishioners were spoken through the landscape itself to all who know the Gaelic tongue.

A young man eager to learn, I loitered in pitiful fields and the mud o' many a poor home to gather tales of the *sìthichean* from the lips of all who bore witness. Folk described the *sìthichean* to me as being of intelligent spirit –

that much you gathered correctly

– and of a middle nature betwixt man and angels. How I wrestled with language to render the picture produced in my mind's eye. Bodies of congealed air, I wrote, light and changeable as a condensed cloud and dwelling in any cranny of the earth where there enters air, the earth being full o' cavities and there being no such thing as a pure wilderness in all the universe.

Ye were not so far wrang there either, were ye?

Making notes in the same wise as my university lectures, I described the uncanny apprehensions o' the humblest peasant as gravely and respectfully as Dionysius Areopagitica's marshalling of the nine orders of spirits superior and subordinate, or the precautions of future dangers that Socrates had from his Daemon. I listened to lassies sobbing that the sickly bairn in their lap was a changeling. I sat by the side of an auld wifie with the wonder o' long ago still glowing in her eye, and heard how she had been lifted from a childbed herself to nurse a fairy child. Into my notebook went tales of seers, who had seen the double of a man enter a house days before the real one, or a winding-shroud creep ower a man's legs and up his torso until it cam at last over the head to signal that he was ripe for the grave.

My beloved wife used to tease me. My book o' spells she called it, and bade me keep it hidden. For who in the Kirk, whate'er their view on bishops, would understand a minister's zest for the world o' faery and second sight? Yet hath not every age some secret left for its discovery? Thus I reasoned. And who knows but this intercourse betwixt two kinds of rational inhabitants o' the same earth might not one day be as mundane as the art of navigation, or printing, or gunning, or the wondrous discoveries made beneath a microscope.

'Ca' canny,' said my seeing wife, 'and delve ye not too deep.'
And you know how it ended, Robert Kirke.
I know how it ended.
So forget the past, would ye, and set to work again on the lady.

39

It was with little surprise and even a flutter of pleasure that on her very first walk along the banks of Loch Chon after her return from Glasgow, Isabel found herself keeping company with Robert Kirke.

'How very nice to see you, Mr Kirke,' she said cheerfully as he slackened his long-limbed pace to match hers. He looked, she thought, pleased to see her too.

'If it's no trouble to you, madam, I'd be glad to bide by you as ye walk.' His pleasant rumble of a voice was as soothing as she remembered. ''Tis a fine time o' year with the trees coming back to green, is it not? And might I ask' – in he sped again before she could reply – 'if your husband is well recovered? I recall ye had bad news of him at the turn o' the year.'

'He is very well, thank you, Mr Kirke. Back to sort out the medical emergencies of Sebastopol with his health fully restored.'

'And you, my lady? Ye seem in warmer spirits and have a bonnie bloom on your cheek as speaks of better health yourself. Am I right?'

Isabel looked up at his face quickly and thought about being affronted. But Kirke's gaze was set on the path ahead, head forward, hands clasped behind his back as he walked. Although the assumed intimacy remained unsettling, there was nothing glaringly untoward about his attentions, nor even much to suggest any great interest in the answer to his questions beyond his usual grave courtesy, save for the slight tension in the air between them into which his words had dropped.

'I'm in fine health and glad to be back. The city has its attractions, but I've missed my walks.'

He said no more, and they meandered on in undemanding silence. Breathing in the earthy smell of Robert Kirke with the light scent of the young leaves clustering about their path, Isabel was sorry when it was time to turn back.

They met frequently as April blew and showered its way towards May. With Alexander fully occupied again, Isabel found she was glad of Robert Kirke's bracing companionship. In a way that she had no desire to explain to Kirsty or for one second broach with Alexander – indeed that she barely understood herself – this grubby-looking character with the lovely voice, who looked and sounded as if he had stepped straight from another world, felt as if he belonged to her. He drew her to him as the landscape did, bestowing comforts threaded with danger, a form of exhilaration to which she had become increasingly receptive.

Sometimes they met by what was almost an arrangement. 'Tomorrow promises to be fine. I shall be at Loch Dhu,' he might say. Or, 'I may chance to gang towards Katrine if the rain hold off in the morn.' But it was never quite an arrangement, and it is even possible that when Kirsty began interrogating her like a tenacious police inspector, Isabel believed what she so stoutly and impatiently maintained: 'Really, Kirsty, it is no business of mine or yours where Mr Kirke walks. And only to be expected that our paths will cross occasionally when I am so much out and about.'

He had begun in these encounters to tell her something of himself – unwillingly, as she often felt, sensing a tussle behind the watchful eyes. A mention of his childhood in Aberfoyle brought forth a veritable rhapsody about the boyish delights he had experienced on some hill he used to climb, followed by a sharp intake of breath when she asked if he went there still.

No, he intimated. He no longer made a habit of going there.

'Then shall we not go together, Mr Kirke?' she asked in a burst of spontaneity.

Isabel had a tendency to be impetuous in the company of Robert Kirke, who defied the rules of social inhibition so flagrantly himself that she kept being tempted to follow suit. The same rush of gaiety seized her as had made her want to dance to the music of the ice bells. She would go with him to his childhood haunts. She would learn his story. She would find out what lay behind these troubled eyes. If her suggestion had a faintly improper ring in her own ears (which it did), she rather enjoyed the sensation.

'Nay, my lady,' Kirke countered, ''tis too far for you to walk.'

As anyone who had studied Isabel Aird might have calculated, this elicited the retort that she was able to walk for hours and would like nothing better than to explore somewhere new.

'Then let us meet on the morrow, my lady, and we shall gang to Doon Hill. I dare say it might suit us both.'

40

The day she went off with him I was outside my house on the slope above Sebastopol. Of course I knew fine she'd been meeting him all over the place already. I'd spied them together on the Katrine road a few days before – him black as a crow with his head bent to listen and her standing there simpering. Well, I'm assuming the simpering.

'Kirsty,' she'd told me that time, 'it's only by chance we ran into each other and I wish you would stop going on about it.'

But at least that was close to home. It was nothing to seeing the pair of them strolling off for Aberfoyle, side by side like some respectable couple out to take the air. Well, I put down the kindling and went rushing out the camp after them.

'Will ye no' turn back, mistress,' says I. 'Ye know the doctor doesna like you to stray.'

'Stray?' says she, flaring up the way she could when you crossed her. 'You think I'm a dog to be kept on a leash, Kirsty?'

And by that you'll see how difficult she could be for the doctor to handle at times, or anyone come to that, never mind her sorrows which nobody was denying. She had spirit when she was roused, Mrs Aird. It used to burst out its cage every which way in those days, and no' always so wisely.

Kirke is busy hopping from foot to foot in that bird-like way o' his, impatient to be away and looking at me in such a shivery way. Oh, the way he looked at me from those black eyes, though when he turned them on her he was nice as ninepence.

'You must go back if ye will, my lady,' he says. That's the way he used to address her, like something out an old ballad. And I knew that polite tack would work nicely – just enough of a challenge in it, but oh so understanding. He always seemed to have her measure.

'Pay no attention to Mrs McEchern,' says she, giving me a cool look. 'Where I choose to walk is no concern of hers.'

And nor was it, when ye think about it. Maybe this is what the wifies felt like who were aye warning o' this and that in olden times. They knew what was coming and nobody ever listened to a word they said.

41

You dare to come to Doon Hill again?

Why should I not? I am winning her trust. Here she walks by my side with roses in her cheek and signs – I have observed her sae lang that I know how to interpret the smallest flutter of hand on gown when she thinks I see not – signs, I say, of hopeful developments to come.

Ye fear not to come to Doon Hill of all places?

The hill is not to be feared, but only those that live within it. And you have done your worst. Will ye kindly leave me in peace.

Ye will pass your own grave, man.

Taunt me not, vile voice.

'Linguae Hiberniae Lumen' you will observe on the stone. Is it not gratifying to know your efforts for the Gaelic tongue have been remembered?

You are cruel.

So are you, Robert Kirke. Have you forgot what ye intend for this woman?

What you intend.

Are you afraid, Robert Kirke?

I fear what you have done to me. Does that count?

42

It was a warm, rain-freshened day, and they walked briskly along the banks of Loch Ard. As the way lengthened and the trees thickened, it did cross Isabel's mind that she was alone in the middle of nowhere with a man she hardly knew for no better reason than her own curiosity and the novelty of acting on impulse: no calling card, no carriage, no mother, no chaperone, no husband.

Kirke had barely addressed a word to her since they set out, except to caution her to tak care over this burn or watch out for the briars in yon bosky hollow. He seemed to be arguing with himself. Sometimes his lips moved and she thought he was about to speak, but no words came. She was becoming used to it. She never minded the silences.

They skirted the clachan of Aberfoyle, traversed a length of knobbly pastureland and drew near to a plain oblong church which stood alone, dilapidated and surrounded by graves under a sky the colour of over-milked tea. A short distance beyond arose a perfectly round hill, covered in trees. Kirke stood observing the church amid its tombstone host without expression.

'This was my father's kirk, and mine too after I left Balquhidder,' he offered. 'I preached in there every Sunday for seven years – and long before that listened to my father in the same pulpit. It has been sore neglected. The manse where we lived is hard by.'

Isabel waited for him to say more. As she did, it started to rain – violently, in the theatrical manner of the season, and without notice. Kirke grabbed her arm.

"Twill pass soon. The kirk is closed up and lockit, but we can tak our shelter under that tree by the wall.'

He hurried her around the side of the church, giving a wide berth to a gravestone more prominent than all the others. It rested flat above the ground on two boulders. Isabel glimpsed ornate Latin lettering. She felt Kirke's grip tighten as he steered her past.

'Whose grave is that?'

'Mine,' he said brusquely.

Isabel laughed. 'Is it a family plot?'

'Ye might say that. Although my wife rests in Balquhidder kirkyard.'

She glanced up at him quickly. 'I am sorry to hear it, Mr Kirke. Is she long deceased?'

'Aye, my lady. Lang, lang gone.'

They reached a spreading sycamore at the edge of the church-yard and stood together under its leaky spring canopy, looking out at the rain.

'What was her name, may I ask?' Isabel said softly. Coaxing information from Robert Kirke was a delicate business.

'Isabel.' He cleared his throat and tried again. 'Isabel. She had spirit enough for the two of us and a wiser head than mine. And if I'd not buried her so young she would maybe ha' stopped me . . .'

He looked suddenly uncertain. Isabel waited. The hectic patterings continued overhead.

'Nay, 'tis not helpful to be talking about the past,' he said at last. 'I'm aye having to warn myself about it.'

Isabel shifted to avoid a rivulet of rain. 'What would your wife have stopped you from doing, Mr Kirke?'

The lowering glare also arrived without warning. He brought his face so close to hers that she could see the dirt in his wrinkles and tawny flecks in the dark eyes. Taking a quick step back she thought suddenly of Alexander, his open face, his cheerful grin.

'From losing my soul,' Kirke said coldly.

'Ah,' Isabel said.

'And my humanity.'

'I see,' she said, and wished very much that Alexander were here.

43

Now. Bring her now.

Nay, this goes too far. 'Tis not my commission.

You are weak, Robert Kirke. Ye know fine the bargain we made. Fail to carry out your part and there will be no fond reunion with the one you choke to name. No heaven, Robert Kirke. Remember that. Nor any peace on earth neither. Only us.

This that ye would have me do now is no part of that bargain.

But it reveals your weakness. See how you cavil, see how you quibble.

It is no part of our bargain, I say.

Show some mettle, man. Bring us the lady.

44

There was no sign of Kirke's earlier gruff solicitude as he led her up through the close-entangled trees that encased Doon Hill. The way was winding rather than steep, but it was strewn underfoot with lumpy roots and mushy leaves on which Isabel tripped and snagged her skirts while he strode remorselessly ahead. Shoving an overhanging branch out of the way, he left it to swing back before she could pass herself. This was plain rude. When she protested, he grasped the next knot of briars in her way so fiercely that blood spurted from his bare palm. His face was closed, angry even, so different from his confiding mood in the churchyard that Isabel began to feel unnerved.

A deep fatigue was weighing on her now. She had eaten nothing for hours and her head was light, her thinking cloudy. Reluctance was growing with every step, although she could not have said whether her companion's mood was responsible or the hill itself and the cloying disorder of its ancient shrubbery, which shut out the sky as they climbed and seemed to draw the very air into itself.

A solitary chee-chee-chee rose in the rinsed air. Where were the rest of the birds and their whisking springtime industry? Isabel listened, holding her breath as if the whistle of her own exertion had extinguished the song of Doon Hill. As they wound higher the trees grew ever thicker, rowan twisting into birch, oak choking elder, dead hawthorn stunting young leaf-bursts of holly. Giant ferns thrust at her face and thistles aimed their spikes at her dress. A broken-backed pine held out such pale, supplicating arms as they passed that she had to avert her gaze in case . . . Well, in case what? Isabel made herself pause to admire the delicate feathering on a young fern that Kirke had just flattened, which had been thrusting at no one. Honestly, she was getting worse than Kirsty.

Looking back with a click of agitation, her companion told her to make haste.

The trees stopped. They were at the summit.

'Oh,' said Isabel. 'Oh.'

After the tangled abundance of the ascent, the flat, wide circle at the top of Doon Hill was shocking in its nakedness. Sky rushed to meet them as she followed Kirke across the mossy floor. But this was sky without light, or rather light without radiance, brownly diffused by a single pine tree, which stood immense and alone in the centre of the circle, the centre of the domed hill. It was so tall that Isabel, tipping back her head and screwing her eyes towards the topmost branches, could see no end to it. Lichen the shade of peppermint grew between plates of red-brown bark and among the cones on the ground. The beardy tendrils made the place feel very old. Unease clamoured again in her chest.

Kirke stood with his back to the tree, his face harrowed with some private emotion he was so obviously trying to master that

Isabel would have considered it impolite to look if she had not urgently required his full attention.

'Mr Kirke,' she said firmly, 'I must thank you for showing me your hill—'

''Tis not my hill,' he growled.

'Your boyhood haunt then. It was kind of you to bring me here, but I am tired now and would ask you to take me home.'

He did not reply. Nor move. Only stood in front of her with his eyes darting around the empty circle enclosed by its silent trees, as if expecting something to happen. Isabel looked around again herself, infected by the nervous anticipation radiating from him. Nothing. No sound. No flicker of the light. No movement, but for a heart-palpitating gust of tardy raindrops from the leaves above, which halted her breath and sent a shiver snaking through a colony of ferns on the rim.

'Look around you, my lady,' Kirke said.

'I have already looked around,' Isabel snapped, her temper on the rise now. 'And I've seen all the sights I wish to, thank you very much, and am ready to leave.'

He paid no attention. His gaze had not settled.

'Imagine, my lady, that 'tis coming on for dusk as ye are leaving the manse,' he said, looking past her at the tall pine.

'Oh, for goodness' sake. What manse?'

He ignored her. ''Tis the same time o' year as this. The white blossom is out on the rowan, and on the hawthorn, too, blithe as a wedding bower, and the air is sweet with the scent o' wild eglantine.'

'Is this a childhood memory, Mr Kirke? I don't wish to seem rude, but perhaps you could return to it later? I really do wish to—'

'Imagine,' he continued in his low, mesmerising voice as if she had not spoken, 'that ye climb the hill as you've done hundreds o' times before. Ye have finished a heavy task and the hill is calling you. Can you imagine sich a thing, my lady?'

Yes, she could imagine such a thing. Loch Chon calling her. Water glimpsed through trees. Bejewelled sunlight on the surface. A Dog hidden beneath.

'But something is wrang this e'en. The birdies are gone too early to their rest. The light seeps away too fast. And when ye stand at this great pine looking around, ye sense you are not alone.'

Isabel's heart was thumping hard again, her stomach lurching and swooping, a prickling sensation at the back of her neck. She affected a careless laugh. 'Are you trying to frighten me, Mr Kirke?'

'Then you look up,' he said softly, now wholly focused on her face, those wanting eyes boring into hers. 'Look up now, my lady, just as I did then.'

'Mr Kirke,' she said, staring him out. She had had enough of this. 'I am not going to look up just because you tell me to.'

At which Robert Kirke, to her great surprise, came as close to a snort of laughter as she had heard from him yet.

'Ach, my lady, you're as contrary as she was. May I suggest, then, that ye look down.'

Isabel frowned at him for another long moment and then shrugged. Slowly she raised her head to the tall tree and looked straight up into the brown light. And as she did so, the branches began to whirl and she had a sensation of falling – down, down – until everything was black.

45

There, are ye satisfied? I have done as ye bade me.

Calm yourself, Robert Kirke. Think of it as a way of testing yourself.

A test?

To prove ye can act when we require it. Our bargain depends upon it.

Ye know fine this nonsense on the hill has nothing to do with our bargain. She is not ready.

But she soon will be. Remember that, Robert Kirke. She soon will be. And then must you be ready also.

46

Isabel came to herself with her nose pressed against the damply odorous wool of Robert Kirke's coat and a strand of lank hair tickling her cheek. Sunlight flickered through the canopied glades of oak through which she was being inexpertly bounced. Now and then his loping stride slowed to edge them both around a protruding bough or tackle a steep decline and then he was off again, clutching her in his long arms like some rescued damsel. The damsel in this case was feeling extremely foolish and wanted to be sick.

At the bottom of the hill he eased her to her feet and turned away while she smoothed down her skirts and reassembled her dignity.

'Thank you, Mr Kirke. How very embarrassing. I must have fainted.'

'Aye, madam, you did,' he said curtly, still looking away. ''Twas best to get ye down the hill at once before anything else happened. Tak your rest a minute and I'll see you hame.'

She sank on to a stump of tree trunk at the end of a straggling line of aspens, and might have closed her eyes if she had not become conscious of a tremble in the undergrowth at her feet. Cautiously she toed the vegetation aside. Staring back with panicky eye was a woodpecker, the first bird she had seen on Doon Hill today. One black and white wing was struggling feebly; another lay at an awkward angle, quite still. Isabel leaned down to stroke the warm, scarlet tip at its head. Such a lovely thing. At her touch the bird thrashed more desperately.

A swift movement at her back and Isabel froze. The long fingers of Robert Kirke grabbed her wrist.

He whisked the bird into his hand, swung his arm back and slammed its head against the nearest aspen. Then he hurled the corpse back into the grass.

Isabel gazed at him, speechless with shock. Kirke glowered back.

'Ye think I like to see a harmless creature suffer?' he muttered, whether to her or himself she could not tell and was past caring. 'Do ye? Do ye?'

47

Home she came on a cart. A cart, would you credit it? Mighty flustered she was too, being helped out at Fairy Knoll by a big Irishman none too steady on his feet.

'This man was good enough to give me a lift from Aberfoyle,' says she, a bit embarrassed if I know Mrs Aird. 'He was coming this way anyway and my companion kindly suggested it – though I'd be in your debt, Kirsty, if you didn't mention it to Dr Aird.'

Well, I knew what that was about. The doctor was aye worrying about the way she wandered about the place. Just that last winter there'd been a navvy driving a coal-cart back to the camp from Aberfoyle and likely he'd been into the Teapot on his way, which was a bothy along by Loch Ard, or was it Loch Dhu, I can't rightly mind, but I do know it didna sell much tea. And anyway the night came on before the afternoon was properly started, the way it does at that time o' year. The cart struck a stone and off went the navvy straight into the path of a turning wheel. The doctor had only a body to carry back in his own cart that night. He was aye bringing this up when his wife was on about walking out, and she never got very far asking how likely it was that she'd be found drunk in possession of a cart.

So I could see she wouldna be wanting to rush to her husband wi' the story o' this jaunt o' hers. Mind you, the minute I had her in the parlour with a cup o' tea and her feet up I made sure to get the whole tale myself. Seems it was a longer walk than she'd thought it would be. Went too far, she said, and felt a bit faint when she'd climbed some hill. Oh-oh, I thought. Isabel Aird is long past coming over all ladylike giddy at a wee bit o' exercise, so what have we got here? Well, no point fretting, I thought to myself, and we'd have to see what came o' that.

On she goes. 'And you had nothing to worry about, Kirsty, so don't think it. Mr Kirke only wanted to show me a tree he used to like.'

Aye, that'll be right, says I to myself. What kind o' gentleman has an upstanding woman walk for miles to look at a tree? And never mind a gentleman. If my James propositioned a wifie he barely knew like that and then dumped her in a cart, I'd have him strung up by the oxters. What was he doing wandering about these wild places anyway and *happening* to meet Mrs Aird all the time? Did he no' have a home to go to, or a pulpit to keep him busy?

Right, Kirsty, says I to myself, it's up to you. I'll ask around, I thought. There must be folk from these parts who'll hear the name Robert Kirke and can tell what he's about. So I started asking questions. But it was gey difficult, let me tell you. Everyone I came on was an incomer brought in by the waterworks or a tourist in a hired coach rattling hither and yon to see the sights. The sights! Not a one of them ever came near the Sebastopol middens, I can tell you that. The only clue I did get was from my James, who'd been at the Teapot himself this day I'll tell ye about. The navvies all used to go there on payday and blew the lot, most o' them, although I'll say this for James that he wasna the worst. There was a local man distilled his own whisky and he was the most popular man for miles around. Tam was his name, if I recall, and he was aye coming up wi' ploys to disguise his still from the excise man.

Well, James was there one e'en and got talking to a gloomy man called Wattie Hunter, who was sitting in the corner wi' his plaid over his shoulder looking as if all the woes o' the world were upon him the way Highlanders do wi' a dram or two of *uisge beatha* in them. Told James he had a wee bit croft ower the other side o' Loch Chon and they had a good old blether together in the Gaelic. Seems this Wattie spent the whole time complaining to James about the mess the water folk were making o' the ground over there.

Then they got on to the *sìthichean*, and how that happened I don't know, because it wouldna have been James introduced the subject. I got the impression Wattie started going on about the works disturbing the land o' faery itself, words to that effect. Anyway he said, jokey-like – though there's always a serious vein in every bit o' light talk about the *sìthichean* – that there'd maybe be a few folk escaped from the place if they were drilling down that deep.

James knocks back his dram and says he's never been in a place wi' so many fairy names as round here – even coming from the Hebrides, which have got plenty.

That's because they're here, says Wattie, quite matter o' fact – everyone knows the *sìthichean* are here. And he wouldna be surprised, says he, if there are folk walking again that you and I might not like to meet going about our business, because that place corrupts you. It gets a grip on your soul and you're not the same again. As Wattie says to James, these folk are human all right, but they've still got faery deep engrained. Some o' them have made bargains to get out. I was going to say bargains wi' the devil, but he's from the other place and I'm not sure whether he's doing his worst in faery too, though I wouldna be surprised.

'Do ye know of any such folk yourself?' says James to Wattie. I know exactly how he'd ha' said it, stroking his jar, his face that rosy way it used to go when he was getting merry, and probably none too interested in the answer. James was the sort o' man who'd rather be having a conversation about the exact length and point of a jumper.

And that's when Wattie told him there were stories about a kirk minister in these parts who'd been taken by the *sìthichean* long, long ago for writing some sort o' book about them, and there was plenty of auld wives hereabouts who would swear for a fact he'd been trying to get out ever since.

Well, my blood ran cold at that. The words 'kirk minister' put a chill running right the way down my back.

'What was his name?' says I to James, hardly breathing till I get the answer.

'Och, I never asked,' says he.

See men! Never think to ask the one thing you need to know. Oh, I was fair mad at him. I nagged him for every detail o' that conversation, because you didna need to be a seer to notice that our Reverend Kirke did have an old-fashioned air about him. Which wasna to say he was the character this fellow was talking about, but it looked mighty suspicious to me.

What I can tell you for sure is that nobody else was worrying about it. Dr Aird, he just rushed about the site as usual trying to mend folk, though he seemed happier in himself and came back that bit earlier in the evenings. He and Mrs Aird would talk more about what had gone on in his day, and I'm thinking he maybe didna put her down so carelessly when she had an idea or thought she could help. He was a gentleman born and bred, o' course, with all the usual ideas o' his class about what a lady could or couldna do (no problem wi' the likes of me doing them), and he took his time realising that she was learning about herself and beginning to be good at things he'd not got round to thinking about.

I mind how pleased she was one day when he let her help a young lad, no more than a bairn, that had to get his finger off. Black as soot it was. He'd had him brought in and laid out on the dining table, and the lad was that feart he was howling the house down. Well, we all rushed to see what the carry-on was.

'The finger's got to go, Issy,' says the doctor.

'Then let me talk to him,' says she, 'while you make ready.'

The doctor had something brought from Glasgow that was to put the boy to sleep, but he was swithering about how much to give him, for there were dangers to it as he explained after, and this was an awfu' small laddie. The boy was yelling and trying to leap off the table.

'Now what's your name, son?' Mrs Aird asks him, and out the corner of her eye she's seeing me at the door and beckoning me in. 'John, is it? I had a John once and it's a fine name. Is it after your father? What part of the works is he on? Keeps you busy, does he? I'll be bound you have to run fast carrying things. Are you a fast runner, John?'

And all the time she was signalling to me to hold the one arm down, and his legs too, and taking a grip o' the wrist herself that had the bad finger. And with her other hand she was tender-like stroking the fair hair back from his brow which was wet with sweat. And her voice was no more than a sea-murmur now.

'Everything's going to be just grand, John. You're going to be fine and well. You're going to have a lovely sleep and wake up with a bandage on that you can show off to the other boys. You'll like that, won't you?'

And while the boy was listening and looking up at her wi' his big frightened eyes, Dr Aird was pouring this chloro-thing into a big white handkerchief and bringing it to the lad's face.

'Do you like to smell a flower ever?' she's saying. 'Or bacon frying with an egg? Just have a wee sniff of this. That's the way, Johnnie, that's the way. Off you go to sleep.'

The finger was in the dish in a flash. He was certainly quick with a knife, Dr Aird. That was from the days when he had to tie the patients to the table wi' a rope and cut fast when they were wide awake. But that boy knew not a thing about it after she'd calmed him down, and when I left them the doctor was showing her how to bind up his hand.

When the boy woke up she made a fuss of him, and then insisted – as I've said, she could be determined, Mrs Aird, when she put her mind to something – she flat insisted on seeing him safe to his father. Turned out to be a Yorkshire blacksmith and none too happy to get a son back wi' just the one working hand. Mrs Aird was angry as a wasp about the wallop he gave the lad. It was Dr Aird had to calm *her* down when she came back.

'Thank you for your help with that boy, Issy,' he said. And I mind to this day the way her face shone.

48

On a warm, blue day in the June of 1859, a sharp-eyed watcher, of which there existed at least one in Sebastopol, might have spotted Isabel Aird and Robert Kirke sitting side by side on the broad saddle of moorland above Fairy Knoll that separates Loch Chon from Loch Katrine. This ridge, from which three years ago a line of celebratory flags had descended the hillside through a mass of shrubbery, was a transformed landscape today, strewn not with trees but with mounds of excavated rock and masonry where the shafts for the tunnel had been sunk. Thanks to the might of gunpowder and the industry of men the earth itself was now turned inside out, its deep, secret parts thrown up to form new ranges from the slate and quartz that had once lain smooth and untouched five hundred feet below. Isabel wondered if the surface of the moon might appear like this, all upside down and dusty white. Here and there could be seen a discarded hammer, a drill, iron handles, broken wheels, bits of bridle, ends of rope: the detritus of a job moved on and a stage very nearly emptied.

With the most intensive labouring at this northernmost end of the works over, other forces had begun to assert themselves. Summer, caressing Isabel's cheeks, luring midges from their lair, was at work across the blasted moor. Roots were testing the ground. Straggly patches of heather had appeared (or survived – it was difficult to tell) around the rim of the spoil heaps. Grasses were creeping faster than rust over the scraps of machinery. Tiny young ferns had burst into life from nowhere and already looked set to riot next year. Lazily Isabel watched a buzzard circling overhead, back in the hope of prey.

Below them, far underneath, was the tunnel.

'An ingenious place to put it, Mrs Aird, quite ingenious,' Professor Rankine had enthused at the not unsuccessful Bath Street supper party she had tentatively thrown in Glasgow.

'And if you ever have occasion to be up there,' he had said, sounding as if he really did imagine that a lady might find herself up a pathless hill without harm or impropriety, 'look around you and remember the name Lewis Dunbar Brodie Gordon. It was his idea to put the tunnel there.'

'Is Mr Bateman not the man who designed it?' she had replied, congratulating herself on being in a position to say something intelligent about tunnels.

'Not entirely. Gordon had the idea of bringing water from Loch Katrine in the first place. He was professor of civil engineering at the university before me, and in those days I was his assistant. He tramped for miles looking for a place to run the tunnel through from Loch Katrine. And then one day he was standing at the head of Loch Chon – you'll know exactly where I mean, Mrs Aird – and he was looking round for inspiration when he noticed a place where the ridge to the north-east dropped down to a kind of saddle. You recognise where I'm talking about?'

She had indeed recognised it: it rose right behind Fairy Knoll.

Rankine sucked on his pipe and prepared to continue. I'm enjoying this, Isabel had thought. I'm enjoying a conversation about water.

'So off Gordon went to climb this hill and when he got to the flat bit at the top what did he discover but that, just as he hoped, he was looking straight down at Loch Katrine on the other side. Near miraculously close in fact. Now if it had been me' – Rankine's capacious chest expanded in exaggerated fashion – 'I'd have rushed around crying "Eureka!" to any passing horse-fly.'

Isabel smiled. She could imagine it.

'But a gloomy sort of chap, Gordon, he's never been one to let himself go. Anyway, he wrote up his report saying this was the shortest, easiest place for a tunnel and what a jolly good idea it would be to build one. When the Glasgow Corporation got over its hurdles, he had high expectations of being appointed chief engineer. Crushing disappointment, of course, when the corporation gave the job to Bateman, streaming clouds of glory from Manchester. Poor old Gordon wasn't at all happy to be overlooked.'

Isabel had laughed. 'Then you may rest assured, Professor Rankine, that I'll think of him if I ever find myself up there.'

As it happens, she was not thinking of Lewis Gordon today (which was rather the story of his career), although with so much spoil around it was impossible not to remember the tunnel itself and marvel at its depth as the land arose between the two lochs.

Isabel leaned back on her elbows and tipped her face to the sun. Sharing a cushion of heather that had just about escaped the industrial plunder, Robert Kirke sat beside her with his thin, endless arms wound around his knees.

After the debacle of Doon Hill, Isabel had not gone out of her way to meet him again. That at least, under pressure verging on the impertinent, is what she had assured Kirsty. Once the new pregnancy could no longer be denied Alexander had also become annoyingly persistent about limiting her movements.

'You must rest and not strain yourself, Issy,' he kept saying, with Kirsty's smug approbation. 'For God's sake, will you do for once what your doctor recommends.'

But as May squalled into a serene June, Isabel had to be out. What was the point of lumpenly waiting for the weeks to pass? Rest had achieved nothing before. What book or needle could defend her against the thoughts and hopes, those infuriating guerrilla hopes, that threatened to drag her back to the precipice of the old despair? She had to experience the stretch in her legs and the rain on her face. She had to feel her body alive to keep her mind strong. Climbing the ridge behind Fairy Knoll could not, she reasoned, open her to the accusation of wandering far; nor was it particularly strenuous if she watched her step and took a lazy angle. There had been no attempting it at all when the area was being blown up all the time and turned to mud by horses and a hundred wheelbarrows; but now that most of the navvies were working further down the line, the views from here over piled hills and graceful waters gladdened her spirit and made her feel, for a few hours at least, that she could bear whatever was to come.

She was feeling emboldened in other ways too. Alexander often let her help with patients at the house now, trusting her not to collapse at the sight of blood or distract him with what he had once made her seethe by describing as 'womanly blether': this to a wife who had never been any more inclined to chatter than sew. The times when she had proved herself steady and resourceful – capable assistant, competent nurse – had watered the seeds of a more resilient sense of herself: Isabel Aird, a woman who could do more than lose babies.

And was it really her fault if Robert Kirke also visited the ridge behind Fairy Knoll and could sometimes be found strolling about up here or waiting in his intent heron pose to greet her? Oh, very well, perhaps she did feel drawn to the places where she thought, even (whisper it) hoped, he might be. She was unwilling to inspect the reasons too closely – doubtless in case the exercise forced her to conclude that spending time with such an unpredictable companion was as unwise as Kirsty insisted and as Alexander undoubtedly would if he had any idea where she had been with him already. But there had been no further manifestation of the shifting moods and sudden furies that had so unnerved her on Doon Hill, and after all it was something to do.

No, it was more than that. She enjoyed Robert Kirke's company. There, that was it. She found his directness as liberating as it could be irritating. His unexpected sympathies often moved her. His company soothed at least as often as it unsettled. She occasionally had the impression, intriguing and not unflattering, that he knew some aspects of her personality better than she knew them herself, and approved. How ridiculously angry he had become at her wish to dance that time by the shore, yet there had been something else, something he had recognised in her behaviour and liked about it; she had fleetingly glimpsed the feeling behind the glare, knew it instinctively for a gentle emotion that held nothing more improper than a longing swiftly extinguished from sight. He was always surprising her. Perhaps that was also it. Whatever else, Robert Kirke could be relied on to ruffle this mind of hers that was slowly opening to experience again, and to thinking, and to life.

Behind them, blue in the sunshine under a puffy sky, Loch Katrine was gathering itself for the signal that would one day soon send its waters rushing under this very hill and on to the city. To pipe and to pump. To mansion and tenement. To Nancy, Isabel thought, imagining a hand in the shadows cupping sweet, clear water to her lips. A good deal of hammering and clattering could be heard from that direction. Sluice-gates were being built by the mouth of the tunnel and there was a house under construction for the sluice-keeper and visiting commissioners from Glasgow.

In front of them lay Loch Chon, its waters out of sight from here although the slopes on its further shore could be glimpsed, as bald along the tunnel line as the ridge they sat on. Fifty yards away a group of men on ladders were placing stones on a tall, chimney-like structure, the latest in a series being constructed over the mining shafts to bestride the ridge like giants.

Kirke was gazing into the distance, where mountains folded into one another all the way to Loch Lomond and beyond.

"Tis good to be free of the thunder,' he observed, suddenly moved to converse. 'I have been interested to observe the many new tunnelling skills and implements, but the noise was not pleasant. The booming may be heard as far hence as Inversnaid.'

The Loch Lomond pier, that awful road.

'Are you often at Inversnaid, then?'

As she spoke Isabel stretched her legs and smoothed out her

skirts, running her hand quickly past the swelling belly lest she be tempted to let it linger there. Kirke's eyes followed the hand, flicking a glance there and away. His legs, encased in his grimy black breeches and even filthier black hose, were so long that his knees reached his chin. His head was as usual bare, the dark brown hair silvering at the temples, a wave in it where it met his shoulders and curled messily about the loose-tied cravat.

'Aye, I'm at Inversnaid often enough. Close by at least. In some seasons ye might say I live there.'

'Really?' Isabel clapped her hands. 'Why, Mr Kirke, I have learned something new. Where is your house?'

'Oh, I wouldna be calling it a house exactly.' A flicker of the stern, melancholic smile. 'There's a cave o' sorts further up the Lomond shore where the rocks have tumbled together in ages past. It maks a dry enough shelter.'

'A cave?' Isabel stared at him. Kirsty's home was bad enough, and it had a door and a chimney. 'You live in a cave?'

Kirke withdrew his gaze from the far peaks. Again his eyes rested on the grey folds of her gown, before rising to meet her own. She detected in them not the intensity they so often held, but indecision.

'I am thinking, my lady, that the time has come for me to tell you a story,' he said slowly. Then, seeming to make up his mind in a rush, he added: 'And when 'tis done, I would ask of you a great boon. Will ye listen?'

'Of course I'll listen,' she said.

49

I knew what she was up to all right, traipsing off up that slope at the back when she thought nobody was looking and the doctor telling her all the time not to exert herself.

'Alex,' she says to him, 'what's the point of keeping me cooped up? We know it's not rest I need but a miracle.'

And that always used to annoy him – hurt him too, I'd say – because he knew he couldna work miracles and all his medical know-how amounted to nothing when it came to breeding live bairns.

'Just do as I say, Isabel,' he'd say, all stiff.

Then she'd wait till he was away out and off she'd go anyway. The times I could have shaken that woman, begging your pardon. I knew fine who'd be waiting for her. It was that bare up there that you could see the two o' them easy enough if you squinted a bit. I wondered if I should mention my fears to the doctor, but he was a scientific man and would likely ha' scoffed that this was just some poor fellow down on his luck. Saying that, the Queen's husband was no' so daft either and I'll swear Prince Albert knew what Robert Kirke was about. But that's to get ahead o' myself. All I'm saying is that if I'd told Dr Aird my worries and badgered him to get a good look at Robert Kirke, maybe he'd have got a right sense of him too. I'll never know to the end o' my days if it would ha' made a difference. But you can't think like that, can ye, or you'll drive yourself mad.

Anyway, I kept on asking around. Anyone in my path I nabbed for interrogation. No exceptions.

'Would ye ever have heard of a Robert Kirke, Mr Clark?' I asked the young minister when he passed me outside the Sebastopol store one day, his eyes on the ground and picking his feet very daintily.

Funny wee man, he was. Very spruce and earnest. Looked like he would ha' trouble saying boo to a goose. Mind you, I wouldna be inclined to say much to a goose either. What I'm meaning is he always seemed a bit timid and apologetic, and even when he had to thump his message home on a Sunday you felt he might have to mop his brow straight after and apologise to the pulpit. But that was a happy meeting all right, because what does Mr Clark say to me when I've got his attention but, 'Robert Kirke? Robert Kirke? Now where have I heard that name?'

'You know him?' says I, ready to faint clean away at such an answer after all this time pursuing my enquiries.

'Why do you ask, Mistress . . . er, you must remind me,' he says.

'Och,' says I, 'it's McEchern,' says I. 'I've a couple o' bairns come to your school when I need rid o' them. Ye'll be thinking I'm no more than a daft Highlander, but there's a man by that name been seen round here these three years past and I'd like to know who he is.'

Well! Did Mr Clark not say he'd go right back to his house and look up a book he had. He thought the name seemed awful familiar.

'Call upon me later, Mrs McEchern,' he says, 'and I'll tell you what I've found out.'

By the time I knocked at his house I was fair jittery with excitement. I'd just seen Mrs Aird go off up the hill, ye see.

'Come away in,' says Mr Clark when his maid let me through the door. Sonsy lass, but a bit sharp when she saw what was on her doorstep. The minister was nice, though. He was in a wee parlour place with some bookshelves that looked a mite crooked to me. I told him my James could ha' done a better job, and he said I might be right at that. He was dressed very smart in a dandy waistcoat – green and red, I seem to mind, wi' swirly bits – and he had a pinkish look about the cheeks, which were struggling in the beard department and made me think more fondly o' him than I was ever inclined on the Sabbath. I doubt he got that many visitors, Mr Clark, even one like me.

'Will you take a seat, Mrs McEchern,' he says, and the maid looked fair annoyed. 'I have looked up the reference I recollected to a Mr Robert Kirke. It's in an essay in the form of a letter by Sir Walter Scott. Do you know of him?'

'I don't come across many sirs as a rule,' says I. 'Friend o' yours, is he?'

Mr Clark laughed then, a high tinkly thing, not unkind. 'Oh, Scott is long gone to join his Maker in the realms above.' He spoke the way your clergy do – realms this and outwith that. 'Nigh on thirty years that must be,' says he. 'Before my time.'

He said this mannie had been a very distinguished writer and lawyer. Lived down in the Borders and had to write umpteen novels and poems to pay his bills. A fair number o' them, so he said, were set in this part o' the world. 'A rather fanciful narrative poem called *The Lady of the Lake*,' he says, 'has been drawing admirers to Loch Katrine ever since.'

Well, I'd heard o' that one right enough. It was the book Isabel Aird kept going into a dwam over when she first arrived, though she said she never picked it up again after I told her about the Dog.

'I've heard of it,' says I, 'but there's no Robert Kirke in there, or Mistress Aird would ha' told me.'

'No,' says Mr Clark, 'but he's in here.' And he showed me the book in his hand, a neat wee thing all bound in smooth leather with gold lettering that I couldna read a word of, as he must ha' guessed because he kindly went and read it out for me.

'It's called *Letters on Demonology and Witchcraft, Addressed to J. G. Lockhart*.' That was the author's son-in-law, he said, but they weren't real letters – it was just a way to make the book interesting.

'Demonology, eh?' says I. 'Is that what ministers read in their spare time, then?'

Well, he went even pinker at that and said it was a scholarly book that was 'rightly sceptical', I mind that phrase, of the outlandish beliefs o' the Highlanders. And although this man had written wi' a sight too much levity for his taste, the minister reckoned the spirit of enquiry was to be admired because those in possession of Christian truth should know what they're dealing with.

'And what are ye dealing with?' I asked. It was all getting a bit beyond me and I wanted to know about Robert Kirke.

'Heresy,' he says. His ears were red now. 'Superstition. Supernatural nonsense of every kind. People have more enlightened attitudes in this century, may God be thanked, but pockets of ignorance remain in some parts.' He looked straight at me when he was saying that. Said it was important to understand the old beliefs without resorting to credu-something.

'Benighted folk used to burn witches for such things in times gone by,' he says.

'Are the angels in the Bible not supernatural, then?' says I. 'And yon demons Jesus was driving out o' somebody last Sunday, as I mind you were saying.'

Mr Clark sighed, and I felt as daft as I aye do among thinking folk. Mind you, he never gave me an answer, just started turning the pages o' this book as if they were burning his fingers.

'I have it,' says he at last. 'I will read you what Scott writes of Robert Kirke.'

Well, it was language that was not over-easy to understand, I may tell ye. But the minister read slowly for me and my eyes were well-nigh leaping out my head as he went along. I knew there was something not right about that man.

But the truth is I didna know the half of it yet. Not even when Mr Clark had finished with his reading did I know the half of it.

When I heard what yon Walter laddie had to say, I went rushing out that house and ran as fast as I've run in my life before to Fairy Knoll and up the hill behind. Which was maybe not all that fleet, I'll admit, and none o' your cheek. All I'm saying is that I hirpled on up as quick as I could, because now I knew what Robert Kirke was and Isabel Aird was up there with him all by herself.

50

Fair Katrine behind us, the mountains soft to the sky in the far off. The lady snug at my side on the bruised heath. A bairn swelling beneath her dress.

There may not come a better time.

I tell her first about my Isabel. How I buried her in a corner o' the Balquhidder kirkyard by the burn's white water, under a birch that is gone now though the stone remains. Love and life. My love, my life. I tell her how I carved the words with my ain hands o'er her grave and had them inscribed later on the kirk bell. How I made my pledge to the cold tombstone, to the bitter Christmas air, that when my time on earth was done I would join her in the heavenly place our Father has prepared for those who love Him and our two souls would clap their hands again and sing together as one.

The lady's eyes are alive with sympathy. She listens well, this one. No flibbertigibbet she, as first I thought when I spied her in her rich gown with a parasol at her feet and sich a petulant look on her face as gave me cause to doubt she would last a minute in these parts. She has grown wiser since. Ach, but I wish she did not put me so in mind—

Guard thy thoughts, Robert Kirke.

Nay, but they look nothing like. My Isabel was slight and fair, and in indifferent health all the time I knew her, although she complained not and lay seldom abed. This lady is dark of hair, and she glows in these days with a vitality that bodes well for my commission. Is it, then, the smoulder of hidden intellect and suppressed will to which I am sae reluctantly drawn?

My Isabel knew her woman's place: she was loyal to a fault and for the maist part compliant. But when provoked she would blaze forth to argue with me, having grasped a point of debate ahead of me or failed in any other wise to prevail o'er some folly she was ever wont to detect before I did. I accused her once of unwomanly assertiveness, against which she thrust back with an allegation of unmanly ignorance and the slamming of a heavy door. Such is the contrariness of man that this, the trait that would most reliably agitate my own equability and bring my blood to the boil, was the thing I missed most when she was gone. I see hints of it in the lady. It bubbles up through the sadness and –

do not dare to think you like it in her

– I like it in her.

The day is bright and warm. There are men working at a turret yonder, paying us no heed. The lady's forehead creases, as it does when her interest is caught, and her eyes pull the words out o' me in sich a stream as I have not spake since I returned. I tell her how the years passed at Balquhidder after my Isabel had gone. How I poured my grief and longings into my work – 'Aye,' says she, 'men are good at that' – translating the Psalms into Gaelic, revising a printed version o' the catechism in that language, labouring towards my aim ('twas only part fulfilled) of making a library for common people in every Highland parish. The which gave me much pleasure, because there were times when I groaned, groaned to the marrow, for the lack of devout and rousing society nearer home.

The lady smiles at that. 'I sympathise, Mr Kirke,' says she. 'I have groaned for the lack of rousing society myself.'

And at the same time I was beginning to delve into the other beliefs of my parishioners – in particular their tales of the *sìthichean*.

Now, Robert Kirke, do we come to it.

'Twas an interest born of respect for the views o' folk too easily dismissed as simple and credulous – something you in faery have never grasped, not for a minute. To essay an understanding o' what goes on in the head and heart of another is anathema to you.

We know what goes on in yours, Robert Kirke. Forget it not.

The lady grasps what I say, listening and nodding as I tell her about the questions that began to animate me when I moved from Balquhidder to my new charge at Aberfoyle.

Why should Highland folk be scoffed at, I reasoned, whose beliefs only attested the supernatural existence that Christian theology had affirmed from the start, from God and His angels to the devil himself?

Was it any more absurd for a spirit to inhabit a body of air than one composed of dull and drowsy earth like mine?

If there were more to God's universe than man would ever dream, why might not a world of faery exist in a secret commonwealth below? The theology I was proposing would bring all things, all worlds, together under God Himself.

Would ye describe yourself as naïve, Robert Kirke?

I was the biggest fool in Christendom, as ye were kind enough to show me on Doon Hill.

The lady gives me a puzzled look. My silences confuse her.

'Forgive me, madam, if I appear distracted,' I say. 'My head can hardly contain the thoughts that wrestle each other, the remonstrations that assail me when I remember how innocently I reasoned then and the punishment to follow. For I must come now in my account to Doon Hill.'

She looks of a sudden nervous, as well she might. But, eyeing me boldly enough, she prays that I continue.

I close my eyes to gather strength.

'On my return to Aberfoyle as minister I used to walk on Doon Hill every day. The questions would soar and swoop through my head as I rambled. And ever would I rest a minute against the trunk o' that great pine I showed ye, watching to see where this or that glint from above would strike the circle. And thinking, always thinking.'

Her eyes grow big and I can tell she is looking about in her mind's eye as I bade her do that day, staring up and up into the high branches.

'I wanted to know why they call it in the Gaelic *dùn sìthiche*, the fairy fort. I wanted to penetrate mysteries that no man may explore with impunity.'

The lady shivers a little at that. 'Tis no more than a breath, a tremor about the shoulder. She does not remove her eyes from mine.

'And on Doon Hill was I finally punished.'

The strength has drained from my voice. The lady notices it, though she moves not. Her head stays cocked expectantly towards me, eyes eager. A buzzard flaps overhead, but she shifts not her gaze. There are midges dancing about us in the stillness: she waves a hand across her face to disperse them without once taking her eyes from mine.

Nay, 'tis no good. I cannot say more. I have not put words to this before. Not to anyone. Not to myself.

Wise, Robert Kirke. Very wise.

'First, though,' say I, with a sorry attempt at an apologetic smile, 'I went to London.'

At that she shakes her head in exasperation and draws back. 'London? Dear Mr Kirke, I would not hear of London. You must tell me what happened on Doon Hill.'

She is more impatient, the lady Isabel, than my own dear love ever was.

I went to London to supervise the printing of a Scottish Gaelic edition of Bishop Bedell's Irish translation of the Bible. A mighty work I'd had of it to transliterate the Irish script into Roman characters that our Gaels might make sense of. But eventually, staggering under the weight of the manuscript, I was ready to take the stagecoach south. The money to print – for I had none – cam from Mr Robert Boyle, an Irish nobleman and scientific investigator, weel renowned for his discoveries in the line of chemistry, who had an interest in the Church. He shared my view, by the by, that descriptions o' faery were in harmony with the divine plan of the universe.

Did he indeed. Hark at you!

Pray be done with your snide interruptions when I am trying to master my thoughts for the lady. No one knows better than I that there exists no harmony in faery.

But I knew it not then. Among the bewigged finger-waggers o' the London coffee houses I found sich scepticism and near-atheism as shook me to the core and among churchmen a disinclination to tak seriously the proposition of another world at all.

The lady gives a start at the wigs o' London intellectuals. It requires no great insight to deduce that she is calculating the last time horsehair was seen on a man's head outside a court of law. Mine own was a paltry piece beside Robert Boyle's, whose wig was a sight to behold – as long and full as I saw upon King William himself when he passed one day in a carriage drawn by a dozen horses. Perchance the lady's mind is also consulting a rote of the land's monarchs to arrive at the date of the Glorious Revolution.

She gives me a long, searching look but passes no comment, for I have rushed on to tell her how I became fired up with a determination to write down all I had found out and refute the sceptics. I would show these blethering London folk that it was not repugnant either to reason or religion to assume an invisible faery polity, a people with their own commonwealth, laws and economy, made known to us by those seers admitted to their converse.

Tralala.

Therefore on returning from the capital I threw myself into my life's great work.

Your life's very great work.

Writing in the manse from morn till night, I compiled an account of all I had heard and collected in the years before. I argued therein that it was no more necessary for mankind to know, actually to know, that there were such subterranean inhabitants than for us to know the polity of the nine orders of angels or if the moon be inhabited.

'And ye might think,' say I to the lady, 'that I would have

listened to myself. But no, Robert Kirke had to find out. Robert Kirke had to see for himself. He had to fly to the sun and learn what the ancient Greeks meant by hubris.'

As I am speaking these words the lady, who has been turned so attentively towards me, catches sight of something over my shoulder. She peers a moment and then clicks her tongue in annoyance.

'You must proceed to what befell you on Doon Hill, Mr Kirke, and explain with all swiftness the boon that will ease your pain. I fear Mrs McEchern is on her way.'

Whipping around, I spy a trachled figure ploughing up the slope behind the fairy knoll. That interfering wifie again – does she never rest? Panic rises in my throat. I must proceed to the favour. I must secure the promise at once.

'She will be upon us soon,' the lady is saying. 'Come, Mr Kirke, I would not miss the end of your tale.'

Tak care, Robert Kirke. Tak exceeding great care.

'They took me,' I tell her.

Will that do?

'They took me away and left behind – as I must suppose – a double-man dead on the hill in my stead.'

The lady looks at me with stars of wonder in her eyes. No fear though. That much have I achieved.

I tell her that my transporting took place in the month o' May, *anno domini* 1692.

'One hundred and sixty-seven years before today,' I say, looking her straight back in the eye, 'although time passes differently in the place I spent it.'

Her mouth drops open, but she is glancing over my shoulder again. Making an effort to calm my own agitation, I lean towards her. 'I must tell ye something important, my lady.'

Her hazel eyes upon me.

'Three years ago I was released from faery in body, but they bargained for my soul.' My mouth is dry. 'To be free of faery and die like any other man, I am to fulfil a commission. And to do that, to join my Isabel in eternal union, I will need the help of another.'

She reaches for my hand, which she clasps most fervently in both her ain.

'And it is from me you seek help? Is that why you have sought out my company these many months and years past?'

I cannot look at her.

Go on, then. Answer her.

I cannot speak.

What's keeping you, man? Remember what you are. Robert Kirke first.

'Well, I shall do whatever I can,' says she, reading the plea from my eyes alone. 'Your story is a strange one' – she laughs then, but kindly, as my ain Isabel might have done – 'and I must think on it further. But you may depend on me, Mr Kirke. It will be my pleasure to help.'

And then arrives the wifie, trundling across the brow of the hill towards us and screeching, 'Keep away, Mrs Aird!' as you might warn a body from a creeping wasp. 'I know what he is. Robert Kirke lived two centuries ago. He was stolen by the fairies.'

The lady makes to stand up. I scramble to offer her my hand, which she accepts lightly. Dusting a powder of heathery soil from her skirts, she steps forward.

'I know, Kirsty,' she says, most cool and collected. 'I know the whole story.' Then she stalks straight on past the wifie and down the hill.

No, my lady, not the whole story. That ye do not know. But were you my very own lady I could not in this one moment, in this sweet space between truth and omission, be more proud o' you.

Oh, Robert Kirke, you stupid, stupid man.

51

You'll be wondering what this Walter Scott said that had me running up that hill as if the devil himself was behind me. Or likely you've had a read yourself by now, so you'll know. He made it clear that the Reverend Robert Kirke had been a minister a long, long time ago in Aberfoyle, which was frequented, as we're not needing any book to tell us, by the *sìthichean*. Turns out Kirke had been busy writing about them himself and got a bit too close. And the *siths* didna like that one little bit, him going prying about in their nasty business.

So it seems Robert Kirke gets carted off to faery himself for his trouble. It happens while he's up some hill near his manse, and when the body's found everyone thinks at first he's been struck down by the apoplexy. But, see, the body folk find on this Doon Hill is not really him. That's what this Walter Scott was trying to say. (Toss a coal on that fire, would ye, for I'm getting cold as cold.) He ends up by stating plain enough that he fears Kirke is like to be captive there yet.

Except he's not, is he? Robert Kirke isna dreeing his weird in faery any longer. Robert Kirke is out. He's out for all to see, sitting in the sunshine bold as you like beside our Isabel Aird.

When I got to them at last – my, it was a climb all right – she looked none too happy to see me. Got to her feet right away and marched over. Kirke was left standing there, and there was an ugly thing in those glittery eyes o' his. Just exactly like a creature thwarted if you ask me. It fair froze the cockles o' my heart, if a heart's got cockles to freeze, which is a thing I do wonder about.

I was shivering that much when I got down the hill I had to go straight home and stir up a fire. And thank ye for getting this one going again. It was an awful waste o' kindling in June but there you are, there was such a deep cold in me I thought I'd never get warm again. But Mrs Aird? Couldna be happier.

'Oh, Robert Kirke lived a good life,' says she. 'Translated the Scriptures, cared for his parishioners, adored his wife. He deserves our pity for his misfortunes, Kirsty.'

Heaven preserve me! You'd think it would be enough to know the man had spent the best part o' two hundred years in faery.

'He's been below!' I says to her, near to screaming wi' frustration. 'It's no' his life you need to worry about, it's his death. And why it didna happen and what he's become since.'

At that she gave me her remember-your-place look and refused to talk one word more about Robert Kirke.

52

That night by the great pine. A warm May evening, grown of a sudden cauld. The birds quiet. The light sickening.

The manuscript was done. I had written and written till my fingers were sore. But I was restless. Uneasy in my bones, my head full of whispers. Doon Hill calling me. Come climb, Robert Kirke. Come learn the secrets you covet.

Climbing the hill. The light bleeding away. Where is it going sae quick and urgent, only weeks from midsummer?

Standing in the circle with the light nearly gone, fear at my throat. Looking up at the high branches o' the great Scots pine.

Falling, as if struck from behind. Falling. No pain, though. And no ground. I canna bring to mind the mossy feel o' the ground.

Descending into darkness all alone. Why hast thou forsaken me, my God, alone and cauld as any stone?

A whirling of colour through the dark. Not the natural shades o' fern or speckled foxglove; not the salmon's silvered pink or the singing purple of a thistle; not the honest brown of a dod o' peat. Here were greens to make you ill, blues hard as ice, scarlets like metal, yellows ne'er seen at a siskin's throat. I thought I had died and come to hell, till the colours became forms and I saw the dancing. And then I knew I was alive and had come instead to faery.

Sick

sick

to the pit of me sick.

He lifted up the Christ in His agony of aloneness on the rugged cross, but He cam not for me. He never cam for me.

53

At least I had the doctor on my side. He was as angry as I ever saw him to hear that his wife had been climbing that hill, though it was only because he was anxious about the bairn she was carrying, as anyone could see.

Of the two he was the one that could never hide his feelings. As the weeks went on I used to see him looking at her, sort o' yearning like, as if he'd like to reassure her but couldna think what to say or do. But a man's never happy if there's not some doing to be done, so he gave himself something to do by stopping her doing a single thing herself – don't stir, don't walk, raise your feet, watch ye don't catch a chill, take care on the stair, close your eyes a minute – which I dare say was the best he could think of and done for love. He was more often at home himself by that time, with the site being quieter towards the end, and there were times he patrolled that parlour like a policeman.

Now I think on it, he did bring her books. I mind there was one he found by Florence Nightingale – a name you and I know these days all right – which Mrs Aird went fair starry-eyed over and he came over all pink to have pleased her. Seems it was a load o' notes on nursing. And bless me if she didna have every window in the house open day and night after that.

'Pure air is what we need, Kirsty,' she'd say, wrapped in about a million shawls in her own parlour. 'Pure air, pure water, good light, proper drainage, cleanliness at all times. Miss Nightingale teaches us that without these no house can be healthy.' She quoted the book that often I knew it back to front myself.

Poor Annie was near off her head wi' having to wash things the whole time and try to keep the damp out. Mind, I had my doubts about how helpful it was in Mrs Aird's condition to be reading that one in seven infants perishes before it's a year old. Well, I could have told her that for nothing – and it's well seen that nurse was never in a Glasgow tenement or she'd ha' watched way more babes than that die. 'Och,' says I, 'do you have to be reading that kind o' thing right now?'

But it was a funny thing about Mrs Aird this time round that though she never once talked about her own bairn that I ever heard, or gave away her feelings more than usual, she had a new toughness to her that ye had to admire. Not a tight shutting-out like before but, as ye might say, looking outwards more. I had a feeling she was thinking past her own travails to the time that would come after. She kept going on about the things that needed to be done for other folk's bairns, and how she was realising that posh women like her were just as ignorant as the likes o' my Nancy about how to keep a bairn alive.

'I always had my doubts about playing the piano, Kirsty,' she says. Well, I wondered what was coming here. 'And now Miss Nightingale makes the point for me. She asks how it can possibly be better for a woman to learn the pianoforte than to apply herself to the laws of the sanitary conditions that will preserve our offspring.'

Mrs Aird did give a wee gulp as she was saying it, mind, and

I knew what else she was thinking. But she held up this wee book in her hand and shook it at me and for a minute she looked all fierce. 'There's work to be done when I get back to Glasgow, Kirsty,' says she.

Anyway, the main thing is that all this reading and thinking and planning took up her time as the summer went on, which suited the doctor and me fine. We'd become allies in a way, each one of us trying to keep her safe at home.

It started to look to me as if she was maybe a bit bigger and maybe a bit further on than last time.

'Would ye take it amiss if I enquired when the bairn is due?' I asked Dr Aird, very careful and polite, choosing my moment.

'It's always difficult to be precise, Kirsty,' says he in his best doctor voice, only he didna look at me, 'but I would expect full term to be into December.' He gave me a wan sort o' smile. 'We have a long time to go yet, do we not?'

54

An ancient tale is told of Thomas the Rhymer, the laird o' Ercildoune in the Borders. 'Tis said a beautiful Queen cam to him on a steed hung with silver bells, which made music to the wind as she rode. She led him to the land o' faery, where knights and ladies were dancing by threes in a great hall. Afterwards this Queen bestowed on Thomas a tongue that could only tell the truth.

Nonsense. The tale is nonsense.

Blethers. Fiddle-faddle. Trumpery.

There was no Queen on a white steed. There was no reverence for truth. No dances of stately co-operation, two or three folk together, stepping back as another glides forward, hands held, eyes fixed on a partner. None, I say.

Every person in faery was alone.

In every mad swirl o' colour they were together but single, each obeying an inner eye, not one of them animated by the common weal. They danced and whirled and bumped and trod one upon the other, moving to some anxious tune which I warrant rang different in every head and let not one of us be still. There was no truth that all would honour, but only what each man and woman proclaimed for their own purpose. 'You lie!' we hissed at each other, passing in the dance. Into my head poured a lifetime of slights disregarded and offences once cheerfully ignored. What word of poison would slay my fellow dancers in return? Quick and vicious arrived the spit of anonymous venom in my mouth. There was no barrier of social grace or moral qualm or fellow feeling to prevent insults and lies from spilling into a passing ear. 'Robert Kirke first,' I sang out, elbowing the next person from my path.

The commonwealth I sae fervently imagined? As much a fiction as silver bells on a white steed.

Benignly governed for the well-being of all? An illusion conceived in the all too accommodating image of Robert Kirke himself.

Out at last, ejected in the earth's great upheaval. I lay on the grass, stunned by light.

Between explosions I heard the cheering of men above me on the hillside. Nothing could be seen of them but their hats, such strange hats, lined up tall as chimneys before a mighty banner.

Spring sunshine poured o'er my face, warming up the chills o' faery. All the beauties of the earth were shining for me in those holiest of moments.

The sight of Loch Chon was like a splash of icy water on burning cheeks. Like a young alder leaf new arrived when winter has stayed ower lang. Like the scent of the redcurrant bursting into bloom. Like the taste of warm milk. Like the night sound of my beloved's soft breath, the rise and fall o' her breasts, the way she would aye know when I was watching her and open her eyes, and I would see their gleam in the half-light and kiss her lips and pour into her all that I was and wanted to be and hoped for and loved most upon the earth.

The sunlight showered its blessings upon me that May morn like everything beautiful and giving there ever was, everything faery would never understand, everything I had thought lost for ever.

But the moment tipped and the vision of loveliness fell away. In an instant of understanding I knew I was changed. Faster even than the light dimmed in the smoke, the lurid colours o' faery returned to dance before my mind's eye and the taste of those mean cruelties were back on my tongue, most sickening of delights. There was a strange odour hanging about my body that I could not place.

Then, low and insistent, cam the first words of faery I ever heard outside, offering me a way to be free.

55

Isabel submitted more or less gracefully to the weighty alliance of husband and self-appointed spiritual guardian. If it was not Alexander hovering like a moth to murmur, 'Would you sit at peace, Issy, and let Annie do that,' it was Kirsty blowing in to check she was not out hobnobbing with Robert Kirke.

Swathed in shawls, she spent most of her time by the open window in the parlour watching summer slipping away: the last of the wild raspberries gone; tight-balled brambles spilling over the wall in readiness for autumn; the purple heads of the Fairy Knoll thistles exploding into tufts of down that drifted past the window and snagged on the tall grass, populating the garden with battalions of wraiths. When she gazed out at these downy spectres, Isabel thought irresistibly of double-men emerging from earthy graves and fleck-foamed dogs snapping through the waves. She thought about the legions of fairy *siths* who had given their names to copse, knoll and pebbled bank in every nook of the Trossachs and had once, long ago, entranced a curious man. And then, of course, she would think about Robert Kirke.

She had not seen him since their extraordinary conversation on the ridge between the lochs, but he was rarely far from her mind. His revelations had neither shaken nor, somewhat to her own surprise, greatly troubled her – perhaps because they seemed in keeping with the palpable sense of ill-will she had experienced herself on Doon Hill and the timeless oddity of the man himself. His story fitted a place where a monster could lunge out of a serene loch and steal a child away for no reason, just as life did, and where thistles that made your fingers bleed could grow kissable crowns of fluff in another season.

In the weeks after their conversation she went over it many times. What Robert Kirke had been telling her was incredible, literally so in one sense, but she could not persuade herself that he had simulated the gnawing signs of inner turmoil and bouts of tormented silence, nor, surely, the tenderness for his late wife, to whom he so movingly wished to return. Isabel's ideas about heaven were hazy, but she sympathised passionately with the longing to be reunited in some other dimension with those who had left you. He had sought her out, Isabel Aird, the woman who met her babies in the milky vapour smoking from a far hill, the woman who shared his beloved's name, the woman whose deep-buried desire to be happy she had allowed him to see. She would help him if she could, when the time came.

She was also busy sharpening her intellect on Alexander's medical books, which she kept on a table by the window. From these she learned that physicians had not the faintest idea what caused a woman to miscarry or how to prevent it. In the absence of a better proposal most advised doing more or less nothing, paying particular attention to the dangers of straightening a high picture, pedalling a sewing machine, bathing in the ocean, having a tooth extracted, taking a warm bath or being excessively happy.

No danger of any of those. More interestingly, one or two experts inveighed against the constriction of a corset, which at least made sense. Isabel promptly threw hers off with the assistance of a scandalised Annie. Another school of thought maintained that a woman who expanded her mind thereby sucked the energy from her reproductive system, a theory that caused her own mind to rock with energetic annoyance. At least Alex had not tried that one on her. Liberal with his books, he was happy for her mind to take the strain as long as her body did not. The most common assumption was that losing a child before term must be – stands to reason – the woman's own fault for something undone or overdone. As, presumably, was dying of blood poisoning or a haemorrhage in the process.

As Isabel mused on the expert opinions one empty afternoon, a slow fury, long in the boil, began to bubble. How dare these men blame her for ten years of grief! How dare they! Where was her fault to be located? Had she committed the same one eight times over? Looking down at her rounded belly she began to stroke it. Deliberately. Mutinously. Even to talk of 'losing' this child was a calumny, as if she might one day mislay it in a fit of carelessness. Tentatively at first and then more confidently, she began to press down with the heel of her hand – here, there – feeling the skin yield and a shiver of movement within.

'We will beat them, little one,' she whispered fiercely.

It caught her unawares, that whisper. Isabel's tried and tested rule of pregnancy was never to imagine the child inside, never to think of it, never to dream of it, at least until it had left her to join the others in the grass and the mist and the stony burn. In this rule lay her mind's protection. But just now, just then, for the first time since Johnnie and Sarah, she had addressed a person. And with that realisation came such a rush of fearfulness and panic and sadness that her face was suddenly streaming with tears and she wept for ten minutes without pause, sitting there by the window in the dreary brown parlour, her fists in her eyes and no one to hear the howls.

Afterwards, when she had shuddered herself quiet, Isabel thought about why she had cried like that, and how long it had been since she had done it, and how emptied she felt now and yet refreshed, too, and ready to march forward.

'By the way, your name is Florence,' she said, and blew her nose.

56

As the weeks passed and autumn came upon us, the babe was still in there and growing. I even caught Isabel Aird giving her belly a wee stroke once or twice when she thought I wasna looking. And that's when I started to get worried. I'm not saying I wished the grief o' miscarrying on her. Don't be so daft. But my feelings were in a terrible fankle, because I have to be honest with you: the longer she held on to that child the more feart I was getting.

Robert Kirke was biding his time. I could see that all right. It's well enough known to those that live among them what the *sìthichean* get up to, aye wanting to steal human folk away for their own wicked purposes. So if it wasna Isabel Aird he was after – and he'd had opportunity enough, God knows – then it had to be her bairn.

I thought and I thought about what I could do. And then it came to me that if Robert Kirke had got himself infected wi' faery, a wee bit o' iron might help. Nothing scares that lot as much as cold iron. Mrs Aird had a giggle herself once when she found out there were huge big swaggering navvies from Ireland that wouldna dream o' stepping outside without a knife in their breeks, in case they should meet the *sìthichean* on the way back from the Teapot and need some iron to see them off. Says she, 'Kirsty, if you or I were weaving our way home in the state these men get in, we'd likely be seeing fairies too.'

It's no' very wise to laugh at these things, though. And don't you be thinking I canna see you smiling to yourself as well. It's all very fine when you're sitting in the city like us, the gas lamp on and a nice bright fire in the grate. It's different when you're by yourself in the dark – just you and the trees and the loch stirring out there in the gloaming. It's a foolhardy soul doesna think about what you'll do if ye meet one that's really got it in mind to hurt you.

So I was thinking, could I maybe smuggle a wee something into the Airds' bed? No point relying on the warming pan if it needs to be cold, and the pair o' them would likely ha' spotted a mangle. That's a joke, by the way. In the end I found an old tap and stuck it under the mattress. No knowing if its powers would reach through all that horsehair, but it was better than nothing and there was not the devil's shadow of a chance that Annie would ever get round to turning that mattress. As soon as the berries on the rowan were full red I added a few o' them too, since they've aye been useful against sorcery.

I did my best. After all this time it's still what I'd say to you. I did my best. How was I to know I was going to all that trouble for the wrong bed?

Part Five

October 1859

And renownèd be thy grave

Cymbeline

57

Queen Victoria to Victoria, Princess Royal and Princess of Prussia

Balmoral,
October 1859

My dear Vicky,

I cannot begin to describe my delight in being at Balmoral, though perhaps I need not try, since no one save your dear papa is able to divine my feelings in this regard better than you.

Do you recall our driving up Corriemulzie once by the Linn of Dee? You spied a thick cluster of berries on the mountain ash, intermingling very prettily with the spruce and larch. 'Mama,' you cried, 'it looks just like coral growing on the trees!' Now the mountain ash (which Brown, who has no sense of the romantic, insists on calling the rowan) is out once again in full glory. The berries are magnificent this year after all the rain, and I think of you fondly when I look at them. You will like to imagine the scene in your dismal German palace.

I am glad to have seen you this summer during your brief visit to Osborne, although why you could not have stayed longer by the side of your mama, despite my most firmly expressed wish, I cannot fathom. As I explained with utmost plainness, there was no need to hasten so importunately back to Berlin to see Wilhelm: a child will do perfectly well without his mother in constant attendance.

However I was reassured by how well you looked and to learn that in the months after such a difficult confinement you had followed my advice to take plenty of air. Opening every window thrice a day cannot be too highly recommended if you are not to become sickly and old before you reach twenty, and I hope I have made my views clear on the necessity of having water-closets installed.

I was sorry to hear from you that the complications of the birth resulted in a deformity to the child as the doctors were attempting to extract him. Childbirth is an appalling indignity for women and you must on no account blame yourself for anything that goes wrong, although it is a weakness of both the medical profession and the female condition that one often does. Our own doctor is of the opinion that Wilhelm's left arm may improve in time and I cannot think you should worry unduly about the number of minutes that passed before he drew breath. I have stressed to you before that motherhood is in general a most trying condition. If you should find your child's charms eluding you, be assured that it is quite normal. The company of an infant is greatly overrated, although I confess to having derived a most unexpected pleasure, after many years of avoiding the pastime, from observing our own little Beatrice being bathed. Your youngest sister is such a dear little thing.

Your papa has also been much refreshed by the wonderful Highland air. He had a particularly acute stomach attack towards the end of August, when he could keep down only milk and water and fainted while attempting to dress. Really, Vicky, he looked so fearfully ill that my heart became quite chilled with dread. But he seems reasonably recovered and has had a very energising time of it since we came north, not least in the delivery of a highly acclaimed lecture to the British Association for the Advancement of Science in Aberdeen. You will agree with me that nobody could make a better or more assiduous president of this august body, which is in every way attuned to Albert's ideas. He returned to Balmoral very much gratified that all had gone off so admirably. He had met numbers of learned people, and everyone was delighted with his speech. The chief engineer of the Loch Katrine waterworks, a Mr Bateman, also spoke eloquently at the meeting, one hears, making no secret of his satisfaction that within just three and a half years of the works being commenced no less than fifty thousand gallons of water will shortly be flowing the considerable distance to Glasgow every day. Quite extraordinary!

Which reminds me that your papa and I are looking forward to visiting these works later this month. The invitation to perform the opening ceremony was delivered to us here in Balmoral some weeks ago by Mr Bateman in person accompanied by the Corporation of Glasgow's chairman of new works, who proved to be extremely personable if somewhat thick in his Scotch accent. (One becomes used to the Aberdeenshire version, as you know, but even the more educated Glaswegians do rather test one's comprehension.) Mr Bateman, while not speaking precisely the Queen's English as regards vowels, does form most of his consonants without excessive strangulation of the throat, which is always a relief. The Glasgow Rifle Volunteers are to form a guard of honour on the day, a most patriotic initiative which one is glad to encourage. We shall make the visit on our way back to London.

Oh dear, even to write the words 'back to London' makes me feel quite ill. Balmoral feeds me so, and to contemplate being parted from our home again is an agony. While your papa was on his way to Aberdeen, I drove out with your sister Alice and my two ladies, accompanied by Colonel Toplady and the usual ghillies, to Morven, a mountain to the east of the Cairngorms. It is exceedingly high and very steep. We mounted ponies at the foot and halfway up took luncheon on plaids laid out on the fine springy turf. We walked about and sketched for a while, after which we remounted and rode to the top. The view from the summit was so very beguiling – such a sea of mountains, such wonderful lights and colouring. In the extreme distance one could see the blue sea, and even the ships on it, while below was the tableland between Tarland and Ballater, and indeed the whole of Deeside. I thought then, as I repeat to you now, that I cannot bear to leave this place. I cannot bear it. My spirits are already sinking as the leaves turn yellow and the day of our departure draws nearer.

Your father bids me not to think of dreary Holyroodhouse awaiting us in Edinburgh, but to look forward instead to the glories of the Trossachs and to seeing Loch Katrine for the first time, of which I have read and heard so much. It is indeed a cheering thought. I had Lady Toplady look out for me the following words from The Lady of the Lake, *which always brings such fine pictures to mind:*

> *One burnished sheet of living gold,*
> *Loch Katrine lay beneath him rolled,*
> *In all her length far winding lay,*
> *With promontory, creek, and bay,*
> *And islands that, empurpled bright,*

The Ninth Child

Floated amid the livelier light,
And mountains that like giants stand
To sentinel enchanted land.

I very much doubt that any such giant can compete with Morven,
but it does raise one's spirits to think of the enchanted land that
awaits us. Write soon, dear child, and pray do not forget to open the
palace windows in EVERY weather.
   Your loving
   Mama

58

Word went out that there was to be some kind o' grand opening on Loch Katrine. Big fish expected, so folk said, and they'd be needing housemaids and floor-scrubbers and coal-carriers and cutlery-polishers and the Lord knows what else to get the Commissioners' Cottage ready. That was what they called the big stone house they'd been building next to the loch for the sluice-keeper to bide in, wi' rooms aplenty for the water commissioners when they were up to inspect the works. But everyone knew there would be nothing like this fuss for a few Glasgow gentry.

Seeing as I did a fair bit for her round the house – I was in and out o' Fairy Knoll most days by that time – I thought I'd better ask Mrs Aird if she'd mind me taking the work. Och, it'll be fine, she says. She could tell I was interested in what was going on along the road, not to mention the wage for some good long hours. I chose my moment well, mind, because she had her nose in one o' the doctor's books.

'On you go, Kirsty,' she says quite the thing. 'Annie will manage fine here.'

I had a wee smile to myself at that, though to be fair to Annie it's more of a labour than Mrs Aird ever realised to be up at the crack to set the fires and keep them going all day and lug the water in and get it boiled and all the rest of it, never mind the scrubbing and washing I used to do for her. I don't suppose she gave a thought to how her own chamber pot got itself back under her bed each day, nice and empty and polished to a shine, which was another of Annie's jobs. Anyway, I took my older lassie out the school to see to the wee ones and cook for James, and before I knew it I was tramping off to Loch Katrine every day.

Most o' the time I went round the long way by Stronachlachar. You could get there quicker by going over the ridge behind Fairy Knoll, but you needed a lot o' puff for that and anyway I didna fancy meeting you know who again if he happened to be hanging around. I must ha' been working over there a fair few weeks when you count it up, there was that much to be done. See the silver I polished! Whenever a nice-looking spoon comes my way to this day I get an ache in my fingers.

Then came the great day when we got told who'd be coming. Well, it's not often I have news o' that quality to spread.

'Ye'll never guess the folk I've been polishing all these forks for!' I go shouting into the Fairy Knoll parlour on my way home.

Mrs Aird was fair excited to hear it. After that she had me pick up every bit of information I could and be sure to report back so she could argue her case wi' the doctor.

'An easy carriage ride to Stronachlachar,' she tells him. 'A quiet seat in a boat a couple of miles round the bay to the Commissioners' Cottage.' (Only those and such as those were getting ferried that last bit, I may say. The rest of us would be walking as usual.)

The doctor rubs his nose that way he used to and looks awful doubtful. Between you and me I had my doubts as well, since I knew I'd be too busy in the big house to go keeping an eye on her.

Mrs Aird has her dander up, though. Eyes a-flash, she says she's stayed at home for weeks and done everyone's bidding as well as she could and nobody is going to stop her going to the first social occasion the Trossachs has produced ever.

'I thought you didn't like parties,' the doctor says, looking weary.

She bridles at that all right. 'Alex, there'll be thousands of folk there,' she says in that purposeful way she was getting all too good at to my mind. 'I'm not going to be the only one for fifty miles who doesn't get to see her.'

So there ye are. Isabel Aird was going to see the Queen and that was that.

59

The captain of the little *Rob Roy* steamer, charged with ferrying the royal party up Loch Katrine later that afternoon, could find no grounds for optimism. As he muttered gloomily to his first mate, 'Tak my word for it, man. It'll be pissing like this all day.'

And so it proved. The rain that arrived on 14 October 1859, the day appointed for the ceremonial turning on of Glasgow's new water supply, was not a collars-up autumn drizzle or even your average Trossachs head-to-toe drenching. It was the heaviest, windiest, most umbrella-savaging, face-slashing deluge that Scotland had experienced in twenty years. Nobody missed the irony or much appreciated the symbolism.

Water poured through birch and oak woods as if the heavens were tipping out giant jugs of the stuff. It oozed out of sphagnum mosses expressly designed to keep it in. It gushed into burns, dripped from bronzed ferns and streamed down the black rocks in a million rivulets, drowning the brambles beneath and turning the whole earth – so it felt to the city-bred hordes who had seen nothing like it – to mud. It played miserable symphonies on the umbrellas gathered by the Commissioners' Cottage (dubbed from this day forth Royal Cottage), where those who had risen before dawn in town and city to trail here by some testing combination of horse, carriage, train, steamer, rowing boat and very wet foot were gazing between other people's brollies at lethal clouds and furious waves, counting the hours until royalty arrived.

The Queen herself had at least enjoyed the luxury of breakfasting in Edinburgh at a civilised hour, although that might fairly be described as the sum of her enjoyments at Holyroodhouse that morning. Victoria had failed for years to warm to the gloomy palace of her ancestors, with its dark, draughty rooms and a gallery of the most frightful portraits of the kings of Scotland. So she was not at all unhappy to board a train to the village of Callander at a quarter to ten, even if the weather was a trifle inclement. Albert, grateful for a diversion from the recitation of what they might have been doing in Aberdeenshire today and the imputation that it was somehow his fault that they were not, was looking forward to the uncomplicated company of engineers.

From Callander, damply *en fête* to receive them, the royal party was transported towards the craggy head of Loch Katrine by four muddy horses and an escort of dragoons. Victoria, appreciating the tenacity of the well-wishers, was sorry to have to order Albert to order the carriage to be closed over. Although she was not a jot concerned for her tartan dress and grey mantle, or her white bonnet secured (with her usual lofty indifference to the frivolities of fashion) by a black veil, the rain really was getting worse and there was Helena's peacock hat-feather to consider. The people greeted them with touching cheers and halloos, springing up in the mist from tussocks of sodden heather as the carriage passed exactly like Roderick Dhu's clansmen in *The Lady of the Lake*. Dear Sir Walter. One really did feel oneself right in the middle of his poem here: such enchanting creeks and inlets, such an abundance of trees and shrubs growing right to the water's edge.

On board the freshly painted and newly betartaned *Rob Roy*, panelled (how perfect!) with carved vignettes of scenes from *The Lady of the Lake*, the captain duly assumed personal responsibility for the weather and apologised handsomely. Victoria was charmed by the specially erected glass pavilion on deck, declaring, as moisture beaded down the glass, that what she could see of the loch was all she had imagined – although she did consider privately that the mountains in these parts were really rather *tame* compared with Balmoral's, as she was sure Albert would agree if only he would pay attention and stop staring at those wooded crags as if he had seen a ghost. Really it was too vexing. Mr Bateman was waxing lyrical about gneiss rock and aqueducts and she required her husband's help.

But Albert was not paying attention. He had just been assailed by a memory, unbidden, long buried, of the man he and Brown had caught by the Dee. It must be all this chatter about fairy dreams. It must be the mist. It must be the effect of a train journey with Victoria, always trying on the nerves. All the same, he could not quite stop himself imagining the man emerging from the sodden foliage along the bank as the boat steamed past, calling out impudent questions in that shockingly beautiful voice. Albert swallowed hard and tried to restore his attention to the triumph of Frederic Bateman and the great British labourer over slate, bog and Highland brook in a feat that exceeded the nine famous aqueducts of Rome and would last until the end of time (Mr Bateman was beginning to get carried away), as indestructible as the very hills themselves.

Albert stroked his chin a little too sagely to convince the one who knew him best. Victoria glared at him.

Captain William Macquorn Rankine had been awoken at the crack of dawn by an importunate bugle below his window. The men of the University Company 1st Lanarkshire were a motley sight marching to Queen Street Station in their second-hand uniforms, each bearing an antique rifle borrowed from whatever hoary soldier could be parted from his Brown Bess and persuaded to submit to close questioning on how to present arms for a royal salute. Along with the other Glasgow companies the University Volunteers had been drilling night and morning for weeks to prepare for royal guard duty. They were proud to be part of the swelling nationwide citizen movement pledged to defend the land from foreign aggression, the precise nature of which remained largely unspecified but France had better look out. As a diversion from the centrifugal theory of elasticity as applied to gases and vapours, Rankine found it all tremendous fun.

Which was just as well, because even his invincible cheerfulness was put to the test. On the open deck of the Loch Lomond steamer rain struck the men like nails. At Inversnaid pier, readying themselves for a seven-mile trek along a road which the Crimean veterans among them would shortly be comparing unfavourably to the one between Balaclava and Sebastopol, they found an eccentric collection of brakes, carts, traps, carriages and coaches waiting to transport their fellow steamer passengers to Loch Katrine, there being hardly an owner of four wheels and a serviceable nag for miles around who was not making a killing today. Alas, nobody had predicted the numbers who would embark on this Highland adventure, and there proved to be room in the vehicles for only the ladies and a few of the more bullish husbands. Well over a hundred gentlemen were abandoned to labour behind in the mire. The guardsmen left them wrestling their upturned umbrellas in the wind and set off themselves in a squelch of bugles.

The rutted track between lochs Lomond and Katrine had been built as a military road by General George Wade, despatched north by the government in London more than a hundred years earlier to suppress rebellious Highlanders. The riflemen marched past the grey ruins of an old fort, its walls mantled in ivy, the drill-yard colonised by nettles and foxgloves. Rankine, ever prone to romantic musings, wondered if this was the first time these hills had heard the measured tread of armed men since the days of the wily rebel Rob Roy MacGregor, who was reputed to have hidden from government troops in a cave on the Lomond shore nearby. Measured was stretching the point, however. After a few miles of violent drenchings the step staggered between the Double and the Dead March, and only a brisk fusillade of puns preserved the men's good humour. At their head Rankine was called upon to agree for perhaps the fourth time that this road was indeed a general wade.

Ahead weaved the line of improvised transport and behind them trudged the unfortunates who had missed out. From time to time other travellers, those who had bivouacked in the hills perhaps or happened upon some other devious route to Loch Katrine, staggered on to the road to join them. Together this bedraggled stream of humanity wound along the high passes of the exposed heath with but one hope beating in every breast:

that they might arrive in time to join their Queen in celebrating the copious blessings of Highland water.

At last the pallor of the sky ahead met a line of darker grey which might (hallelujah) turn out to be water. Shouts of 'Loch Katrine! Loch Katrine!' rumbled along the line of guardsmen. Rankine had the painful task of passing the message back that although this was indeed the aforesaid loch, the tunnel itself began a further two miles along the shore. And he should know. Damn near designed the thing.

As he was about to order a right turn off the road, a small carriage rattled up behind. The line of guardsmen swayed aside to let it pass. A woman inside was waving.

'Ye know that lady, sir?' asked the company ensign, a fresh-faced Greek scholar who was feeling the strain.

Rankine laughed. 'That was Mrs Aird, the doctor's wife here. I'm glad to see her enjoying the day. Her husband is a fine fellow.'

'Where are they off to, sir?'

'To the boats, my lad, the boats. The easiest way to reach the tunnel is by water, and there's a pier down there at Stronachlachar. But that's for the lucky few. We, Niven, are going this way.'

He swung to the right along a roughly cut path running above and parallel to Katrine's shoreline. Between the trees they caught glimpses of agitated water, upon which a ragged flotilla was making heavy weather of the short voyage to the same destination. Sinking into mud and moss, scratched by brambles, soaked to the skin, the guardsmen pressed on. Then, just as Niven was deciding the moment had come to fall to his knees and sob for his mother, the path plunged to meet the loch at last. Perched above it on a spit of land stood a squat grey house. Give or take the royal standard flapping frantically from a flagpole on the roof, it could have been one of those plain seafront holiday residences that served indifferent kidneys for breakfast.

Already there seemed to be thousands here. Some must have overnighted in a pierhead hotel and got here early. All were milling about the craggy slopes around Royal Cottage beneath such a sea, such an ocean, such a veritable planet of umbrellas that the Queen could at that moment have landed, danced a jig and departed again without her loyal subjects being any the wiser.

The special guests were meanwhile settling into tiered timber galleries on the far side. These afforded a bleary view of the loch, where the rumour of hills on the opposite bank remained currently unconfirmed, and over to an octagonal dais got up like a rustic temple, its roof thatched with drooping arrangements of juniper, heather and oak leaves surmounted by a royal crown. The dais faced away from the loch and towards a semi-circular alcove that had been gouged from the rock to form a basin completed by the sluice-wall presently holding the waters at bay. Around and above this alcove another high wall was knitted into the contours of the remaining crag. Here in all its glistening obduracy was the rock of black slate streaked through with white quartz that had so tested the skill and endurance of the Corporation of Glasgow navvies.

Seeing it, the spectators understood why it had proved such a mettlesome adversary. Had men really hacked at that with hammer and chisel? To those ratepayers who had queried the sluggish pace of the excavations and the eye-watering expenditure on gunpowder, the progress of the tunnel seemed of a sudden no longer slow but amazing. They gazed at the hewn alcove, craning and straining to see in it the opening that the rain was doing its best to obscure. And there it was. Yes, there it was. Set within such pillared stone grandeur as would rival one of the more ostentatious mausoleums, the misty mouth of the great tunnel itself.

Macquorn Rankine headed straight for a large refreshment hall behind the house. Along with every furnishing, every square foot of upholstery, every plank and nail of the timber galleries and every hothoused bloom from the Botanic Gardens, the wooden tea-tent had made just such an inconvenient journey to get here as everyone, its parts transported down the River Clyde, up the Leven, along Loch Lomond, down the road to Stronachlachar and finally around the bay on a series of rafts. Rankine strolled about in his steaming rifleman's uniform, legs afire with itches from the unfamiliar cloth, greeting friends and smoking a restful pipe. The mood he encountered seemed, in that bracingly British way of which he much approved, to be mostly rather jolly: och, it's only rain, there's tea aplenty, we've got sandwiches and a nice pigeon pie in the basket, and the Queen, God bless her, will be here within the hour.

A portly banker of his acquaintance, nursing a badly stricken umbrella and a mood which, on second thoughts, could not be described as jolly, waylaid him to report that he would on no account be venturing north of Glasgow again as long as he lived. Another man, a poor, reedy fellow without even a hat to fend off the worst of the rain, looked so pinched with cold on his own at the back by the grazing horses that Rankine thought he should stroll over and say something.

'Have ye no umbrella, man?' he asked affably. 'I'd give you my own if I had one, but all I have here is a musket.'

'I thank ye, sir, but I'm used to rain,' returned the man in a remarkably self-assured and resonant voice for a tramp. His ill-cut hair was plastered tight to his head and dripping down his cheeks.

'Will ye not let me get you a cup of tea, then?' Rankine felt rather moved by the man's dignity. Royal occasions brought out all sorts. 'They have a good urn going over there. Or are you waiting for someone?'

'I wait to attend upon royalty. I am an acquaintance of Prince Albert.'

'Are you now, my good fellow?' Rankine twinkled. 'Well, you'll have to wait a while yet. The *Rob Roy* is not expected till nigh on two. Come now, how about a wee refreshment?'

'You are kind, sir,' said the man, 'but I am lang used to waiting.'

Rankine clapped him on the shoulder and went off to make sure that none of his men had inadvertently stabbed anyone with a bayonet.

The rowing boat wobbled as Isabel reached for her husband's hand under the proffered umbrella and lumbered ashore. Alexander's face was thunderous. The short voyage had been rough and he was furious at himself for allowing it.

'Oh, cheer up, Alex.' Isabel was looking about her with pleasure at the jostling umbrellas, the kilted pipers, the bunting whirling from every eminence. 'A bit of rain and a bumpy boat ride won't do me any harm.'

Tucking her arm in his, she made a stab at winsomeness: 'And don't I deserve this one outing?'

Alexander raised her hand in its wet glove to his lips, smiling despite himself to be flirted with, adoring the gleam of unaffected relish in the bright eyes that met his own. 'Aye, you deserve all sorts of good things, my Issy.' He rubbed his nose. It was russet-hued with cold and made her want to laugh. 'But I have to say it. This was a mistake when we've come so far.'

Isabel laughed a shade too gaily. It was not the time to mention a minor misgiving of her own. 'We've been through this endless times. A trip down the road to see the Queen won't make a ha'penny of difference one way or another.'

She jiggled his arm and they set forth on a gingerly navigation of the puddles. Rain beat down on the umbrella and leapt up her skirts.

'Will ye tell me one thing truthfully,' he said as they headed for the stands, making sure to catch the reaction out of the corner of his eye. 'Why did you rub your side back there? You know, when we were being buffeted about in the waves. You were holding yourself as if it hurt.'

'I was not.'

'Truthfully, Issy.'

'Alex, are you policing my every move? Did you happen to notice that I also patted my cheek and tweaked an ear? For goodness sake, I can't remember. Maybe it was a twinge of indigestion. I don't know what Annie did to that porridge – the girl has been half crazed with excitement all morning.'

Alexander's heart lurched at how fast she was talking.

They found a place halfway up the gallery, where the consensus among their fellow spectators seemed to be that the weather was easing at last: 'Is the loch not a wee thing calmer now, would ye say, Mary? I'm wondering if that might be a hill over there.' The Airds peered over the waters, following the pointing fingers of the most optimistic commentators, who had convinced themselves that yonder was no cloud but, as anyone could see (which nobody could), a puff of exhausted steam in the distance.

A large, voluble man one row down was explaining what was going to happen when the Queen arrived. There was a small pillar rising from the floor of the octagonal dais to which was attached, he asserted, a lever. 'All Her Majesty will have to do,' boomed the gentleman in confident tones, 'is touch this lever and it will set in motion a small hydraulic engine above the sluices. Do ye see it along the platform there? No, my dear, the other way. It will raise the sluices and we'll see the water pouring in from the loch.'

'Aye, if we see anything at all,' muttered a diminutive man on Isabel's left, whose ill fortune was to be seated directly behind the speaker's mighty hat and formidable brolly.

'Are you an engineer, sir?' asked a lady in front admiringly. Isabel winced to notice that her maroon silk bonnet had bled down the grey stripe of an expensive-looking mantle.

'He read it in the *Glasgow Herald*,' piped up the large man's wife from the other side.

Her husband's shoulders huffed and he turned to the admiring neighbour. 'I am not an engineer, madam, but you may rely on me for the details. The way it works is that a tiny stream has been diverted from the mountainside ninety-five feet up and by the power of gravitation will open the sluice. Think of it, madam. The column of water performing the initial work to move the waters of this great loch is not much thicker than your finger.'

'That was in the paper too,' his wife interjected, with the air of a woman who has heard more about hydraulic power this morning than flesh and blood can bear.

Looking about him for relief, Alexander was delighted to spot Professor Rankine among the crowd on the lower slopes.

'Will you be all right here if I go and bid good-day to Rankine, Issy? I nearly didn't recognise him there, pretending to be a soldier.'

'Of course I will.' Isabel was relieved to be free of the anxious sidelong glances. 'Just as long as you leave me that umbrella.'

By the time Alexander caught him up, his friend was almost at the covered pathway that stretched from the house to the landing platform and as far as the royal dais.

'Dr Aird, what a pleasure,' cried Rankine, pumping his hand vigorously. 'I wondered if I'd see you. I'm just planning my manoeuvres here.'

Alexander grinned. Rankine was squeezed into a dark green military uniform set off by two rows of straining gilt buttons and a pair of trousers marginally on the safe side of indecent. His curls were spilling from a peaked pillbox hat that was also too small. He acknowledged the picture with a genial shrug: 'All borrowed, my dear fellow, and I'll be glad to get the things off.'

He tapped the bayonet at his side. 'Just about to go and attach this thing to the rifle. I think I've got the hang of it now. My men will be lining this part of the covered way up to the house and presenting arms as Her Majesty walks past after the ceremony. Quite an honour, you know, and—'

There was a commotion under the umbrellas, and a cheer began to ripple through the massed ranks of onlookers. Few could have seen for themselves the white smoke of the approaching *Rob Roy* steamer, all but impossible to distinguish from the sickly sky, but a blast of bugles confirmed it and the cheer was soon a mighty roar. With a 'Good heavens, it must be them,' Rankine rushed away, and Alexander began excusing himself back to the stands. He was still negotiating a path to his seat when the band of Stirling Castle's 79th Highlanders started on the Queen's anthem and the guns of the Athole Highlanders responded with a royal salute from the cliffs.

Any minute now, although hardly a soul would be able to vouch for it personally, the tiny sovereign would step ashore on the arm of her Prince Consort, followed by the Princesses Alice and Helena and some lords and ladies nobody had heard of. What everyone could most certainly attest, however, was that the rain, in what was generally agreed to be a royal miracle, had stopped.

As he worked his way up past the collapsing umbrellas, Alexander could see Isabel looking out towards the landing platform, craning her head this way and that to see what was going on. As he watched, her hand moved to her side.

He edged along to his seat. The instant she saw him Isabel dropped her hand and welcomed her husband with a careful smile. He sat down beside her, queasy with foreboding.

60

The servants were allowed out the house to watch the Queen arriving, though not a thing could we see with so many folk packed all the way up to the cottage and over by the tunnel and away up on the heights behind. The whole place was thick with umbrellas. Mind you, the sky did clear up a bit just as the cheering began and they started to be taken down. Saying that, all those top hats and bonnets in the way were just as bad.

You could hear all right, though. What a noise when the boat pulled up. Bands playing, guns booming, folk shouting their heads off. There was this gravel path going down from where we were standing outside the house to a funny wee platform done up in flowers that I'd seen them put up the day before, and there was a load o' soldiers lined along it. Folk all the way up were passing on what was happening, saying that was her stepping up to the platform now, and what a nice voice she had, and was that no' a long prayer from the minister and suchlike, so that you got a fair enough sense o' the thing. And then we heard the Queen had turned a handle that sent the Katrine water in and away. There was another big burst o' cheering at that and we got 'Rule Britannia' from the band and more big guns. Seemingly there were guns went off at the same time in

Edinburgh Castle and Stirling Castle and a telegraph sent to Glasgow so they could ring the bells there, not having a castle o' their own. Quite a to-do when you think about it. We were told to get on with our jobs after that, but I hung about outside anyway and there were that many people around that nobody noticed.

The news was passed back that the pair o' them wanted a closer look at the water coming in through the sluices and how it swirled about on its way into the tunnel, which was this big, gaping hole in the rock – I'd had a good look before. There were steps down and iron railings around and some fancy lettering along the top that said 'Glasgow Corporation Water Works'. And even though I couldna exactly read the words myself, it gave me a proud feeling to look at them, never mind that I'd only stayed that time wi' Nancy and fair hated the place. So the Lord Provost leads the Queen along this platform and Her Majesty has a keek down at the water rushing in, and a wee while later there's this great stir in the crowd and someone yells, 'She's coming, she's coming,' and here she came up the pathway under a long red cloth.

The whole way was lined with soldiers who looked half dead wi' nerves, and they were holding these rifles close to their chests wi' long bayonet things sticking out the top. Well, here comes the best bit. Somebody shouts out very stern, 'Royal salute! Present arms!' – and these knives shoot all the way up and right through the red cloth. It was like a forest o' dirks coming up in a bed o' blood – just exactly like. The laugh everyone had! I bet the Queen had a giggle afterwards too, if royalty does that kind o' thing which I suppose they do.

All this while I'd been keeping an eye out for Mrs Aird. I

knew the doctor would be sore afraid for her, going on boats and that. They used to argue about it. More than once I heard her tell him there was no evidence in a single one of his books that moving about made any difference. She'd tried every which way to carry a bairn and thought she knew as well as anyone. And maybe she did. Nobody ever told me to stop walking out and carrying things and won't you put your feet up, Mrs McEchern, and I still popped those babes out like peas.

There was no sign of either o' them, so back inside the house I went. My, but the folk in charge had done well with it. They had six rooms all ready for Her Majesty. A dining room overlooking the loch that we could have fitted the whole o' Nancy's tenement in no bother, all done up in green and gold wi' crests of this and that all over the place, and sitting rooms, and a dressing room for the Prince, who was dressed already as far as I could see, and bedrooms for folk that had no thought o' staying over. And what would you be needing a bedroom for if you've only to powder your nose is what I wanted to know, but the serving-man who brought the dishes to the scullery looked shocked and said it was weary work being a queen and you needed to rest.

I'd tell you what they and their party ate if I knew. Eight courses I mind it was, but I was that busy I only saw the leftovers, which would ha' done us a month in Sebastopol. I slipped half a pheasant into my apron from somebody's plate, thinking it would do nicely for James's tea, but that wasna to be.

When the meal was done, it went round that they were getting ready to leave. Well, I was out that scullery in a flash to see if I could get a proper look this time, and there they were just beyond the front door and about to walk back down the covered way to the pier and, funny how things work out, I ended up just as close as I am to you now. Fair overcome I was, to be right there next to them.

She was not all that bonnie, the Queen, being honest, but she had a spark to her eye that I liked, and she was leaning on her man's arm and looking up at him now and then as if she was actually quite fond of him. He was handsome for a foreigner, I'll say that. Stood very erect, moustaches at attention, but he looked straight at folk in a real thinking sort o' way when they were speaking. He wasna looking at me, of course, but I'll tell you who he did notice. He was having a word at the top o' the covered path with the captain fellow in charge, when I saw him glancing over to the folk looking in from outside, behind the guardsmen, and his face went so pale I thought he was going to keel right over.

Was it not Robert Kirke standing there on the slope just off the pathway! Kirke was tall as a stork, so that even with all the folk around he seemed to stand out in the crowd. It gave me quite a turn to see him there wi' his drookit hair, the only man in the place without a hat on his head. And I can't think the Prince got any less of a shock, because he just stood there staring back and his eyes, such a nice blue they were up close, they just froze to ice. When I think back it seems a long time the two o' them were just drilling into each other like that, though I suppose it was only seconds. But I looked from one to the other and I thought, the Prince knows. How does the Prince know? What does he know about Robert Kirke that's made him look so troubled?

Neither of them moved, and I doubt the Queen even noticed. She was having a sly keek at the crimson cloth overhead that was so torn and tattered, and the captain, bushy-haired fellow, was looking mighty embarrassed if I'm not mistaken. And before you knew it, she and the Prince were being ushered down the line and away.

When I looked back Robert Kirke had slipped into the crowds himself. I wondered for a minute if I'd made it up, the way ye do when a thing is there and gone and you're not sure after if ye can trust yourself. But with every year that passes I mind it better. That's the way it goes when you're an old woman. You forget where you've laid your bonnet five minutes ago, but these big moments from the past shine out brighter than ever. No, I didna imagine it. These two knew each other, the Prince shrinking into himself in a kind o' horror and there was Kirke, gobbling him up wi' those same greedy eyes I'd seen him lay on Isabel Aird. And all I could think then was, where is she, where is she, and what's he got planned amid all these folk?

The *Rob Roy* got away again with the same carry-on wi' guns and salutes as before, and back came the rain. Right on the dot o' them going, would ye believe, back on it came. I felt sorry for the guardsmen. They were saying to each other the rain had waited for the exact moment they had to start again on the long march back to Inversnaid, and I'll tell you I wasna looking forward to getting myself along that path and back round to Sebastopol in such wet either. The posh folk started scurrying towards the boats that were dancing about on wee white waves to pick them up, but from where I stood I couldna see the Airds among them.

I was looking in the wrong place, though, for the call o' 'Kirsty! Kirsty!' came not from the pier but from the slope up to the house. Dr Aird had a big umbrella over her and an arm about her shoulder.

'We'll need a room, Kirsty,' says the doctor as they're drawing near. He was calm enough, but I'd seen that tight stretch to his cheekbones before and knew what it meant. 'My wife must lie down,' he says.

I led them towards the front door. The flunkeys were all out the way by then and we went straight for the porch. Mrs Aird was walking not so bad, but she had to stop just outside and breathe through gritted teeth and I could see it was costing her to keep quiet. Being a man ye'll not know that feeling when the labour pains grip so hard you want to yell the house down but you feel it wouldn't be over-polite so you do your best to swallow it. After a while ye couldna care less, but that's by the by.

'It's too early, Kirsty,' she says when this one is past.

That's all she said to me, bleak as bleak. And what else was there to say? The three of us all knew it.

'Can ye manage some stairs, Issy?' says the doctor. And she nods and we go up this grand staircase, red carpet and all. I'd passed it many a time getting the house ready those weeks past, but I'd never been up. First door he comes to, Dr Aird pushes it open and it's a bedroom, huge affair and very elegantly decorated. Curtains o' that deep shade I think they're calling maroon all edged wi' gold, pretty washbasin and jug, a bed the size o' Sebastopol. He steers her across to this bed and she sits on the edge a minute, getting on wi' the next pain, then sinks into the pillows. I've never felt pillows like them for softness before or since.

I'd been wondering how long it would take for someone to notice we were there. The place was at such sixes and sevens, everyone rushing round tidying up, that I thought we might get a while to ourselves. But no, this nervy character in a kilt suddenly bursts in, shouting, 'What in the name o' the wee man are ye all doing in here?'

'My wife requires medical assistance, which I am administering,' says the doctor, very posh-sounding. And when the man opens his mouth to protest, he's straight in there with, 'I am the physician to the Corporation of Glasgow Water Works, appointed by the commissioners themselves, who, I believe I am right in saying, own this house.'

I always did like to hear Alexander Aird being the doctor. He was mild as could be for a man with such red hair, but he had that bit o' toughness underneath you could never mistake. I mind when our Lily had the croup I had sich a strong feeling of being safe in his hands. This man in the kilt sensed it right away, the authority. You could practically see his feathers folding themselves down one by one, but for a last wee ruffle.

'But it's Her Majesty's bedroom,' he says in a pained voice. 'Her Majesty the Queen *has been in here*.'

'Aye, and she's now halfway to Callander,' says Dr Aird. 'Which means the bedroom is now vacant, is it not?'

The man, a sleekit fellow wi' thin hair and a pointy nose, just shrugs.

'Now,' says the doctor, 'my wife will soon be giving birth. Pray assist my nurse here' – he nodded towards me, would ye believe – 'with anything she may request and be kind enough to leave us in peace.'

Between us the doctor and I got Mrs Aird out most of her clothes and into the bed. Her dress was wet through and I thought it was the rain until the doctor said her waters had gone.

'Ach, Issy, Issy,' says he, stroking her head in a tender way. 'You mustn't blame yourself.'

Mrs Aird was not feeling tender at all, though what woman is when you're labouring. 'I'm not blaming myself,' she snaps right back. 'If this was the day the bairn was to come, she'd have come wherever I was.'

'But at least we'd have had you safe in your own bed,' he says with a sigh.

She managed a bit of a laugh at that. 'Well, I'm in the Queen's bed now, Alex. And you can hardly get safer than that, can you?'

61

Save a friendly salutation for auld times' sake there was naught I desired of the Prince. But friendliness was there none in the look he fixed upon me. It disturbed me, the fear in it. Worse, the revulsion.

So you are turned hypocrite now, Robert Kirke.

He saw only the canker in me. Nothing else of what I am.

He saw you as you are. Speaking of which, your attention is required elsewhere.

The lady. I know not what her husband was thinking of to let her go traipsing about another loch sae close to her confinement.

She is gone in the house. Watch for her. She is very near.

By the house is a stone hut. Empty. Coal piled in great heaps.

Sitting on the floor, my back to the wall and my head at rest against the cauld stone, I listen to the thundering rain on the roof and the shivering rattle of the windows.

A boy comes to the door. A servant o' some ilk, all gangly-limbed, chin smooth as a babe's. When the light of his lantern falls on me, huddled against the wall in the midst o' the shining coal, he nearly faints at my feet.

'Whit are ye doing here in the dark, man?' he stutters out.

'I but seek shelter from the storm,' say I. 'I will be gone 'ere lang.'

He gapes at the sight and sound o' me, as folk do. Then says I am not the only one grateful for a roof tonight: there is a gentlewoman having a bairn –

Hah!

– in the very bedroom where the Queen rested this afternoon. And he the unlucky fellow sent out in all this to keep a fire going through the night.

Well, well, well. 'Twould appear, Robert Kirke, that our time is truly nigh.

I lay me down, using coals for a pillow. I can scarce take these tidings in. My escape is at hand. My salvation, my reunion, my eternal happiness.

And her harm. And our profit. Ye have it exactly.

I close my eyes, trying to shut out the voice. A bone-deep ache is creeping through every limb.

'Tis not sae easy to shut us out, Robert Kirke. Has it occurred to you that Katrine is the wrang loch?

I know my commission.

Then kindly bestir yourself and bend your thoughts to the Dog Loch.

I will. God knows, I do.

And to what ye are going to do now.

62

Rain is a weak kind o' word for the hurly-burly tempest that worked itself up outside the windows that evening. So much water banged against them you'd have thought the whole loch was flinging itself at us to get in. When it grew properly dark outside I got the candles lit and the heavy curtains drawn.

I can't say there wasna just a wee bit of me that was happy to be toasting my feet quite the thing at the Queen's own fireplace instead of having to tramp home in weather like that, for all the ill luck that placed me there. I heard after that the guests and the guardsmen and all those day-trippers had an awful job getting back along that terrible road and away. Not a room to spare for miles around, and folk were all but coming to blows for what space there was. At the Stronachlachar Hotel they were crammed up staircases and into outhouses and a few had to sleep in the brakes that had come back empty after dropping off folk in Inversnaid. Those that made it down Loch Lomond on the *Prince o' Wales* steamer found themselves not as lucky as they thought, for the light was that bad it nearly ran aground on an island. Another steamer refused to go further than Tarbet, across Lomond's other side, and the hotel there got so crowded there were many had to sleep on tables. By all accounts a few gentry made the close acquaintance of a barn floor.

So Mrs Aird could ha' been in a worse place when you look at it that way, labouring through the night with a great fire roaring away and more candles around than I'd seen in one room in my life before.

'Her Majesty is fond of candlelight,' says yon sniffy man in the kilt, Mr Aberlour by name, when I was saying as much in the kitchen, 'and we had to be prepared in case it was decided the royal party should stay the night.'

He was fine and helpful, all the same, Mr Aberlour, once it was clear that Dr Aird was in charge and nobody was moving from that room. Made sure we had enough sent up from the coalhouse to keep a furnace going all night and hot water and towels aplenty, and three supper trays wi' bread and butter on and some very tasty cold meats which I was heartily glad of (me, served on a tray!), though the doctor only picked at his and Mrs Aird, well, she was past eating and waved at me to have hers, which I did.

She did well that night, Mrs Aird. Kept calm through the most of it, breathing very slow and steady and not yelling more than any flesh and blood would when the pains came so fast they were running into each other. She gasped out that some o' yon thing-amajig that put you to sleep would come in very handy about now, and the doctor said shush now, shush now, he hadna thought to be needing it when they were only here to see the Queen. He sat by her side the whole time murmuring, 'Good for you, Issy. I'm proud of you,' and suchlike endearments that kept her going.

Must be a right funny thing to have your man around when you're in the throes like that. Last place on earth I'd ha' wanted my James, seeing me in a state and getting in the way, not to mention he'd likely ha' been in his cups from start to finish. But Dr Aird had that quiet doctory way about him that was good for her and you felt she was trying to do it well for him, too – be brave, ye know, show him she could do this. She had laboured before wi' some o' the bairns that had made it that bit further, and there was this to be said for it, that they were aye small. The doctor muttered to me that at least he saw no sign of complications: the labour was going nice and steady. There was nothing for me to do but sit by the fire and listen to the coals shifting and sighing, and his quiet murmurings from the bed, and the rain battering to get in.

Sometimes, even today, I can see them together in the glow o' fire- and candlelight as they were that night. Her propped on the bed with her white face upturned to his and her eyes fast on his eyes, pulling his strength into herself. And him holding both her hands in his and whispering gentle words and feeling his own heart swell – I knew fine to look at him – with what he got back from her, which was maybe strength of a different kind and more like the sort a father needs. That's how I've liked to think o' them all the years since. And that was how they brought the babe into the world together.

It was born just before two. I remember the time, for there was a clock in the house chimed softly into the pool o' silence that grew after she had pushed and groaned the wee thing out. I thrust a towel at the doctor. It was warm from hanging by the fire for hours for this moment and he lifted the bairn into it, all slithery and wet. I had the scissors ready for him too. I'd washed my hands about three times over in the Queen's washbasin, knowing how particular Mrs Aird was about such things since she'd been reading the Nightingale lady, and the scissors had a good clean too on the doctor's instructions. He had the cord snipped in a second. And then, ever so gently, he wrapped the top flap o' towel around the bairn and jiggled it around a bit in his hands. I got a keek of a teeny face wi' skin you could nearly see through.

Then, as I looked, just that very moment that I looked into the towel, it gave a gasp, and then a gulp, and then – oh, you'll have to forgive an old woman's tears – then it gave a wee frail little cry. And the doctor just stands there with this mewling bundle in the crook of his arm, looking at it in a wondering way, and then looking at his wife, who'd been labouring away to pass the afterbirth and nobody paying her a bit of attention. But she could hear. She could hear that sound all right, and she just gazed back at him wi' hardly an expression on her face.

'Well, Issy,' says he at last, 'would you like to meet our son?'

I plumped up the pillows and helped her to sit up, and he laid the wee thing on her breast and watched as she took a finger to its cheek and traced the blue veins under the skin. And then she peeked under the towel and checked he was all boy and counted toes and fingers, like any mother will. But Dr Aird's face was more severe now. I don't think he expected the bairn to breathe very long, and it was as if he was setting his guard against another such gust o' wondering happiness as had caught him on the wing wi' that first breath.

But when she glanced up at him he managed a smile, and then he busied himself ordering me to stoke up the fire and bring over a shawl we'd been sent up by the housekeeper and prepare a warm wet cloth and make ready to change the sheets and this and that, until Mrs Aird calls him to leave all that to me – 'Kirsty knows what she's doing, Alex' – and come and sit by her side.

Still the child is breathing and his eyes are open, beady wee things like a bird. And she takes the doctor's forefinger and guides it into the tiny fist, and it's as if he just forgets himself, for the babe grips it and they both sit there wi' smiles as big as their faces.

'Florence,' she says suddenly after a long while o' this. 'He was going to be Florence.'

'You can call him Florence if you like,' says the doctor, not moving his finger, not taking his eyes off the child. 'You can call him anything in the world. Though he might not thank us.'

'Will he live, Alex?' she says quietly.

He took his gaze from the bairn and gave her a level look back, respecting her understanding of hard things in that way I'd seen him do more often of late. 'I don't know, Issy. He's bigger than I feared he would be, and his lungs are working. We should try to get some nourishment into him.'

She nodded.

I turned my back and went over to shovel more coals on the fire. I should ha' been blithe and hopeful for them. But there was something muttering at the back o' my mind that had started to grow louder, for all that I tried not to listen. At first I thought it was just the same dull feeling I'd caught on the doctor's face when the excitement of a live birth was over: realising that the bairn shouldna be here yet and was likely going to struggle. Ach, but it was more than that and I knew it. Somebody else was interested in this bairn. That's what was going on in the back o' my mind. And I'd seen him not twelve hours ago just a few steps from the front door.

I stirred the fire till it took again. Then I laid the poker aside and stayed a while on my knees looking into the flames.

63

The slope above Loch Chon on the day I was spat out of faery. The voice in my head offering a bargain.

Search out a newborn, they said.

Are there not newborns aplenty? (Thus I answered.) Are you not well accomplished in snatching them? Why must I procure one?

I heard the querulous note in my voice. Heard it as if from without, with the vague interest of a man contemplating some boil new erupted beneath his skin. No principled expression of outrage from this Robert Kirke, fresh from faery.

You are to christen this newborn. After the ceremony ye will place it where we instruct you anon, for removal to faery.

You would mak a mockery of a holy Christian sacrament?

'Tis you who will be making the mockery – a task for which ye will agree that faery has equipped you most handsomely.

And if I do not as ye instruct?

Then, Robert Kirke, will heaven be closed to you and your love lost unto eternity. And we will keep our nails in your soul for ever.

I made no protest. I knew then that the best of me was gone and the mouldy odour hanging about me was the smell of the grave.

64

Day after day the October sunshine, insouciantly back as though nothing had happened, danced through the windows of the Queen's bedroom. Isabel was happy. One day she would identify a splinter of dread in that happiness, although perhaps it was not dread – easy to imagine afterwards – but only some sad little intimation, buried deep within her contentment, that happiness so exquisite must pass. Day after day Alexander dripped her laboriously squeezed milk into their son's tiny red mouth with a syringe, crooning the while that he was a bonnie babe, a fine boy, the best his papa could have wished for. Day after day, with every rise and fall of the tiny chest, her own swelled with such love she wondered that her body could contain it.

Alexander had been constantly by her side, monitoring every breath the baby took, checking his temperature, feeding him until he was strong enough to suck. Isabel had made Alexander laugh by reminding him that her mother still boasted of having secured the same wet-nurse as the Duchess of Buccleuch and would require a week's recuperation in Rothesay if she heard they were doing this by themselves.

The family in the Queen's bedroom provided a welcome diversion for the Royal Cottage household, now working with a will to return the house to drabness. Outside, workmen were busy dismantling everything that had taken so many weeks to transport and erect. The octagonal temple was stripped down and the punctured crimson cloth wrapped up. Down, plank by plank, came the grand wooden hall, along with dozens of trestle tables, all the spectator galleries and thousands of fittings – each to be loaded on to enormous rafts tied up by the pier for the journey back to Glasgow or set alight on a lochside bonfire. Isabel's dozes were punctuated by the clang of poles being deposited along the causeway and endless stop-and-start hammering. She lay in bed listening to jaunty whistles and snatches of song. Sometimes she glimpsed wings of glowing cloth and scraps of charred paper drifting past on the breeze. When she wrestled the window up there would come rushing into the room the earthy smell of burning wood, and in years to come just one whiff of woodsmoke in autumn would bring her back here, to the gilded room, the glistening loch, her perfect, sleeping child.

Mr Aberlour, who ran the house for the water commissioners with his housekeeper wife, had resigned himself to an extended stay for the duration of Mrs Aird's lying-in. He asked one of the carpenters to hammer together a cradle and Mrs Aberlour sent up a crocheted bonnet so small it would have fitted an apple. Young Billy Hamilton continued to supply them so diligently with overflowing scuttles from the coalhouse that Kirsty complained the room was like a Turkish baths, a convenience she had never tried personally but would wager James's life on the experience being hot. Meals arrived for the doctor and his wife with as much ceremony as if they were royalty themselves. The Airds took afternoon tea at a table by the window, through which they could watch cloud-shadow scurrying across the

burgundy hills. When Kirsty plodded along the path to Royal
Cottage every morning to 'do' for the couple, as she described
it to Mrs Aberlour (who drew up her bosom and tutted her hope
that Mrs McEchern was not expecting the Corporation of
Glasgow to pay for any such private doing), she was disappointed
to find herself relegated to the kitchen table.

On the third day the baby took his first slippery sucks from
his mother. Just after first light on the following day he was still
curled at her breast in a milky stupor when there came an urgent
knocking at the door. An agitated Mr Aberlour enquired if the
doctor would be kind enough to attend a worker who had fallen
while attempting to unfasten one of the stands. Alexander
beamed that it would be his pleasure: his wife and son were
doing well and it was about time he made himself useful. When
he was gone, Isabel changed the small napkin, swaddled the
child tight and tucked his bonnet around his ears. Such pleasure
it gave her to do all this, such bliss to press her lips to those
pearly cheeks that were less transparent now, filling out, softer
than thistledown.

She laid him in the cradle by her bed and sank back sleepily
into what Kirsty, who all but genuflected when she had occasion
to fluff them up, insisted on calling the Queen's Pillows. Kirsty
should be here soon. Isabel was looking forward to telling her
that a name had at last been decided upon, although it could
be predicted with some certainty that she would not approve.
And what's wrong with a good Scots name, she would retort for
sure – or better still a Gaelic one. Kirsty had already unburdened
herself of the conviction that the baby looked like an Angus.
'Do ye not think Angus Aird has a ring to it?' she badgered
Alexander. And he had laughed in the easy, open-faced way that

Isabel loved to see returned and said he was personally wondering about Genghis Khan Aird. 'Which has an even better ring, would ye not say?' And Isabel had giggled and told him not to tease Kirsty, who didn't seem to mind at all (these two had always been thick as thieves), only saying that her father had been called Angus and he was a very fine man.

When Isabel awoke next, full morning sunshine was pouring through the window, bright on her eyelids. She took a long, contented breath and stretched her shoulders, once, twice, blinking in the rush of light. She turned towards the cradle by the bed. It took her a bleary second or two to register the shadow that lay across her woolly white bundle.

65

Hair a-stream on the pillow. Eyes befuddled a moment with sleep and the sun's dazzle.

So, too, looked my love as she stirred in the morn. It is of her I must think now. Only of her.

66

'Mr Kirke!'

She hauled herself up the bed and drew the sheets around. 'What are you . . . how dare you . . .'

He was standing in heron pose a few steps from the bed, twisting his hands. The cravat was more loosely slung than usual and his exposed neck looked pasty and vulnerable beneath the weathered face. The material was perhaps a shade closer to white than Isabel remembered, which made her wonder if he had tried to wash it before this most outrageous of social calls – a thought that, as she recovered her poise, she found first amusing and then unaccountably moving. Kirke swallowed. Finding outrage as hard as ever to manufacture in his company, Isabel was transfixed by the nervous bobbing of his throat.

'Pray be not offended, madam. I would only that we speak thegither a while,' he began.

He was bone-pale, an effect accentuated by smears of black coal-dust below one ear and across a cheekbone. Clearly Robert Kirke's toilet had been a hasty one. Isabel put a hand to her hair and attempted a perfunctory tidy where it had escaped her cap. Her guest had smoothed his own hair somewhat and this morning wore it tucked behind his ears. Again Isabel experienced an unexpected surge of tearful sympathy. What was wrong with her? She had wept yesterday on spotting an unseasonal duckling.

Even Kirke's black coat looked as if he had made an effort. It had been largely divested of shrubbery, although the usual wet-leaved aroma lingered amid a more pungent confection of sweat and general seediness. She hoped he would keep his distance from her sweet-breathed baby.

'It is not appropriate for you to visit me in my bedchamber.'

Even as she said it, Isabel reflected that in the time she had known him nothing Robert Kirke had said or done had ever been appropriate. Indeed, now that the surprise had passed, she was less shocked than she supposed she should be to see him at her bedside. It was almost fitting that the figure who had first appeared on the disgruntled day she arrived should be at hand now to witness her joy, should be here when the fear was ebbing that every breath her son took would be his last, when Alexander was relaxing into fatherhood, when they had just that morning dared to bicker over which room in Bath Street ought to serve as the nursery, when they had chosen a name.

'I hope ye will forgive me for importuning you thus, madam, but I am so lang out of society that I forget my manners.' His voice was recovering its confidence. Glancing towards the cradle, he murmured, 'The bairn thrives, I hope?'

'He came very early, but our son does well, Mr Kirke, and' – the elation burst its banks – 'after all this time I am so very, very happy.'

He offered one of his awkward smiles. 'May I ask where you plan to have the bairn baptised?'

Isabel blinked. He was so very direct, Mr Kirke. 'We have

not thought of it. Our minister Mr Clark has already departed. I imagine we'll wait until we return to Glasgow.'

Kirke gave her one of his beadiest looks. 'Nay, 'twere better the bairn were christened here. A bairn sae small ought to receive the sacrament without delay.'

It was Isabel's turn to swallow. 'Well, I dare say we could get the minister from Aberfoyle to do it. Alex could despatch someone to fetch him. I shall ask him when he returns.'

'I was thinking, madam, that you might allow me to be of service?'

'You, Mr Kirke?'

'I am an ordained minister, my lady. 'Twould be an honour.'

Isabel looked at him sharply. Kirke smouldered back.

'I fear your . . . your credentials may be out of date, Mr Kirke. Why are you so anxious to do this for us?'

Kirke was silent a moment. His thin throat bobbed again, and he shifted his weight from one foot to the other. 'Ye mind when we met last upon the ridge above the Fairy Knoll? I said I wished to ask of you a great boon. Ye mind, do ye?'

Isabel nodded doubtfully. The two of them side by side on the heather. Kirsty panting up the hill. The warm desire to help him. Which, now that he was here, had begun to cool.

'Aye, weel, now is come the time to keep your promise.'

'But what a time to ask it of me, Mr Kirke. What can I possibly do for you at a moment like this? I am confined to bed.'

He looked past her and through the window. In profile his face was skeletal, the skin pulled tight over the sharp cheekbone and hollowed by the smudge of coal-shadow.

When he spoke it was so softly that she strained to hear him.

'You need do nothing, my lady. I wish only to christen the bairn, that I may be released.'

'Released?'

'So that I may die like any other man. So that I may return to my Isabel.'

Isabel felt suddenly very cold, though the sun shone on.

'Who are you, Mr Kirke?'

'Ach, who are any of us?' He turned back from the window with a grimace of a smile. 'Ye need not fash yourself wi' such questions, my lady. All that may usefully be said is that Robert Kirke is not who he was.'

His throat bobbed again. She no longer found it sympathetic.

'Ye should know that faery is a malign influence on human-kind. It taks the worst of us and calls it good. It maks us believe that truth is only what we would have it be. It puts ourselves at the centre of our own dance and stops us thinking o' what it means to be another. Faery has changed me, I will be honest with you. Corrupted me even. 'Tis what they do.'

He took a step nearer the bed. Isabel shrank into the pillows. The sheet at her hand crept nearer her chin.

'But, madam, there is a way out. I have the chance to become myself again, and to die the way I should ha' done near two centuries ago. Help me restore my humanity, my lady. I ask again, will ye let me christen your bairn?'

He looked nervous again as he pleaded. There was a twitch at his cheek, a pulsing under the skin that was beginning to repulse her. His hands would not keep still. Fold, unfold, rub, twist.

'I did want to help you,' she said uncertainly, stealing a look at the makeshift cot in which lay her life's treasure. 'I was set upon it. But it comes to me after all that I don't know you, Mr Kirke.'

'My lady, I beseech you.' Kirke clasped his hands together and held them tight before his breast in an attitude of prayer, though it might have been to stop them shaking. His eyes stayed steady on hers. 'Let me only christen your bairn and . . . and be gone. 'Tis cruel of you to withhold this boon when you promised.'

'Cruel? Well, it's hardly fair of you to accuse me of—'

'Time is short, my lady. What say you that I splash the babe now and say a brief prayer over it? See, I will but dip my fingers here and the thing will be done in seconds.'

He reached towards the porcelain jug by the washbasin. Isabel's body crackled with alarm. She swung her legs over the side of the bed and launched herself between him and the cradle.

'You will not come near my baby, Mr Kirke. I'm sorry but I don't trust you.'

Kirke glowered at her, but made no further move for the jug. His hands hung irresolutely at his side. His lips were moving rapidly, as if in some urgent conversation with himself, which unnerved her further. They were still regarding each other uneasily when the bedroom door inched open.

'Are ye awake, mistress?' An untidy head poked around the door.

Kirsty's stentorian attempts to lower her voice were a standing joke between the Airds, but when she saw who was in the room she managed a true whisper.

'Robert Kirke! Dear God, man, what do ye want here?'

'Mr Kirke has come with a kind offer to baptise our baby,' said Isabel, studiedly light, airy as an aspen leaf. 'Go and bring Alex here at once.'

'I canna leave you with him, Mrs Aird.' Kirsty did not advance any further into the room, though. Her face was grey.

SALLY MAGNUSSON

'At once I say!' Isabel commanded in a high voice, not so light. 'Fetch Dr Aird.'

Kirsty turned on her heel. She could be heard thumping along the corridor and down the grand staircase.

Kirke scowled after her. 'That woman. Do ye never get a moment's peace from her?'

'She wants only the best for me and my family. As I'm sure you do, Mr Kirke.' Isabel took a careful breath and tried to keep the tremor from her voice. 'Why don't you take a seat by the fire and wait for my husband. He is the one to deal with any christening.'

'Thank you, madam, but I would not sit.'

He took a step nearer the cradle and Isabel flung out her arms. Every instinct screamed threat. She eyed a glass paperweight on the desk against the far wall. It had the Queen's head on one side and Prince Albert's on the other. Kirsty had dusted it every day with reverence. If Robert Kirke touched her baby she would smash his head to pulp in a heartbeat.

But even as she throbbed with fear and readied herself for murder, Isabel was listening to that low, sorrowing voice saying, 'I have waited a lang time to baptise this baby, sich a lang, lang time,' and she was filling up with a confusing pity for the half-life that had harrowed his face and made his eyes burn. Should she let him carry out this simple ritual that he seemed to think would bring him peace? He had been an ordained minister in his time, and by his own account a devout one. What harm could it do?

They looked at one another in silence, Isabel confused by contradictory impulses but with her arms still held wide to protect the cradle, Kirke looking irresolute again, muttering to himself, plainly beset by one of the thinking storms Isabel knew of old. From below there came sounds of commotion.

67

She will not let me do it. Her arms thrown wide before the cradle. Such a wild light in her eye.

I cannot think for the thud o' my heart and the whispering in my head, soft at first but rising to fill it. As it always does, cruel voice. As it ever has since the day they let me out and I saw the lady. If I act not, it will never leave me in peace in all the ages to come. Never. Never. Never. Never.

Act then, Robert Kirke. Tak the baby, Robert Kirke.

But her husband is sent for. Her husband is coming.

Tak the baby, Robert Kirke. The Dog awaits.

She has done me no harm.

Tak the baby, Robert Kirke. There will come no other chance.

68

From the hallway below came the clatter of feet.

'That will be my husband,' Isabel began, looking towards the door. 'He—'

And then Kirke moved. Leaping past her he seized the baby in one scoop and was making for the door before the shock released her. 'I will baptise the bairn in private,' he said over his shoulder.

There was a moment when he paused to look back at the bereft mother hurtling across the room after him. For as long as she lived Isabel would not forget the gloating triumph, the beseeching agony, of that look.

As Alexander thundered up the main stairs, Robert Kirke was running with spindly strides along the corridor in the direction of the servants' stair, the swaddled bundle tucked inside his coat.

69

Down the stairs. Out through a side door. Turn in the direction of the ridge that leads to Loch Chon.

There will I kneel in the shallows and cup my hand in the cold water and gently splash it upon the soft head as I speak the holy words o' the sacrament, making a sign and seal of the bairn's ingrafting into Christ and regeneration to walk in newness of life. Then will I lift the babe in both hands and hurl it, long and high, into the dark waters of Chon. And the black Dog of the *sìthichean* will rise up and catch the bairn in its unholy maw and carry it below.

And I will be free.

70

Thank the Lord, the doctor was on his way back to the house when I rushed out to look for him. Strolling up the path with his black bag in his hand and not a care in the world. Such a braw day it was – the trees autumny bright and Katrine shining so fair you could just about see why so many folk wi' nothing better to do would go to such trouble to visit. Dr Aird's step was as light as I'd seen all the time I'd known him. I've a notion he was whistling to himself. But when I shouted that there was a man in the bedroom trying to steal his bairn, well, he broke into a run and surged past me with a face on him that was awful to see.

He was too late. By the time he made it up there Kirke had taken the babe and was away down the back staircase. When I got up to the top o' the stairs myself, the doctor had gone racing off down the corridor after him, and Mrs Aird was outside the room with his leather bag at her feet where he'd dumped it. She was leaning against the wall in a crumpled way. You have to mind she'd hardly walked two steps on her own since the birth. White as white she was, but more collected than me for all that.

I made to help her back into the room, but 'Run and help Alex,' she says. 'Don't worry about me.'

THE NINTH CHILD

I left her bending down to the doctor's bag. Poor soul, I thought, rummaging in there like a madwoman, her nightgown trailing and her hair all streaky across her face – there's no bandage nor pill will help that bairn now.

71

Men at work. A knot o' them blocking the way to the ridge. Someone behind shouting for me to be stopped. The men downing tools to look, one or two moving in from the left.

Run the other way. Can I reach the rafts? No, too many folk. Unless . . .

This way, Robert Kirke.

A gate.

Stone stairs.

On you come, Robert Kirke.

Water pounding in my ears. Pursuers behind.

A great black hole in the face of the rock.

We are waiting for you, Robert Kirke.

They are waiting for me.

Come straight on through the middle of the earth to the Loch o' the Dogs.

I am coming.

72

Mrs Aird caught me up outside the house just as I was getting my breath and trying to work out where Kirke and the doctor had gone. There were workmen all over the place and I'm guessing he must ha' been cut off from going up the back and over the hill to Loch Chon because there was no sign o' them that way. I had an idea he might ha' run to the rafts, but there were men over there loading up and others wheeling barrows up the causeway, so he wouldna have got very far there either.

Mrs Aird looked fair wild as she gazed about her, and no wonder. She kept saying her babe was only just born and too small to be outside and where was he, where was he. But she had her wits about her all the same, for she was the one to spot her husband and Kirke in the far-off.

'Away over by the waterworks, Kirsty,' she says and begins to hirple down the gravelly path in her bare feet. And sure enough, there was Robert Kirke fleeing through the gate to the sluices, and there was the doctor with his hat fallen off and the red hair you could never mistake all ablaze in the sunshine. He was almost upon him, for he was the younger man, Dr Aird, and he had the fury of a father's love in him.

All the way down the path Mrs Aird is shouting, 'Help us.

There's a man run off with my baby,' so that soon enough we had a few folk rushing with us to the big stone bowl where the Queen had set the water going. There were iron railings all round and a wee gate that was open when we got there, and oh my goodness, the shock when I went through it and looked below.

Twisty stone steps led down to a stone platform going round this deep, deep basin cut out from the rock. Do you mind I told you the Queen went down there to watch the water come in through the sluices under her feet? Well, in that exact same place was Dr Aird, staring down at the swirling water as if he was made o' stone himself. For there below – oh, dear God – there in the midst o' that gushing water was a wee boat, a flat-bottomed thing that a couple of navvies had carried there, so I heard after, so they could sail down the tunnel and make sure the water was flowing right. They'd hefted it down a ladder set into the wall o' the basin, tied it up and left the thing bobbing in front o' the sluices while they went back up to smoke a pipe in the sun, calm as you please, though they'd likely be nerving themselves for a voyage they wouldna be fancying that much.

And there, staggering to keep upright in the boat, is Robert Kirke. He's trying to loosen off the rope, and the boat is going up and down, up and down, in the whirling white water. And here's why the doctor couldn't move, nor a couple o' men that had rushed down the steps behind him and were for swarming down the ladder till he shouted at them to stop: the tiny babe is tucked in Kirke's coat. You can see its wee white bonnet peeking out. Kirke's hands are in an awful fankle wi' this rope, which nobody above could reach, and the boat kept tipping and dipping and the water was roaring out from the three sluices with the force of the whole loch behind it and not a thing could anybody do because as any fool could see, if Robert Kirke fell into the water the bairn was lost.

Mrs Aird reached the doctor's side and took it all in. Oh, and I did too. And I see it now, that wild, jiggling boat and Kirke struggling to keep his balance while those long panicky fingers o' his were fumbling wi' the rope, and the babe stuck inside his black coat just exactly like a butcher's parcel but for that wee hat peeking out the top, and the doctor gripping the rails in an agony of not knowing what to do for best. And I've got the sound o' that roaring water in my head again and over it a thin, trembling, newborn cry that would have any mother half-crazed to hear though I thought to myself, well, he's alive then, at least he's still alive.

Then Mrs Aird plucked something from the sleeve of her nightdress. I'll swear my heart stopped when I saw it was the doctor's own knife, the one he used for cutting folk, six inches long with a black handle and so gleaming sharp he would never let a soul near it. He tore his eyes from Kirke and the thrashing boat.

'No, Issy!' cries he. 'You'll strike the baby.'

The doctor was not the sort to know about iron and how it works against the evil o' the *sìthichean*. All he thought of was his very own bairn lying next to the heart o' Robert Kirke.

But she knew. She knew that much about faery.

At that moment the rope jerked free and Kirke fell to the seat with a jolt that, oh, my heart, all but sent him over the side. But he righted himself and grabbed on to the sides o' the boat. Whether there were oars in there I don't know, but he had no time to be looking, for the boat whisked round a couple of times and then it seemed to buck with pleasure to catch the current.

That was it off. It rushed straight for the tunnel wi' Kirke inside, crouched over his stolen treasure.

But Isabel Aird is still trying to throw her husband's hand off her arm, and they're struggling with each other. With a mother's roar, terrible to hear, she hauls herself out his grasp and hurls the knife with all her strength. It flies through the air just as the boat is leaping the few yards to the tunnel mouth. Straight over Kirke's head it goes and clatters bang into the arch above, which was all done up like a fan in nice creamy stone with a big plaque over it. I can picture it now.

Right away I could see what Mrs Aird had been trying to do. She knew she couldna stop the boat, but she could maybe stop the *sìthichean*. She knew it would be folly to strike Robert Kirke, but she knew she didna need to. One throw straight over his head was what it would take.

A second or two later Kirke was whooshed into the tunnel. I suppose the knife will have ended up in the water, but I had no eyes for that because now Mrs Aird is the one screaming for her husband to stop what he's doing. As I think back, it might have been more of a wail than a scream. When I turned, the doctor had his frock-coat torn off and was halfway over the railings and she had her arms about his waist.

I caught the look on his face the moment before he jumped, and I've thought since that in a strange, desperate way it was what you'd call eager. Dr Aird was glad to go after his bairn. Glad and eager. I like to think o' that and maybe you will too. I don't suppose he gave a thought to the speed of those waters or how any man could chase a boat.

My bonnie doctor. He flung himself into the middle o' the basin and went flailing into the tunnel after Robert Kirke, pushed on by all the new water pouring out the sluices behind him. At first the white of his shirt flashed back at us from inside the tunnel. Then the darkness gathered him up and he was gone.

Not a soul spoke. I have a memory of the workmen who'd watched it looking at each other in a sombre way, and I seem to recall one o' them saying after a long minute that they should seek the navvies who'd brought the boat and ask where the tunnel would spit the men out. Another was for finding the sluice-keeper to see if he would turn off the valves.

So off they ran up the steps again, and it was just me and Mrs Aird left down there as the water went thundering on through the tunnel that had swallowed up her family. I mind to this day how high these walls o' rock and stone were around us, too high for the sun to get in, and how they seemed to be leaning in on us, and the heartsore weight of them. I mind the empty feeling of having no hope inside you, and not being able to think of a single thing to do.

A violent shiver took hold o' me at last. I put both hands on the wrought-iron railing – painted a nice mossy green it was – and bent my head and sobbed out gusts of useless tears, until I felt a touch at my back. Mrs Aird was beside me with the doctor's coat in her arms. She turned me very gently towards her and laid it around my shoulders. It was heavy and smelled of his pipe-smoke. Her eyes were dry and blank.

'He can't swim, Kirsty,' she said, tucking the collar very precisely round my neck with her cold fingers.

73

I see not what is thrown. Only catch its flight at the corner of my eye.

But I hear the ring of iron on stone as I am borne into the tunnel.

Hear it.

Feel it.

Feel it like a blade through the heart.

Feel it as an unwinding of the soul, a deep shifting within.

Simple, honest iron. In my enslavement to the bargain I had forgot there are other ways by which a man may become free.

74

Mrs Aird would not go back to her bed. Not for a minute would she do what I'd seen many a lady o' that class do for a lot less excuse and take to the pillows with a swoon. Which, I'll be frank with you, would have been a lot easier to deal with. No, she had to footer about getting her clothes on for the first time since the birth. And to make it worse, poor soul, she was bursting wi' milk and awful sore. You'll just have to excuse me if I'm not choosing my words too delicately, but you've got me reliving all this as if it's there in front of me, my heart bumping away in my breast all over again, and when all's said I suppose you're a medical man.

I helped her into some undergarments and she pondered for long enough over the dress that would fit best and a shawl that matched. We'd already had a load sent over from Fairy Knoll. Then she had me brush her hair out and coil it about her ears nice and proper. She even took her time choosing a cap, comparing this pretty bit o' nothing with another: 'Now, Kirsty, what do you think to some lace this morning?' Every movement so precise and orderly that I nearly drove myself daft trying to mind my tongue, for all I wanted was to weep and wail loud enough to drown the sound of the water bearing the doctor into the tunnel and the sight of him going under and bobbing up again and the eerie curl o' vapour about his head.

And here was she doing all that careful mulling over whether this bodice was going to button all the way down or, what did I think, would this one here serve better for now, while I would have torn fistfuls out my own clothes if I could, like those women in the Bible that used to rend their garments. I think that's the word Mr Clark used. Aye, rend. I wanted to rend and cleave and tear and rip till my apron was in shreds and my skirts no more than rags in my fingers. And as I ripped I would imagine it was Robert Kirke's heart I was plucking, whole and bleeding, right out that place in his chest where he had tucked the bairn. There was such an anger building in me, and such a sorrow. Yet on we went, pinning hair and exclaiming over gloves as the sun streamed on the folds o' soft cloth that framed the cradle, which we were both trying not to look at though I'm sure I'd be right in saying that neither one of us saw much else.

And all the time another sort of anger was gathering under my breast as well. It had a nearer focus, this big red welling of rage, and there she was in front o' me: this footering, pernickety, high-falutin lady handing me the hairbrush and bidding me take special care with in God's name the tangles. She that had never paid heed to a single warning about Robert Kirke, she that liked to think she was in tune with nature yet was so blind to the human version. For what's the supernatural telling us if it's not what we are and what we're capable of?

Och, I'm getting myself all het up again just thinking about it. But it's not fair to blame her. I liked Mrs Aird in a lot o' ways, and had aye been sorry for her woes and admiring of how she was rousing herself to deal wi' them when she'd been bred to do so little. But she had a strain of romance in her thinking that cost us all dear. I suppose that's what made me sae furious to see her worriting about dresses when her child was that very hour stolen away and her man surely drowned, her sweet man wi' those freckles that made his face look like a song thrush, who treated me more like ally than servant. I wanted to tug that lustrous hair out by the roots wi' frustration and grief and guilt that I could ha' done more.

Only I never did get round to exploding with all that feeling, for I caught her face in the mirror as I bashed the brush through her hair. Her narrow chin was set so tight you'd ha' thought her head had been stuck on her neck like some Hallowe'en turnip and the eyes just empty holes. And my hand was stilled by a gush o' pity. And along behind the pity came an inkling that just because what I needed was to shout and tear and gnash my teeth (which the Bible is also keen on and I can see why Mr Clark drew our attention to it), and most urgent of all I could ha' done with a swig o' gin, it didna mean there were no other ways o' steadying yourself before your mind broke. And if clothes was how Mrs Aird did it, then fine.

After she was ready I went and got her a cup o' sugary tea from the kitchen. She was still chittering cold and pale as a swallow's breast, so I pulled the table to the fire and loomed over her till she'd drunk every last drop. And then what does she do next but wave me into the chair opposite, pull the bell and ring for another cup. Up comes a hoity-toity parlour-maid looking as if she's got better things to do – and what, in the name o' the Lord, might these be? – and Mrs Aird, would ye believe, gets *her* to pour for *me*, and there I sat by the fire drinking from porcelain or something so frail I thought I was going to crush it just by touching it to my lips. Well, yon maid looked so black affronted I almost enjoyed myself.

Mrs Aird, though, she had taken to walking up and down the room, her mood changed. Up and down, down and up, saying over and over she had to be out doing something.

I said, 'Listen, mistress, there are men sent all over the line o' the tunnel. They'll check every place it runs in the open and there's a message sent to the reservoir at Milngavie if they get that far.'

I didna tell her what else I'd learned in the kitchen. When I went down for the tea, I'd found the navvies that had brought the damn boat busy telling their tale to an audience o' maids and boot-boys and I don't know who else, although I seem to remember even Cook had sat down at the table. Aye that's right, Cook was there, because I mind that when she put her hand to cover her mouth at what she was hearing, she left a mark on her chin that looked like bramble juice, a reddy-black streak o' something anyway, and I just stared at it and stared because I didna know where else to look. The navvies said that anything carried on the water would be a good ten hours or more getting all the way to Milngavie, but nothing of that size could ever pass whole across the first really big bridge that crossed a valley six or seven miles hence. There were bars going straight up through the high pillars that supported the aqueduct over the valley and the tube across was so narrow that it filled right to the brim. No boat would make it, nor no human being either.

'How were you meaning to get safely by, then?' says Mr Aberlour, who was looking all pinched and worried, striding round the kitchen in his kilt and these wee thin legs: he probably thought he would end up being blamed for the whole thing. Well, those navvies said they'd been charged with inspecting no more than the first sections. Seems they knew where and how to get out before that high bridge, though they hadn't been looking forward to the job over-much because while you'll not find a navvy who'll say he's scared – and to be fair, they're brave men, the most o' them, who never do think about danger – the first time down that tunnel in full flood was always going to be risky, according to them.

'Will they no' turn off the valves?' the coal-lad they called Billy piped up. Mr Aberlour frowned at him for the cheek of opening his mouth, but then, since we were all looking at him for an answer, he sighed and said no, the sluice-keeper had told him it would be a waste o' time shutting off the water, and they'd be better waiting for the boat and (oh, to hear myself saying this) for any people to be flushed out as quick as could be.

'So there's nothing you can do, Mrs Aird, but pray,' says I in the bedroom, gentle as I could and thinking I could do with Mr Clark's help here. 'Maybe we should both just spend the next wee while on our knees.'

The pacing stopped. 'I can walk the tunnel line,' says she suddenly. A flush had rushed into her cheeks that I didna like the look of at all, and her eyes had a dangerous-looking glitter to them.

'You're just out your childbed – and too early at that,' says I, though maybe not very convincingly. After any birth o' mine I'd ha' done a washing by this time, carried up the water, lugged in the firewood and boiled up half a dozen meals.

'It's not an illness,' she snaps. 'The birth was normal and I can still walk.'

SALLY MAGNUSSON

'Aye, but the walking's hard. Even just that first bit over the ridge to Loch Chon would finish us both the state we're in.'

'There's no "both" about it, Kirsty,' says she. I knew that brisk note to her voice and that there'd be no stopping her now. 'You are to pack up here, and then I bid you go and warn Annie that I'll be returning to Fairy Knoll when I'm done. I'm going to walk till I find them. Or till someone does.'

'Oh well, Mistress Aird,' says I, hauling myself out the chair by the fire in the Queen's bedroom with my heart sinking right down to my cousin Jemima's boots that were too big for me, which was half the trouble when I tried to walk anywhere. 'In that case, if ye wouldna mind waiting till I get some sandwiches made up down the stairs, I'll be coming with you.'

75

The light is quickly left behind. No longer can I make out the tunnel wall and the roof's curve, nor see my fingers clenching the side of the boat or the babe's mewling mouth.

What to do now?

My head is empty.

A sharp turn to the left. Thick black. Judging by the route that the stone towers marked above ground, we must have crossed the head o' Loch Chon and are being borne along its southern bank.

The quivering cries beneath my chin have not ceased, and a lang-forgot remembrance stirs: my Isabel nursing our only bairn; a father's wonder at how strong is the lust for life in the newest and frailest of beings. I raise one hand and guide a knuckle to the hungry mouth, the while bidding the babe hush and desist from its protest. Which, after a brief exploration of the knuckle, it does not. Alas, dear wife, I still have not the knack.

Then, a thought. And with it a choking sensation of peril. Into my mind's eye arise mighty aqueduct pillars. I have seen them striding out o'er the wide glens. I observed their construction with awe. Surely no boat may pass betwixt them intact.

But here is a puzzle. Why fear I to be dashed to certain death?

If it be true that the flight of iron, hurled straight and true o'er this foolish head, has unwound the clutch o' faery, then let me only perish now, crying out to my God for forgiveness and salvation. 'Tis heaven I long for. Why such horror at what lies ahead for our frail craft?

Our craft.

Ours.

Understanding strikes like a shower of clean winter ice.

In the distance a glimmer o' light appears. Below the babe's heart mine own is pounding hard. The light grows bigger.

Hold fast, bairnie. Hold fast.

Aye, they are gone all right. They are gone. And tucked within this coat is my humanity.

76

Following the line o' those huge tower markers up and over the ridge between the lochs was something I'd done before when I had to. It was the nearest route between Royal Cottage and Sebastopol if you hadn't a mind to trachle all the way round by Stronachlachar and back on yourself by the waterworks road. And it was heavy going, as I'd warned her. But we managed all right at first, though the spoil from the tunnelling works had our feet skittering all over the place and the grass was slippy yet from the drenching it had taken.

Another time she'd likely ha' been exclaiming at the sun glinting through the trees and the hawthornberries hanging so pretty as to make you forget that those twigs they were on would pierce you to the heart, as they nearly did more than once on the way. But Mrs Aird had no eyes for any of it. She just plodded on, looking out for where to put her feet next, what with rock and masonry one minute and spiky bushes the next, and I huffed and puffed behind, praying she might be up for a rest soon and a wee something from the basket. I was busy trying not to think o' the water rushing along underneath us, and I dare say she'd be the same. There were flies clustering round the last o' the brambles, all squishy and shapeless from the rain, and I kept seeing Cook's hand go to her mouth and the look o' horror when she heard what was like to happen to the wee boat when it reached the first big bridge.

She did well, Mrs Aird, for a woman that hadna long given birth, which turns your limbs to water and makes you sore in parts I won't be dwelling on. I wasna long in wondering if I'd been rash to come with her. Usually I'd be stopping every five minutes to catch my breath and rub my feet, and I started to think I should ha' stayed put to pack up the Airds' things, as I was bidden, and then got one o' the men to row me round wi' the bits and pieces and fetch me a trap. I could ha' travelled back to Fairy Knoll like a queen, instead of look at me now, traipsing about the hills for no good reason but to keep an eye on a grief-crazed woman who might do anything.

But not even she could keep it up. As we hobbled our way down the other side to where the tunnel line passes just beyond Fairy Knoll, near enough the place I was standing all those weeks before when I saw her on the very ridge we'd just been on with Robert Kirke, her legs buckled under her and there she was, half-sitting, half-lying in the grass, her face all white and clammy.

I made up my mind right away and took action. I'm good at that when I need to be, as you know to your cost.

'Mrs Aird,' says I, 'you sit here and rest a while. When you're feeling stronger, I want ye to gang down very slowly – very slowly, mind – to the works road yonder. I'll run to Sebastopol and fetch us a cart.'

Well, when I say run, obviously I wasn't meaning exactly that. But I did get myself to the camp at last, which had hardly a soul left in it by then except those that were clearing up. As I came to the edge I yelled blue murder for someone to come and help.

And who should come stumbling out one o' the far houses on the hill, which as it happens was mine, but James. Just woken up, if I'm any judge, though the sun was right above us. I'm not saying he was lazy, my James. He worked every hour he had to, night and day, but the works were quieter now and when I wasn't about he took his chances with his bed as any man will.

Anyway, off he goes with a bit more urgency in his step than I've seen for a while, and while he's away I round up any bairns o' my own I can put my hands on and give each one a wee kiss, daft wifie that I am, for there's something about another soul's loss that makes you long for your ain.

When James and I came clip-clopping up from the camp on to the works road, we could see Mrs Aird waiting by the side. James got down and helped her up beside him and I sat in the back against a knobbly sack that might ha' been potatoes, or maybe coal – aye, coal it would ha' been because, my, it fair stuck into my back. We turned on to the track that followed the tunnel line along the side o' the slope that rises from the head o' Loch Chon. It was no more than a rough path that the navvies had cleared through the trees for machinery and suchlike to be brought along.

Mrs Aird sat quiet as a mouse beside my James, who was very nice and gentle with her, I must say, and I was right proud of him for grasping so quick what had happened and what the lady felt she needed to do, though he understood well enough the hours that were gone already and he knew better than either of us how quick the water would flow on its way to Glasgow.

After a bit, the track took a tight turn to the left and jolted us high along the southern bank. You could see across to here easy enough from Sebastopol, but I'd never been up this side myself before. Well, who would want to? It was aye being blown up. Mrs Aird used to walk our own side as far as Loch Dhu and even away to Loch Ard in her wandering days, but I've a feeling she hadna been up here either and was interested to see her life from the other side, as ye might say.

Mainly, though, she had her eyes fixed not on the loch to the left but further up the bank to our right where the tunnel must be running, as we could tell from the spoil and a load o' trees down. Somewhere up there was where the first o' the aqueducts would likely appear. I mind James used to talk about the palaver it was to bridge the burns that came down through the trees to join the loch at the bottom. The navvies had to cut into the hillside on either side of each stream and then build an iron trough between to carry the water, which meant the tunnel just went on a while in the open air till it was back in the hill again.

I don't know what Mrs Aird expected to find, and maybe she hadna dared to think it through either. All she knew was that somewhere in that tunnel were a husband and a son. The first o' the big aqueduct bridges was still a few miles hence, but she knew that over these burns was where the tunnel would first come into the light and I suppose she just had this feeling that she had to bear witness and pass on, for what else was a woman to do?

'Whoa now. Yonder's the first one,' says James in his slow, steady voice.

And see, you've got me in such a state that it brings a tear to my eye to think o' James now as well, sitting there wi' his cap jaunty atop his big head and his neckerchief that could do with a wash after all the time I'd been working away and the reins in his hand and not sure what he was expected to do.

We look over to where he's pointing and there's no mistaking the aqueduct.

'Thank you, James,' says Mrs Aird, polite as you could wish. 'Be so kind as to assist me down and then wait. I will go and take a look.'

I made to get out with her, but she wasna having it.

'Let me do this on my own, Kirsty,' she says.

77

We burst out into daylight. Thanks be, thanks be, 'tis not the mighty aqueduct but only a paltry crossing. The boat is carried swiftly along a short trough and back into the tunnel. Just before we enter the dark again I glimpse beams across the top o' this trough. Too late it comes to me that I might have tried to seize one.

Right away another ball of light appears ahead. Can it be that we are traversing naught but burns here? That the great bridges lie further ahead?

Wheesht, bairnie, wheesht. There is still time.

I tuck the babe further into my coat, assured by the squawking that it is not a whit short of air. Seizing the cloth from my neck, I bind it tight around us both. The light-ball is become huge now.

Out into sunshine a second time. I jump to my feet and this time reach with both arms outstretched for a beam. Miss it. Lunge for the next beam. Stagger. The boat swings away and hits the side o' the trough, throwing me backwards with legs in the air. Water pours in. I clamber back to my seat and cling to the sides again as we go back into the tunnel.

The boat is sitting lower now, and the water inside laps at my ankles. We are in deeper darkness this time, but in the distance again has appeared another pin's head o' light. I adjust the cloth around us, to be ready once more. The black softens to grey. I wait, senses alert. All that can be heard is the sound of water slapping against wood.

All?

What ails ye, little one, sae quiet of a sudden?

I bend an ear to the babe's head. Damp wool on my cheek. With scrabbling fingers I feel inside the coat.

The curve o' the bairn's back is no bigger than my hand. I pat it and I rub.

78

She was back to the cart in minutes, picking her way down the slope between tree stumps and rubble and all the usual mess. James hurried round to help her climb back beside him. She gave me a quick look as she did, and shook her head.

'There's another one just along a bit, mistress,' says he, 'but we're as well to keep to this navvy track. It's treacherous underfoot.'

He clicked at the horse and we moved on. Not so many yards further we stopped again. James pointed up the slope. There was a second aqueduct, said he, which stood in a direct line wi' the first. Mrs Aird was on the ground in a moment, lifted her skirts and went to have a look.

'Is there anything to see?' says I, when she comes down again and back into the cart. Biding there in the back I was starting a fever of not knowing whether I wanted there to be anything or not.

'Nothing,' says she. 'It was only a wide trough again, with plated sides and beams of iron across the top. The water' – she gave a funny wee half-sob as she said it – 'the water just goes through the trough from one part of the tunnel to the next. This one was longer than the last.'

294

'Are there any more o' these wee ones to come?' says I to James, not being able to ask directly what was on my mind because I'd never said a word to Mrs Aird about the big bridge.

'Just one more, if I mind aright,' says he, not turning round. He was aye good at talking out the side of his mouth, my James. 'I'm thinking that will likely be the longest yet. There's a sturdy burn there that's gouged a fair dip in the hill. Quite a job they had o' it to get an aqueduct laid across that one.'

That was a long speech for James. He wiped his forehead wi' the back of his arm and clicked at the horse to step on. The sun was hot on our faces as we bumped on down the track. I sat back against the coal sack and tried to ignore the prickle of dread that was growing under my skin with every minute that passed.

The boat surges into daylight again and I leap up, taking no care, driven by a reckless pulse of anxiety for this silent bairn who is depending on me.

I reach for the third bar. The fourth. Nay, I cannot grip it and fall back as before. A blessing indeed, as I swiftly understand, for I see now that this will be the longest aqueduct yet. The pair of us would have been left dangling above the water like a man from a cliff's edge.

Peering ahead, my wits better collected, I remark a platform of iron mesh over the far end o' the trough, just before the water enters the hillside again. Most carefully I judge my action this time, marking to myself the last iron beam before the platform. The boat approaches it. As if in supplication, I lift up my arms. I pray for strength and steadiness, and – there! – I have grabbed the beam. I hold on tight, very tight, with both hands.

The boat journeys on into the tunnel without us.

Now must I find the strength to haul myself upon this platform. I reach for the edge with my right arm and cling on there until the other dares join it. Then I throw what strength my shoulders will muster into pulling myself high enough to get a knee to the platform.

This platform is a latticed walkway across the trough – erected, as may be deduced, for men to mak their way along to a wheel at the side, which, to guess, should by its turning affect the water's flow. Waiting for the ragged breaths to become even, I sit with my back to the top o' the tunnel mouth and look about.

The aqueduct crosses a shallow but wide crevice, through which a burn hastens down a steep slope to Loch Chon. On a hillock behind stands a lone rowan. There are oaks further up, and alder holding tight to their cones, and birches in a pool o' papery leaves. Below, stretching from here halfway to the loch, is a great sea of rubble and rock. And beyond lies the loch itself, where –

think of it not,

dwell on it not

– I was to throw the Dog its prey.

A ladder at the side, thank God, to tak me and my bairn to the ground. I am about to crawl towards it, not trusting to these quivering legs, when something enters the aqueduct at the other end and is carried along in the steady flow that minutes ago bore our boat.

On it comes and on, until it passes directly beneath us. 'Tis then that I see, through the holes in the iron, the white face of the man who chased me to the sluices.

And then I know what I have done.

80

Even when Isabel Aird is an old woman, looking back on the moment she noticed what was snagged on the iron mesh above the third aqueduct on the day that Robert Kirke stole her baby, she will see the same image. It is not, curiously, an image of the thing itself but of a thread, or a twine – sometimes it appears as the string of a pianoforte – yanked so taut across her mind that it must surely break. Whether the string or her mind, she cannot tell. But then she was not sure at the time either, standing there on a bank of industrial spoil, looking up at the aqueduct and feeling her sanity stretched beyond screaming.

'There! There!' she said, as Kirsty's husband came hurrying up the slope behind her, leaving the horse with trailing reins and an alarmed Kirsty to clamber down from the cart by herself.

'I'll have it down for you in a tick, Mistress Aird,' he said. James McEchern spoke with a slow Hebridean lilt. 'There'll be a ladder attached round the back.'

Within minutes he had rescued the tiny cream bonnet from between two frets of the grid that covered one end of the aqueduct. It was soaking wet, Mrs Aberlour's proud crocheting matted into felt. Isabel turned it over in her fingers and pressed it to her cheeks and ravished it with her lips, and all the time she was strung out on the wire between wild hope and raw, nauseous fear.

When the scene rises before her, she will sometimes remember the osprey that startled them by whistling past on immense, tattered wings on its way to the loch. Sometimes she will conjure again the pair of crows screeching at each other in the oak woods, or the rowan tree standing vigil. Sometimes it will be the perversely merry gurgle of the burn racing out from under the high, black-plated trough that she remembers, or thinks she does, though surely she could not really have heard it above the sound of the water crossing above. That sound she will have slashed from her memory.

But what Isabel will always remember, exactly, every time, is a little brown birch leaf twirling past Kirsty's shoulder, and then another, and then two more, and the jolt as she realised there was a breeze starting up and, look, these are grey clouds in a sky that's been clear all day, and he doesn't have his hat, her baby doesn't have his hat. She will remember James McEchern poking about in the bracken and toeing chunks of rock aside with his boot to see if anything else has been dropped, and Kirsty making a clumsy attempt to assure her that if the hat got itself up there then likely the bairn hasn't drowned, and then putting her hands to her face as soon as she said it, poor woman, because of the other thing that neither woman is allowing herself to think.

It was James who took charge. He was ill-practised in addressing a conversational gap with his wife within fifty feet, but as the two women went on staring at the limp hat he cleared his throat.

'It looks as if the bairn's been brought out the water here. So we maun think to ourselves where he might ha' been taken.' And, as neither responded: 'How would ye feel, Mrs Aird, about asking at Wattie Hunter's place at Dow o' Chon? It's just a step further.'

Isabel roused herself. A great weariness was dissolving the wire.

'Let's do that,' she said. 'Let us do whatever you think best.'

Wattie Hunter's house, to which they were shortly alerted by a thread of smoke, sat a little way up from the shoreline. It was a stone and turf dwelling of the kind Isabel had seen sunk into the landscape here and there and been thankful not to have need of inspecting more closely. The works road they were on ran above it at first, joined after a few minutes by a cart track leading on towards Loch Dhu. James turned down it and they rumbled into an overgrown yard.

The door was opened shyly by a girl of no more than six or seven in a loose dress of grey plaid that reached all the way to her dirty feet. James exchanged a few words with the child in Gaelic, then took off his cap and stood aside to let Isabel precede him into the crofthouse. The child led them through the byre – Isabel too fraught to register that the people of this house were living side by side with cattle, though she thought about it later – and into a dark room of unplastered stone. It was separated from the cow-house by a wall that stopped well short of the roof. A fire smouldered half-heartedly in the inglenook, and the reek from three trout hanging there to dry, mingled with the waft of dung from over the wall and smoke struggling to find its way out, was for a moment so overwhelming that Isabel swayed. A mannerly touch on her arm guided her forward.

After the brightness outside she could make out very little

at first. The outline of a recessed bed gradually revealed itself, and an upturned crate of some kind with a tin plate on top. In the fire shadows sat a woman, grey herself from top to toe, cradling a baby in her arms. Isabel's heart swooped. And dived. The infant was months old.

Kirsty, whose eyes had no trouble adjusting, barged ahead. Her husband gave way without a murmur, explaining to Isabel placidly: 'The wifie here will have no English. We'll see what Kirsty can find out.'

Kirsty leaned forward, hands on thighs, and rattled off a screed of Gaelic. The woman nodded and smiled. Her face was wizened, her hair under a knotted handkerchief on its way to silver, her mouth pinched for want of teeth. The grandmother, Isabel thought, trying to guess the drift of the conversation. Was this still an exchange of pleasantries, or did the woman have news for them? The habit of the Gaels to take a very long time to get to the point, a familiar irritation where Kirsty was concerned, had Isabel nearly stamping the earth floor with impatience.

'Aye, she says there was a man here all right,' Kirsty duly reported. 'Wet coat and in an awful hurry to be away.'

'Did he have a baby with him?'

Kirsty relayed the question in Gaelic, taking three times as long. Getting into her own stride, the woman, patting the stirring child, devoted an agonising number of minutes to the reply. Isabel's eyes were streaming from the smoke. The little girl, perched on the floor with her back to the fire, regarded the exotic visitor out of big, curious eyes. Kirsty listened, nodding and offering the occasional encouraging aside. The pair might have been discussing the weather.

At last she straightened up.

'She says the man came looking for Wattie, who's her husband, and seems to have had a mind to borrow his horse. Wattie's away wi' the cart, she told him. Seems they've had not a bad harvest this year and he'd just got the potatoes—'

'NEVER MIND THE POTATOES!'

Kirsty threw her a reproachful look. There was no excusing such a breach of manners.

'Well, I'm just coming along to the next bit. The man looked fair unhappy to hear Wattie was away. Seems he'd wanted Wattie's nag to take something back to a woman he'd served ill. Well, we know who that must be, Mrs Aird. So then he says to the wifie here, look, could ye just take a keek at this bairn I've got here and see what ails it.'

Isabel stopped breathing. Behind her James shifted nearer. The infant on the woman's knee was beginning to fuss.

'Och, says she, I'll do that no bother, sir, says she. And Kirke hands her the mite from out his coat. And she takes one look at the size of it and the skin on its head that you can nearly see through and she's thinking to herself, well, God bless this wee soul that never did anyone any harm, there's nothing to be done for it now.'

From the back came a warning growl. 'Get to the end, Kirsty, or I'll tell her myself.'

'Well, I'm just telling her what the wifie here said and how she said it, as you're my witness,' Kirsty huffed. 'But it's glad news, Mrs Aird, for when she took the babe from him she saw it was breathing after all, but maybe on the weak side, as you'd be expecting, what with everything. And she says to Kirke, "Well, I'm going to have to heat up this bairn by the fire" – though it seems Kirke had kept the wee one dry enough and it's been a good warm day till now, so we can be grateful for that. "And I'll need to get some milk into it," she tells him. Which, by God's good grace, she was able to supply, having a bairn of her own not weaned yet. And the man seemed glad of it.

'So she got her girl here to poke the fire and she sat down wi' the babe in her lap, just exactly as she is now with her own, so she says. And she got the bairn to suckle no bother, which is another blessing when ye think it was only yesterday, or was it the day before, that he first—'

James broke in again. 'Just ask where the bairn is now, woman.'

Kirsty leaned in confidentially for another question, and Isabel snatched a half-breath. The woman mumbled something, at which the little girl rose to her feet and skipped across the room.

'*Seall, seo e,*' she said, pointing to the shadowed bed.

'Ah, well, isn't that nice,' said Kirsty, beaming from ear to ear. 'Your baby's asleep over there, Mrs Aird.'

81

The sturdy stone valve house commanded the cavernous Duchray Valley like a heavily eaved fortress. By the time the first of the searchers entered, holding his breath, late afternoon sunshine was leaking through the diamond-paned windows.

As the men at the back pulled the door further open, more light rushed in. And there, illumined like a stage tableau before them, was the scene that everyone had dreaded and everyone privately expected. Nobody familiar with the valley itself (too deep, too broad for a normal aqueduct bridge), who understood that only a narrow siphon pipe could serve here, who had laid eyes on the formidable cast-iron machinery assembled inside the valve house to move the water from tunnel to pipe, had entertained a moment's doubt about where Alexander Aird's journey would end.

By nightfall the body had been disentangled and removed. James McEchern borrowed a saw and hammered up a coffin, and Alexander was brought at last to the Fairy Knoll parlour to lie before the window. Isabel sat beside him, their son in her arms and no tears left, and made her husband a promise.

More days passed before she judged the baby strong enough for the journey to Glasgow. Kirsty sniffed at her caution, taking the view that an infant who could survive an aqueduct would have no trouble with first class on the ferry. As she said to James, the doctor should be given a decent Christian burial as soon as possible, although she did concede that if it meant he would not end up in the Aberfoyle kirkyard a wee delay would just have to be tholed.

Isabel would no more have buried Alexander within sight of Doon Hill than ventured there herself. She shuddered to imagine laying him to rest in the place where Robert Kirke had roamed, whose malice and treachery had robbed her of the husband she was learning to know again and the family they might have been together.

On a crisp morning towards the end of October she went to stand in the garden of Fairy Knoll, feeling the bite of the air on her face and wondering as she looked around for the last time, wondering as she would wonder for ever, who Robert Kirke really was and how she could have accepted him so blithely.

Had she been under a spell herself, blinded to the wickedness that Kirsty seemed so palpably to have sensed? Easy enough to believe in this place of celebrated enchantment, which had communed with her from the start. But it hardly took a spell, did it, to make one person ignore in another what she preferred not to see.

What, though, of the Robert Kirke she had actually seen? His tale was fantastical, but were not his torment and his contradictions all too human, this man who wished for good but was drawn to destroy, who had so plainly exulted in the thing he loathed himself for? That last look he had flung her in the

Queen's bedroom: might it be that neither she nor Kirsty had ever grasped more than a fragment of the truth about Robert Kirke?

Isabel walked across the garden grass, feathery with hoar frost, to the rowan tree where one of her children was buried. Brittle stalks of thistle clustered about the trunk; long gone the downy heads that had drifted in the lazy summer air.

Why had she thrown the knife? It was a question hard to face when all she really wanted was to shriek her loss to the heavens and rage, rage, at the man who had caused it. She leaned down and curled a hand around the nearest clump of thistles. Slowly she crushed them in her bare palm, refusing to wince as the spines punctured her flesh, rejoicing fiercely in the pain. She could do this. She could bear it.

She knew the answer anyway. Of course she did. She had thrown the knife because in that terrible moment at the tunnel mouth she had believed that something could be salvaged from the wreckage of Robert Kirke's soul.

Beyond the garden a morning moon hung low and faint between the trees. She wondered where Robert Kirke was now, and if the knife had done its work and whether he too was staring at a filigree moon in a clear autumnal sky.

Soon the conveyances would be here. Alexander would be borne home to Glasgow in a casket made from oaks grown on the shores of Loch Chon. Annie would carry the child that had also grown here and, like his mother, found a way to keep living. Isabel turned back from the grave of her eighth child towards the house, thinking of all the wasted children who had played here by the lochside, and how this place had saved her, whatever Robert Kirke had done or meant to do. She thought of her tiny survivor, swaddled for the journey and, to judge by the sounds of rising protest within, hungry again already. And of the letter she carried in her reticule.

'My husband has hopes of moving to Glasgow as professor of surgery at the university,' Agnes Lister had written. 'We shall be friends. Let me support you in the days ahead.'

She thought of Alex, and of what she had possessed all along and how much he had been to her when she was too deadened by sorrow and aimlessness to know it. She would mourn him and she would grieve for him, but she would not sink. She would do him proud. That was her promise. Isabel Aird knew the thing she could do and she would find a way to do it.

82

There's not much more I need to be telling, for you know the
rest as well as I do, don't ye? Isabel Aird went back to Glasgow
with her son. She says to me as she's leaving – a bright, cold
October day it was – that if I ever needed a position again I
should come to her. And so, by and by, I did. Not many years
later I found myself at the back door of her house in Bath Street
trying to persuade Annie, who I may say was further up her own
backside than ever (ye know fine what I mean) to let me talk
to the mistress.

Hard times these had been. James got himself another railway
job after the waterworks was cleared up, and the rest of us
trailed there after him, but he sickened wi' something, and got
weaker and weaker. There was no civic-minded corporation to
send a doctor on that job, I can tell you. But there was a foreman
all right, who made clear there would be nothing on his payslip
if James didna go down that embankment every hour he was
meant to. Until one night he just lay down in the mud and died.

So I turned up at the door. Mrs Aird threw her arms around
me and sent Annie off to make us both some tea. You should
ha' seen the face on her. And that's how I ended up here with
a flock o' bairns in tow.

Once we were settled in I had the care of you, my lad, when your mother was off to the hospital. And you'll remember how mollycoddled you were by my Lily and how ye looked up to Lachlan when he came visiting. It was just like growing up with a whole lot o' brothers and sisters, Mrs Aird said, for we filled the house up nicely.

'They just poured up the stairs like frogs,' she said to her friend Mrs Lister, which was some private joke between them. Dr Lister was high up in the Royal Infirmary on the High Street by that time, I mind, finding new ways of keeping folk alive after he'd cut them up, which was something our own doctor would dearly have liked to know too.

Annie was fair scunnered to have us here, as was your grandmother at first, though Mrs Gillies did teach Lily to sing a tune once and had no real harm in her beyond not having a single clue about how anyone else lived. Mrs Aird taught the wee ones to read and write at the same time as she was starting you on your letters, for all that she was so busy in one hospital after another. I've never seen such energy. Once she found her way there was no stopping her.

My, but she had a fight on her hands with her nursing – and not least wi' that mother o' hers. That a lady should go out to earn her own money, and with a bairn at home too! But that's another story.

Just shuffle a bit closer, would ye, as I'm coming to the last part o' this one, and let me look at you properly. I'm that proud of what you've become, Florentine, and so would your father ha' been as well. You've got his nice fiery hair (aye, and he used to blush just like that too) and your mother's frowny brow that I've had to look out for from the both o' you in my time, although you're the one that's aye had the lighter heart – that being from your father, I'd say, lovely man. One thing I'm glad about is that you've not had a day's illness since the day ye were born – who would ha' thought it? – and you've as big an appetite on you still as I've ever seen on a man. Not that anyone would guess it to see you – I've known thinner skelfs. I suppose you'll be wanting me to hurry up and finish so ye can go and prowl round the kitchen like ye always do when you're back here with all your bairns in tow.

And while I'm on the subject, you know that's the best present ye could ever have given your mother, don't ye?. How many are you up to now? Aye, Mrs Aird's had near as many bairns from you and that poor wife o' yours who's had the carrying of them as she ever saw dancing about Loch Chon.

And you know what would ha' made your father happy, bless him? Public health. Nobody made you go that way – 'It's not for me to push him, Kirsty,' Mrs Aird used to say – but she's fair proud to see you become as much a champion o' better housing and water and air and all the rest of it as your father ever hoped to be himself.

Dr Florentine Aird. Now, there's a name I'll grant you does have a ring to it, although to my mind you've still got the look of an Angus, but that's by the by.

Your father would ha' been proud o' your mother too, if I'm any judge, and of the way she threw herself into recruiting nurses and getting them properly trained up and paid: women from the tenements, some o' them, who didna know their arse from their elbow to start with but had a spark o' something she liked. She used to say my Nancy had been the one to get her thinking about folk's chances in life and she'd always be grateful to her, which gave me a warm, sad feeling because Nancy was long gone by then. I chuckled when I heard she'd handed every one o' these nurses a copy o' Florence Nightingale's manual. Aye, your father would have approved all right, never mind his fears about his wife working in these horrible hospitals. We just have to make them less horrible, is what she says.

And of course the next cholera epidemic everyone had been so worried about arrived in, when was it now, 1866 or thereabouts, and was nothing like as bad as the last one. I mind Mrs Aird sitting you down and telling you it was good clean water that had saved all the folk who might ha' died in this city, and your papa it was who had seen early on why it mattered and done his bit to bring it to Glasgow. 'And Kirsty's man played an even bigger part,' she says, looking over to me with a smile.

Och, you're being awful patient to listen to an old woman's memories, but it's good to bring to mind how life got better for your mother. You'd ha' been too young to notice the big effort she made to open the house and have folk coming in and out for parties and the like, for all that she's never been comfortable with idle chat and seemed to lose all the interest she ever had in dressing up. I heard her mother call her a slattern once, which was maybe on the harsh side, but she only laughed. And a merry laugh she has, too, that mother o' yours, when she lets herself go.

Do ye mind yon burly fellow by the name o' Rankine who used to call sometimes? He was in charge of all those poor guardsmen that put their bayonets through the Queen's awning that time. I recognised him at once and we had a good old chuckle about it. One o' the most important men of science of the age he was, so Mrs Aird told me. I used to think they'd ha' made a nice couple, but he never did marry. She said he was aye too busy writing funny poems about being in love to try it. I doubt your mother will marry again either now, unless she takes the notion in her sixties, which knowing her she might, seeing as neither you nor me can tell what that woman will do next. She's always said she's far too busy to think about men.

I might be wrong, but I've a feeling she does still think about Robert Kirke, though. Do ye mind the time she took you back to the Trossachs? You must ha' been twelve or thirteen then, and she thought she'd show you the parts o' Loch Chon she loved, and the rowan tree in the garden, and what was left o' Sebastopol, which I doubt you'll find on any map these days. I know, because she told me, that she was nervous to think she might see Robert Kirke again. She'd tried not to think about him and mostly managed it, so she said, but she kept wondering all the same if throwing that knife had made any difference. Do ye mind I was telling ye about Wattie Hunter's cottage? Was the reason the babe was waiting there safe and sound that day, she was asking herself, because Robert Kirke had found a way through what tormented him in time to save it – to save you, Florentine? 'Did the iron do its work, Kirsty?' she says to me. It's a thing we'll never know, but your mother wanted awful badly for it to be true. Still does, I would say.

She saw no sign of him at Loch Chon that time. And she would never speak of him, then or after, to any but me. And that bothered you, didn't it? I always knew it bothered you. Even as a young lad ye were aye trying to wheedle it out o' me so ye could put the pieces together. You've always had a questing sort o' mind and ye could wrap me round your finger almost as easy as ye could your mother. Only . . . not that. Honest to God,

Florentine, I could not do it. I couldna speak o' that man for such a long time for the hurt he caused us and the feeling that's weighed on me ever since that if I'd said something or done something different your father might be here today.

But you got round me in the end, didn't ye, my lad that I've loved since I saw you take your first breath in the Queen's bedroom. You cornered me here in my own wee room in Bath Street with a flask o' *uisge beatha* in your pocket to loosen my tongue if a pot o' tea didna do the trick.

'Kirsty,' says you, 'tell me what happened to my father, and why, and the hurts my mother won't speak of. Tell me, I beg you, about Robert Kirke.' That's what you said, wasn't it? Just those exact words. 'I need to know,' says you. 'I want to understand. Just start at the beginning and tell it your own way. Forget it's me listening.'

Well, it's what I've tried to do, and you're a good listener, Dr Florentine, I'll say that, though I'm fair worn out now, to be honest. There's just the one thing I canna tell you. Well, maybe two. And that's what lies inside that grave in Aberfoyle and where Robert Kirke is now. It's why I've never been as sure as I'd like to be that this story has an end at all.

Now, would you help me to my feet, laddie. It's time we rescued your mother from all these bairns.

83

In the pale of evening I tak myself back to Doon Hill, hoping that God will come for me this night in the wind that sighs in the oak woods, that my spirit may return to Him at last.

But where I awaken is not for me to determine. There is a cost to the underground dance, which cannot be counted and cannot be paid in iron. It may be that a man never truly escapes, that he can never be saved from what he allows himself to become. Faery has taken me once and may summon me again as, see, the light begins to drain from Doon Hill and the wind stirs the branches o' the tall pine.

Forgive me, bairn, for the father I cost you.

Forgive me, my lady, wheresoever you be.

Now will I lay me down to sleep.

Wait for me, my Isabel. I will come if I may.

Author's Note

Reverend Robert Kirke was an Episcopalian minister whose tolerant views and scholarly achievements have been eclipsed by the legend that curled itself around him after his death. The book written just before he died and published posthumously, *The Secret Commonwealth of Elves, Fauns and Fairies*, takes the supernatural beliefs of the Celts unusually seriously for a churchman – so seriously, in fact, that it was put about that while out walking near his manse on Doon Hill in Aberfoyle on the evening of his sudden death in May 1692, Kirke was snatched away to faery himself as a punishment for meddling. It is rather poignant that this humane, thoughtful, curious man, whose inscription of 'Love and Life' can be seen on the bell that hangs to this day inside Balquhidder church, should be remembered only as the central figure in a fairytale.

Of course, *mea culpa*, I have now added to the burden of legend on Robert Kirke by inventing another. My guilt will be considerably assuaged if everyone who reads this immediately rushes off to find out more about a fascinating man. (And I might as well admit here and now that he had a second wife, Margaret, the first cousin of his Isabel, for whom the constraints of plot left no room.)

As far as the legend is concerned, I've taken quite a few liberties with the one reported and popularised by Sir Walter Scott and would urge anyone interested in the authorised version to read his full account in *Letters on Demonology and Witchcraft*, which is readily available online. My own interest was in using fairytale to explore the notion of psychological duality, a familiar trope in Scottish literature, not least in the fiction of Scott's contemporary, James Hogg.

Anyone who ventures up Aberfoyle's Doon Hill today will discover a great pine at the top hung with ribbons and messages from those who continue to take the news of Kirke's captivity to heart. In the ancient churchyard nearby his prominent gravestone is also much visited. On it, along with a pastor's crook and a Scots thistle, has been carved the unmistakeable outline of a dagger. This stone is assumed to have been laid over the grave some time after his death and to refer, startlingly for a Christian memorial, to Kirke's alleged entanglement with the iron-phobic fairies in the fashion recounted by Scott.

Centuries of fun with the so-called 'Fairy Minister' have eclipsed the beliefs and scholarship of the real Robert Kirke. (His name is found with and without a final 'e' in the sources, but Walter Scott and the Balquhidder bell opted for the former.) In the novel I've tried to reflect these with reasonable accuracy. In her excellent introduction to the 2007 New York Review of Books edition of *The Secret Commonwealth*, Marina Warner argues that Kirke's ministry, his learning and his temperament took him in a different direction from his seventeenth-century contemporaries 'towards a benign and tolerant delight in the breadth of human understanding, imaginings, and possibility'. Kirke's notebooks, which can be viewed in the National Library of Scotland, also attest to what Warner calls the 'spirit of active wonder' that connects Kirke to us today.

Edinburgh-born William John Macquorn Rankine, a genial polymath of eye-wateringly wide interests, is another figure whose achievements are largely forgotten. Rankine was a scientist, both theoretical and applied, a pioneer of thermodynamics, a mathematician, engineer, musician, composer of light verse, captain of the volunteer riflemen who formed Queen Victoria's guard of honour at Loch Katrine, academic teacher and much else. He was known for his enthusiasm, courtesy, warmth, lack of vanity and generosity in helping friends with their own writing while monstrously busy with his own. I am wholly responsible for the sentiments ascribed to him here, but hope to have caught something of his engaging personality. The selected stanzas from 'A Mathematician in Love' are taken from a volume of his *Songs and Fables*, published posthumously in 1874 and accessible online.

In October 1859 a great deal of newsprint was devoted to the opening of the Corporation of Glasgow Water Works by Victoria and Albert. I am sorry to have found no evidence of a story doing the rounds today (and faithfully imparted to tourists) that a particularly exuberant twenty-one-gun salute shattered the windows of Royal Cottage during the ceremony, thus preventing the royal couple from staying the night as planned. Despite the rain and the ample provision of bedrooms, however, the royal party was always due to return to Edinburgh that afternoon: the timetable had been agreed weeks earlier. If anyone has evidence to the contrary, do let me know.

Victoria's diaries, available online at queenvictoriasjournals. org, provide an abundant and delightfully readable insight into their marriage and the restorative effect of their Balmoral home, where they welcomed Florence Nightingale warmly in September 1856. Intriguingly Prince Albert, whose stomach was increasingly bothering him in the last years of his life, did once bury a seltzer bottle at Balmoral with a message inside. He died in December 1861 at the age of just forty-two, to be mourned by Victoria for the rest of her long life.

By the second half of the 1850s Florence Nightingale was already well on her way to being sanctified as a ministering angel, the devoted 'Lady with the Lamp'. Her efforts in the Crimea were followed by *Notes on Nursing*, an unprecedented compendium of practical advice which challenged the ignorance and prejudice of contemporary attitudes. Less well known are her denunciations of the arid, idle lives that upper- and middle-class women of the time were expected to live. In her angry essay 'Cassandra', penned in 1852 although not published until years later, Nightingale inveighs against the amount of time that ladies were expected to devote to keeping a pretty house, ordering the dinner, sending pheasants and apples to poor relations and driving out in the carriage – time that could be poured into work if only it were allowed. She describes sitting among a company of ladies and listening to them reading aloud as 'like lying on one's back with one's hands tied, having liquid poured down one's throat'.

Agnes Lister, wife of the famous pioneer of antiseptic surgery, was one woman who did secure herself a role, if largely out of sight, beyond the domestic. She deserves more notice for the work she undertook at the side of Joseph Lister (no great supporter of the advancement of women in general) as amanuensis and laboratory partner.

The Loch Katrine waterworks was one of the most ambitious

civil engineering schemes in Europe since antiquity, employing the most advanced surveying and construction techniques of the age. To keep up with the consumption of Glasgow's expanding population and industries, a second tunnel and aqueduct system was begun in 1885 at the side of the first, which was completed in 1896. Both still serve the city of Glasgow and its surroundings with Loch Katrine water, which rushes into twin tunnels through adjacent sluices at Royal Cottage. These are now – like many of the novel's locations – at the heart of the gorgeous Loch Lomond and the Trossachs national park, in which many works of Victorian engineering can still be admired. The fairy place names still give the whole area a marked sense of the clash (or synthesis perhaps) of modern progress and ancient traditions.

The idea for the novel's denouement came from an intriguing sentence in the *Glasgow Herald* of 15 October 1859, reporting on the inauguration ceremony the previous day: 'No sooner had [Queen Victoria] left than two navvies, dressed as if in the holiday garb of a London waterman, embarked in a shallow flat-bottomed boat, and accompanied by a young gentleman whose name we have not heard, set out on a voyage of discovery down the tunnel. Where they emerged and what they saw, we have not yet learned.'

Nor have I, but I hope they came to no harm.

Acknowledgements

I am indebted to William B. Black for letting me plunder his minutely researched unpublished manuscript '150 Years of Glasgow Water Supply,' and for all the time spent answering questions and checking the manuscript for historical blunders.

Thanks also to Ian Morrison of Scottish Water, who stood with me above the sluices at Royal Cottage and patiently addressed himself to the practicalities of Robert Kirke's escape route, before helping me to devise a way out of the tunnel.

Thank you to my colleague Darren Laing, of BBC Alba, for help with Gaelic phraseology, and to Eileen Watt for showing me round the lovely home she has made of Royal Cottage.

Sheena and David's hideaway cottage on Loch Katrine provided a perfect oasis of peacefulness for writing. As did Gladstone's Library in Hawarden, Flintshire, and Cove Park artists' retreat near Helensburgh.

My thanks – always – to my Two Roads publisher Lisa Highton and agent Jenny Brown: I hope you both know what your encouragement and patience have meant to me; to editors Amber Burlinson and Morag Lyall, whose skills fill me with awe; and to all the brilliant team at Two Roads and John Murray Press.

Finally, gratitude to my sister Margaret for her tactful advice on the numerous versions that winged their way towards her; my husband, who has been subjected to enough sluices to last him a lifetime; and my children, who still turn pale when they hear the words 'walk' and 'aqueduct' in the same sentence.

About the Author

Bestselling author, journalist and broadcaster Sally Magnusson has written several books for adults and children, most recently her *Sunday Times* bestseller *Where Memories Go* (2014) about her mother's dementia, and *The Sealwoman's Gift* (2018), her acclaimed debut novel.

Sally has inherited a rich storytelling tradition from her Scottish and Icelandic forebears. *The Sealwoman's Gift* was a Radio 2 Book Club and ITV Zoë Ball Book Club selection, and was shortlisted for the Authors' Club Best First Novel Award, the Saltire Fiction Book of the Year, the Paul Torday Memorial Prize, the McKitterick Prize, the Waverton Good Read Award and the HWA Debut Fiction Crown.

Sally lives outside Glasgow. Loch Katrine and the surrounding area have long been a favourite haunt.